Escape to the French Farmhouse

Jo Thomas

CORGI BOOKS

TRANSWORLD PUBLISHERS
61–63 Uxbridge Road, London W5 5SA
www.penguin.co.uk

Transworld is part of the Penguin Random House group of companies
whose addresses can be found at global.penguinrandomhouse.com

Penguin
Random House
UK

First published in Great Britain in 2020 by Corgi Books
an imprint of Transworld Publishers

A CIP catalogue record for this book
is available from the British Library.

ISBN
9780552176842

Typeset in 11/14pt ITC Giovanni by Jouve (UK), Milton Keynes.
Printed and bound in Great Britain by Clays Ltd, Elcograf S.p.A.

Penguin Random House is committed to a sustainable
future for our business, our readers and our planet. This book
is made from Forest Stewardship Council® certified paper.

MIX
Paper from
responsible sources
FSC® C018179

5 7 9 10 8 6 4

To VP, Vicky Palmer, for her passion for books, enthusiasm, laughter and unwavering support in helping me become the writer I always wanted to be and for bringing me to my new home.

And to France, because I have always loved you! Santé!

ONE

Bang! Bang! BANG!

Why today? Of all days? On moving day!

The noise goes right through me, jangling my already shredded nerves, as one of the heavy wooden doors upstairs slams, the wind whipping in and around the house, like a gaggle of overexcited spirits at Halloween, teasing and causing havoc. Except it's not Halloween, it's early June. And it's not spirits causing havoc: it's the mistral wind that blows regularly here in Provence and has chosen to create mischief today, of all days. I can hear it howling, laughing at me.

'You really thought you could do this?'

More doors bang. Glasses I've yet to wrap fall over on the sideboard. I'm exhausted before the day has even begun. My arms, legs and spirits are heavy, as if I'm dragging heavy sandbags behind me, draining my already depleted energy supplies.

1

I walk slowly along the empty hall towards the front door. It was the wonderful terracotta floor tiles I'd noticed when we first arrived. Their red is worn to orange in places, and they seem to tell a story of their own, of the many footsteps that have crossed them over the years. We've made barely a dusty footprint on them, let alone been here long enough to leave an indentation.

I step outside, holding my face defiantly to the wind, which is blowing up dust and carrying it through the just-cleaned house. My eyes stream and I blink. At least we did it, I think. At least we tried. I wipe my eyes with the corner of my poncho. I'm not sure I have a coat to put on later when we arrive back in the UK.

'Don't worry, love,' shouts the removal man over the wind. He's in a dark burgundy polo shirt with 'Broderick and Daughter Removals' in gold on the breast. I nod and try to smile at him, but inside I know I'm out of my depth. My life is way out of my control. 'Me and Lexie are doing moves like this all the time!' he yells cheerily, walking back from wrestling with and eventually tying back the heavy doors of the removal truck.

It's parked in front of the house under the plane trees, their branches waving enthusiastically, like they've seen a long-lost friend. They'll need pruning next year . . . The thought drifts through my confused mind, like a train pulling up at a station exactly on time, despite the weather conditions. Pollarding, I think randomly, letting the word sit in my mind, relishing the calm it brings, as if the wind has dropped, just for a moment, bringing calm. And then it blows up again, with a vengeance.

Why am I thinking about the plane trees at the front of the house? I won't be here next year. I'll be . . . Where will I be? The chaos that the wind brings shreds my nerves all over again as the van doors bang and outdoor pots, gathered together, topple over and roll around.

Ralph barks excitedly and barges past me, catching me on the back of the calves and making my knees buckle. He skids over the tiles to rush out and greet the visitors. Well, at least he may have left a scratch mark or two on the floor, I think sagely.

Mr Broderick walks up the couple of steps to the front door. The shutters, firmly closed upstairs, rattle in their holdings. One breaks free from its tie and bangs against the wall. I look around for Ollie to help, but he's nowhere to be seen. Oh, yes, he is: he's sitting in the dust-covered car, on the phone, making calls. Making plans. I sigh. More plans.

'Honestly, love,' says Mr Broderick, as he kindly touches my elbow, clearly mistaking the dusty cause of my tears. 'We do this all the time! Move people over here for a taste of the good life, then get a call to move them back six months later when they realize what a mistake they've made. They're missing everything about good old Blighty and want to go home! It happens all the time! You can't beat Blighty, that's what I say. Isn't that right, Lexie?' He raises his voice to call over the wind to the woman – possibly the same age as me, late thirties – jumping down from the back of the truck and walking towards us. She's wearing a matching Broderick's polo shirt, smiling. She has short, spiky white-blonde hair and leopard-print jeans. She seems oblivious to the wind swirling around the driveway, the rolling terracotta pots and the clouds of dust pluming around her steel-toe-capped boots.

'What's that, Dad?' she shrieks, over the wind.

'I said,' he shouts, over the banging shutter, 'we do this all the time. Move people over here and move them back six months later.'

'We do.' She smiles widely. 'He always says there's nowhere like Blighty.' She's standing next to her dad now. 'Nice to see you again,' she says, and suddenly her warmth feels like a glimmer of home.

This time actual tears spring to my eyes. Home. Where exactly is home? We sold the house, paid off the debts we'd run up, when we moved out here. Now Ollie is organizing us a house to rent 'back home'. But I have no idea where it will be, or what home looks like.

'Six months, that's the norm,' says Mr Broderick. 'Mind you,' he chortles, 'yours is the shortest I think we've ever done. Six weeks is probably a record.' He chortles some more. 'Now, where shall we start?' he says, clapping his hands together and stepping into the farmhouse.

Six months is the norm, I repeat in my head. But

ours is the shortest he's ever done. Six weeks, from moving in to moving 'home'. Six long weeks. I sigh.

Ralph runs excitedly in circles around Mr Broderick and his daughter. I make a grab for his collar but he swerves past me and thinks it's a game. Then he lies down in the dust, tingeing his cream coat a kind of peach, barking at me. I throw up my hands, despairing at his disobedience.

'Ollie!' I call to him in the car. But Ollie waves a hand to indicate he's busy. He says he gets his best phone signal sitting in the car on the drive. I think he's spent more time on the phone in his car than in the house over these six weeks.

The mistral blows harder. It can send people mad, they say. I pull my arms around myself, holding my face to the warm wind, closing my eyes against the dust, feeling the change in the air on my skin.

'Where shall we start?' says smiling Lexie.

I open my eyes and turn to the packed boxes stacked on the furniture that is going back into a truck, and possibly storage, if the rental house doesn't have room for it. 'Anywhere you like.' I try to smile back, feeling drained and exhausted. The boxes had barely been unpacked before I was packing them again. Some haven't been unpacked at all and I have no idea what's in them. Most of the photographs never made it on to shelves, but, then, that's a blessing as I hate having photographs of myself staring at me when I walk into a room. In our last house, Ollie insisted on having framed photographs in the hall and up the stairs. Us on our wedding day. His graduation picture. A picture of the two of us at his cousin's baby's christening. I thought I looked dreadful in that one but he liked it, said it was lovely of the two of us. To me, it just reminded me of how I'd felt that day: happy for the new parents but hollow and empty inside. It wasn't long after Mum died.

And I'm not sure which loss people meant when they said they were sorry for mine. I was sorry for my loss too. Both of them. Losing my mum and my final chance to be a mum myself. Just before we decided to move out here, which was soon after Ollie bought Ralph. I say we decided . . . It was Ollie's dream. He'd become addicted to *A New Life in the Sun* and *Escape to the Chateau*, when he was made redundant, and thought that this farmhouse, with its peach-coloured stone walls and peeling painted shutters, was the answer to all our problems.

I still had my job at the big department store in town and loved everything about it. I was a department manager. I was good at it. I was respected. It was where I fitted in. I loved talking to customers, arranging the stock, cashing up the tills at the end of a busy day. I knew who I was. Now, I have no idea where I fit in. Not here in France any more, that's for sure. Not that we ever did. We went to a few parties laid on by some of the expats living here when we first arrived, but I didn't meet anyone I really connected with. I found no one who loved the food of the area, or wanted to learn French with me and could tell me about a local class, or anyone who was making a living that might have given me some ideas on how I could start a business of my own, a way of putting my experience at the department store to good use. We met the group of expats every Thursday in the local 'pub', the bar in the middle of the town, on the square, for a few drinks and English quiz night, organized by a friendly, smart woman called Cora and two of her friends. Ollie had loved those nights. I was never one for quizzes. A wide general knowledge has never been top of my list of attractive qualities in a person. But Ollie loved the glory of being on the winning team.

I wander back inside to the kitchen, hoping Ralph will follow if he thinks food's on offer. The kitchen still smells of the ripe melon I had for breakfast, trying to eat up the last of the food from the fridge, and feeling I should have something, although my stomach was tight with tension. I look out of the French windows at the terrace, to the side of the house, where we've yet to enjoy one of those long, happy, friends-surrounded meals we kidded ourselves we would, and the field that slopes to the valley and the river. The other side looks out over the town and the purple lavender surrounding it.

I turn back to the hall. Ralph is circling Mr Broderick as he makes his way outside, whistling, carrying one end of the settee with Lexie at the other. As she bends

I can just see the top of her leopard-print thong and wonder if I will ever enjoy wearing sexy underwear again. Since we left the UK to make 'our life in the sun', I've gravitated to cotton midis and Ollie hasn't noticed, but that may be because he's been sleeping in one of the spare rooms since week one, ever since he did his back in trying to be Dick – Dick from *Escape to the Chateau*, that is – and attempting to sort out our blocked drain, creating a leak, a flood and bringing down the salon ceiling. We had to find a plumber, a plasterer and a decorator, and used up nearly all our savings putting it right.

Thankfully, the doctor Ollie saw about his back thought we were here on holiday and treated Ollie accordingly, without us having to worry about big medical bills as well. And that was how it felt: like one long holiday from hell. Everything that could have gone wrong has gone wrong, including Ollie's plans for working from home, doing business online: our internet is so poor he's had to drive to the next big town to send emails. It's been a disaster.

Ralph goes into a barking frenzy, rushing outside, kicking up even more dust as he goes haring down the drive to whoever might be passing.

'Ralph! Ralph!' He ignores me and carries on careering down the drive. I know only too well that he has trouble stopping and is likely to crash into whoever he is greeting and knock them off their feet.

I run after him, calling his name. Luckily I'm wearing lace-up trainers with a thick, cushioned heel, three-quarter-length jeans and a V-neck poncho over my white T-shirt. But I can hardly see him in the pink dust the wind is creating. I catch up with my dog, who is barking at nothing but the wind blowing in the trees, grab his collar and turn back towards the house.

Halfway along the drive I stand and look at the stone farmhouse and its lavender-blue shutters, rattling in the wind. I think of all the excitement for the future it came with when Ollie brought me here, telling me he'd found and bought our perfect home while I was working out my notice in the UK.

I look at the peeling paint now and think about the crack that had appeared in the salon ceiling before it fell down. The crack that had been covered with a thick layer of paint to patch it and make it last a little longer. That's exactly what this house was: a thick layer of paint to patch the cracks in our relationship . . . and now our ceiling has fallen down.

I watch Ollie talking urgently into the phone, leaving the packing to the people he's employed and me. I watch him, but he doesn't notice me. I turn back to help the removers. There's no let-up in the mistral, making the job twice as hard, the shutters and doors creaking, whining and banging. But, in what feels like no time at all, Mr Broderick and Lexie have the truck packed. They've done it. My entire life is inside it, ready to go home.

Home. That word again. Back to where we started. Back to where the cracks first appeared, after the failed

IVF attempts, Ollie's redundancy and then my mum dying. What exactly is left of our home together? What exactly is left of us? I take a final look around the empty house to make sure we've left nothing behind. I take a forgotten photograph off the wall on the staircase. The only one that made it on to an existing nail. When Ollie tried to put in others, the walls cracked some more. It's a wedding picture, with all the hopes and dreams from before the cracks happened and couldn't be filled. All that's left is me, this picture and Ralph, now sitting at my feet, panting and exhausted by all the excitement.

'Right! All set?' Ollie is standing in the doorway, finally off his phone. 'Think we're all sorted,' he says. 'We've got a couple of houses to see when we get back. They're nothing special but it's a start.' He goes back to trying to text from his phone.

A start. Another new start. Starting over. The house I left was special. I loved it. I thought it was going to be our family home for ever. Just like I loved my job. Now we're going back to our old lives, without the house I loved, or the job I was good at. Now we're going back to the start. And if I was starting over, would I do it with Ollie, knowing what I know now? Is this a fresh start – the words have formed in my head before I know it – or is it the end? Suddenly I feel a sense of calm, of stillness, of absolute clarity among the chaos of the day.

I look at him and say exactly what I'm thinking.

'I'm not coming, Ollie.'

TWO

'What?' He looks up from his phone as if he's misheard me.

'I'm not coming. I'm not going back,' I say. I can't go back to where we came from. Not the house or the job, but us. I can't go back to feeling how I did before we came here. Ollie had moved on very quickly at the end of our IVF treatment. He bought Ralph for me, let him sleep on the bed and decided we should move to France. I can't go back to the unhappiness and the loneliness I felt in our marriage.

'Don't be ridiculous! The van's all packed up! They're just about to leave! Of course we're going!'

I take a deep breath. 'I'm not, Ollie. We have to be honest with ourselves. Our marriage wasn't working in the UK, it didn't work out here and it won't work back there, because neither of us wants to be in it any more.'

He doesn't argue. I think about the ladies we meet at

quiz night who love Ollie and how long it might have been before he gave in to their charms, blaming it on our 'problems' . . . like last time: just the once, he said, back 'home'. Home isn't there for me. I don't know where it is, but it's not back where we came from in a rented house with Ollie.

'Look, Del, I don't know what this is about. We agreed it wasn't working for us out here and that we'd move home.'

'We agreed it wasn't working for us,' I say.

He breathes out, exasperated. 'We're going to miss the ferry if you don't get a move on. I have to drop the keys with the estate agent before we go.'

I hear the banging of truck doors, the engine starting up. And then a crunching on gravel as it starts to edge forward from under the trees. There's a beep. Ollie and I step outside. Lexie is at the wheel, sticks an arm out of the window and waves.

'See you in Blighty!' calls Mr Broderick, from the other window, and they begin down the drive.

'They're leaving! We have to go!' says Ollie, frustrated and angry. The wind whips up around us.

I could stop the truck, tell them to unpack it, that I'm not leaving. But I watch it go, my old life driving off down the lane.

Call it some kind of mistral madness, early menopause, bereavement, all the things I'm feeling, but suddenly a weight lifts off my shoulders as my past disappears down the lane.

Ollie rants at me some more. But I'm not listening. I've never felt more certain of anything. I'm not going back to my old life with him. We're over. Finally, the cracks are wide open and the ceiling is on the floor. Now all I have to do is work out what kind of ceiling I want to put up. Not the same as before, not that awful, miserable one.

'We have to go now!' Ollie says, getting more and more cross.

'Ollie, I'm not going back with you. Leave me the key. I'll take it to the estate agent and I'll let you know my plans.' I hold out my hand.

'Do you need a doctor?' He cocks his head.

Instead of feeling his concern, I feel patronized.

'No, Ollie.' I smile. 'I need what you need . . . I need not to go back.'

'You're being ridiculous! You're . . . upset! You're . . .'

'I'm right, Ollie. This is right. You know it. We were just papering over the cracks, coming here. Now give me the key and you go.'

He stares at me and I know he's not going to argue any more. He's put up a good show, but I sense that he knows I'm right. He looks at the big ornate key in his hand then slowly, ever so slowly, he passes it to me and swallows, hard.

'I need to go,' he says quickly. 'I need to get the ferry. The removal people are expecting us . . . me.'

'You go,' I say, calmer than I've felt in a long time.

'You're stressed! It's just the move, everything else.'

I take a deep breath. There's a trace of the old Ollie now, the one I married, the one I loved, the one who cared. He pushes his hair off his face and attempts a reassuring smile. 'It's your mum, the baby thing. You'll change your mind, realize this is just madness.'

The baby thing was where life took different directions for us, with me unable to become a mum and losing my own. The Ollie I married left me then.

'I'm not coming back with you, Ollie.'

'I'm not staying!' he retorts. 'Mad country. Nothing works! Impossible to make a living. I need to get going. Now, I'm giving you one last chance. Are you getting in the car and coming with me?' He stares at me, challenging me.

I lift my chin and stare back. 'No,' I say. 'I'm not.'

And he throws his hands up into the air. He lets out a huge 'Phhhhffff!' of exasperation and stomps to his car. Then he reaches in and pulls out my holdall, with my clothes and wash things in it to tide me over until we'd found a place to live and unpacked. He dumps it furiously on the drive in the dust. I don't move.

'Madness!' he repeats, standing by the door. 'I mean it! I'm leaving!' He sounds like a parent threatening a child, unsure whether to go through with it. 'I won't be turning back!' Then when I say nothing he gets into his car, turns on the engine and, with only the swiftest hesitation, shoots off down the drive in a cloud of dust. The last of my old life leaving without me. I watch the car disappear down the lane, then look down to see Ralph sitting at my feet. Well, nearly all of my old life.

'Looks like it's just you and me now.' I bend down and rub his ears. He barks happily. I look at the key and close my hand around it. Like a plaster that's been ripped off a wound, it hurts, hurts like anything to watch him go but already the pain is easing. I couldn't go back. But I have absolutely no idea what I'm going to do now.

THREE

The next morning I wake with a crick in my neck to the sound of birds singing. Not a whole morning chorus, but each bird being allowed to sing his own part – except the wood pigeon, which wants to sing over everybody else, and the cockerel in the distance heralding a new day. But apart from that, nothing. Silence. The mistral has gone as suddenly as it arrived. Came in, whipped up a storm, caused chaos and left a whole different landscape.

My phone buzzes in my jeans pocket, catapulting me back to reality. I open my eyes: my cheek is against the cool porcelain of the bath where I slept the night. Instead of what I'd thought was a warm blanket over me, Ralph is lying on top of me, for comfort and warmth. I'm suddenly very grateful to the mad bundle of curly fur. I might not have felt quite the same when Ollie brought him home as a gift after my final cycle of

IVF had failed. For Ollie it was like a full stop on that part of our lives, but to me it was like he was offering me a baby replacement. To begin with, I couldn't accept the dog into my life, especially when Ollie suggested calling him Eddie – one of my favourite baby names had been Edward. Ollie was clearly trying to do something kind – he was kind. He would often do really thoughtful things, like making a drink for me after a hard day, driving me into town to meet up with my friends on a night out, and he always remembered birthdays and anniversaries.

The puppy became Ralph because I would never have called a little boy Ralph. I knew a Ralph once, a long time ago, before I met Ollie. He'd been funny and adoring, not in the least bit reliable, and loved every person he met. It seemed a very suitable name for the bundle that had just landed in my life. Ralph slept with us from the first night, and as he grew and spread, sleeping right across the bed, so did the distance between us with every day that passed.

Ollie threw himself into the idea of France, freelancing from home. I carried on working but now had a dog in my life that needed feeding, walking and apologizing for when he ran off in the park and covered passers-by with muddy pawprints as he threw himself at them. Ralph became another thing on my to-do list. But now here he was, keeping me warm as I lay in the empty bath. Last night, I went from relieved at the decision to cut the cord with Ollie to wondering what the hell I'd done in letting him drive off without me. Eventually, exhausted, I had curled up in a tight ball, my back to the bathroom wall, arms over my head, and wondered if he had been right. What on earth was I doing alone in an empty house, when all my belongings and my husband of ten years were on their way back to the UK? Would I regret this? Was my decision another symptom of my early menopause?

My mind started to replay everything about our relationship, from how we met to how I'd ended up sleeping in the bath in an empty old farmhouse in the south of France.

So, what on earth was I doing there? In a tired farmhouse in the Luberon in Provence. In a small mountainside town, with terracotta-, orange-, yellow-, and peach-coloured houses. With my husband, the one constant thing in my life, back in the UK. Well, he'd been there in body, except when he'd been in someone else's life and bed for that one-off when the stress of our situation had got too much. Sex to us had become about making a baby, not making love. I can't remember the last time I made love. And all the time, as I thought back over my married life throughout that night, trying to work out where it had all gone wrong, the loose shutters banged, banged, banged against the windowpanes. Eventually, when I could stand it no more, I stood up and went to tie the shutter to the wrought-iron railings we'd had made to stop any visitors falling out of the window. But no one had visited in the six weeks we'd tried to make a go of things here. Once the move had happened, our 'fresh new start', once we'd eaten the bread and cheese, drunk the wine, taken down the 'happiness in your new home' cards, once the front door was shut, it was just Ollie and me, alone, our future spread out in front of us, like a long, long night with nothing on the telly. And nothing much to talk about, apart from shopping lists, people planning to visit, Ollie's frustration with the internet and his daily battles with the phone in the car. He'd come back to the farmhouse after a trip into the town furious that he had got no further in improving our broadband and Wi-Fi connection and that no one spoke English.

'Bloody country!' he'd rant. 'And they all stop for lunch! Who stops for lunch these days? How does anyone make a bloody living here? And, honestly, it beggars belief how many of them don't speak English.' The last six painful weeks played over and over in my mind for what seemed like most of the night.

I felt safer in the bathroom than anywhere else in the empty house, in what felt like the tatters of my marriage, with Ralph by my side. Suddenly my dog was there for me when I really needed someone and no one else was.

I thought about Ollie and our life together over the last few weeks. Mealtimes had become fraught as the work Ollie had tried to pick up, then deliver, became more and more difficult to achieve, and our savings from the sale of the house started to dwindle.

So, work was drying up for Ollie, and my French wasn't nearly good enough yet for me to look for work in a local shop. We agreed, over the *plat du jour* in the most expensive brasserie in town, to put the house back on the market and phoned the removal company. Ollie complained at the size of the restaurant bill and that 'nothing in France is cheap any more'. But we were both right. Nothing in our lives was working because our marriage wasn't working. The glue had gone. We'd tried to fix it, but it was broken. It was over. I know I made the right decision for us both. That was how I ended up in the bath on my own.

'Come on, Ralph, up we get,' I say.

He's suddenly alert and scrabbles out of the bath, ready for whatever adventures the day might bring. With every joint and muscle in my body aching, I ease myself out and pull out my phone. There's a message from Ollie.

I'm back. Come to your senses yet?!

I don't reply. I've said all I need to say. There's no point in discussing it any more. I ripped the plaster off our broken marriage and my damaged heart yesterday, which hurt, but it's going to get better, for both of us.

I walk over to the long bathroom window to retrieve my bra, the only thing I could find last night to tie back the loose shutter. I'd seen Joanna Lumley use hers as slippers when she was on a desert island, and mine did a great job last night. I untie it, then push the shutters back. I take hold of the wrought-iron railing and breathe in deeply. I can smell the pine and cypress trees. I can hear the birds singing as they flit in and out of the trees and the cockerel in the distance still heralding the new day. A donkey from up the road has joined in the morning celebrations and is braying. I can smell the rosemary plants under the window and the lavender hedge. The mistral has blown all the dust away and everything is bright and clear. They say that the clear colours after the mistral draw painters to the area, and I can see why as I stare at the valley below. I'm not mad. Ollie and I had come to the end of our journey. Going back to where we'd started would have made us even more miserable.

The sky is streaked with blue and pink as the sun rises over our field behind the house and beyond. I close my eyes. I open them and the birdsong, the smell of the pines, the wild rosemary and thyme on the white rocks make me feel calm. I look at the view, taking it in as if for the first time. I may have nothing in the house but I have this for now.

I smile at Ralph, sitting happily at my feet, and I reach down to stroke his soft ear. Instead of seeing it as a sign to bound around in play, he lets me. And I'm grateful for that. A smile pulls at the corners of my mouth and there's a flutter of excitement in my stomach. Was it mistral madness? Whatever it was, this is a new day, a fresh new day, and there are far worse places I could be.

FOUR

The sun is warm already and I'd love to sit outside and feel it on my face, but with no food in the house, and nothing to sit on, I decide to walk into town. My large basket-cum-handbag, which I bought in the market on our first day, hangs over my arm. I tell Ralph I'll be back with breakfast, and fill an old bucket I found in the barn with water. I think it may be the first time I've ventured into that barn. I also find an old blanket covering what looks like an ancient plough and put it on the kitchen floor for him, promising I'll be back soon. I daren't risk trying to walk him on the lead into town – we'd probably both end up in the river.

I shut the front door and lock it, then put the key into my bag. I stroll down the drive and out on to the lane beyond the metal gates. I can feel the sunshine feeding my soul as I walk. I breathe in the scent of pine and rosemary, trying to work out what I need to buy.

The town seems busier than usual as I walk along, watching an unusual amount of traffic arriving. And now I know why: there's a market, not like our usual Monday market but for antiques, a *brocante* market. I can hear chatter and bargaining from the riverbank as I walk towards the town square. This is an amazing route into town. I knew this path existed but haven't walked it before. Ollie always insisted on driving: he didn't want to walk back with shopping. At the end of the path, I pass a clearing with what looks to be a small hut. Fairy lights are strung from it to the trees, and a blue velvet settee, with gold trim and legs, has been placed under a huge pine. Its beauty takes me by surprise. There's a table and chairs too, with two men playing chess, so intent on their game that they don't notice me.

I smile as I walk towards the busy market. I'm not thinking about last night, or yesterday, the months that led up to it, or what I'm going to do next. I'm just here, walking in the sunshine with all the other Sunday browsers. The bells I can hear from what was our house, Le Petit Mas de la Lavande, are ringing as church-goers pour out. I watch as a group of short women, dressed in black and smart court shoes, kiss each other three times on the cheek, then head off in different directions, probably going home to prepare lunch for the family. I feel a twinge of envy: there's no family waiting for me. I think of my mum and the gaping hole her death has left in my life. I need one of her hugs to tell me everything will be okay. Will it? I wish I was here with Mum, Ollie and our child, getting ready for Sunday lunch at home. But I'm not. I'm here on my own.

The sun is warm on my face as I walk around the stalls filling the square, the streets and side streets of the town. I don't think Ollie would have liked it: he doesn't like 'second hand'. Although Le Petit Mas de la Lavande was picture-perfect, he wanted to replace all its original features with new. It needed work, but I liked it as it was, flaws and all.

I wander among the stalls, piled with mirrors, chandeliers, milk churns, even beautifully carved dark-wood furniture, where the car park usually is, at the top of the town, in the shade of the big plane trees there. I stroll leisurely. The only thing I have to do today is make plans for the rest of my life and, right now, I want to put that off for as long as possible. It's far more appealing to mingle with people, furniture, clothes and bedding, full of stories about the life they had before and waiting for a new era to begin. A bit like me, I think, and tears spring to my eyes. I blink them away. I have just walked out on ten years of marriage and everything I know but I can't let myself crack. I have to keep going.

I used to like the idea Ollie had for our life, our future. He preferred things to be perfect, even though life isn't. But I can be happy, I think, picking up a jug and running my hand over its crackled glaze.

My stomach rumbles. I put down the jug and walk along the main street towards the *boulangerie* we've used every day since we've been here.

'*Bonjour, Madame,*' says the young woman behind the high counter. The baker is pulling baguettes from the oven in the kitchen behind her.

'*Bonjour, Mademoiselle, Monsieur,*' I say.

She smiles at me brightly behind her round glasses, asking me what I'd like.

I look at the pastries. I've been trying to avoid them, but I point to a *pain au raisin*. I take a baguette too. For later, although I have no idea where I'll be. I have to drop the key to the house with the estate agent and work out where to go from there. I take the pastry and pay from the change in my purse. I still have the envelope of cash from the sale of our sit-on lawnmower that I was supposed to pay into the bank before we left France. I push the baguette into my bag and pull it up on to my shoulder.

'I thought your husband said you were leaving,' she says. 'Did you forget something?' She cocks her head sympathetically.

I look at her and see myself, a young woman with all of life's opportunities in front of me. 'I think I probably did,' I say, and smile. Myself, I think.

I step out of the shop, take off my poncho, put it into my bag, then get out my pastry and take a bite. I shut my eyes and enjoy the moment, which takes me back to a time when food was fun, when I wasn't worried about what I ate, before food became a battle, not a pleasure. Right now, this pastry is heaven. I open my eyes, and across the street an old man with a dark lined face, wearing a flat cap and jacket, grins at me and beckons me over to his stall. He's selling lavender bags, bundles of dried lavender and essential oil. He picks up a small bundle and hands it to me. 'Because you have a beautiful smile,' he says, and grins, showing the gap where his front tooth once was.

'Merci,' I say. 'Vous êtes très gentil,' I try in my simple French. 'Au revoir.'

'Bonne journée, Madame,' he calls.

Suddenly I feel really happy. I haven't felt like this before. Why not? But I know the answer. Because Ollie and I had made each other unhappy.

I pass the estate agent's window and see the smart young woman behind the neatly ordered desk talking to a middle-aged couple. I think of the big key in my bag. Surely it wouldn't do any harm to hang on to it for a bit longer, just while I work out what I'm going to do. Give it until the weekend. Then I'll start looking for a job and somewhere to live back home. I can't just stay here, like I'm on holiday. I'll have to go back to the UK soon and look for somewhere to rent while the house sells. I suppose we'll split whatever profit there is, if any. The reality of the situation is sinking in: dividing our small 'assets'. I'm no longer half of a couple. I'm no longer someone's wife. It feels odd. It'll feel strange telling people I'm separated. I sigh. We had lots of friends, but over the years I've felt lonely. The more people tried to sympathize when we discovered we couldn't have children, the more I kept them at arm's length. But now it feels good to smile, and here, in this town, although I'm on my own, I don't feel lonely at all.

But if I'm going to stay until the weekend, I'll need a few supplies. Everything went into that truck, except my bag with toiletries and essential clothes. At that moment I spot a pair of big double doors down a side street, inside a courtyard, behind wrought-iron open gates. I've never noticed it before. A large *brocante*, by the look of it, with all sorts of furniture, bedding and even a clothes rail. I need some bedding, maybe something to sleep on, a cup and a pan. Looks like I could get everything I need right here. Perhaps even sell it back to the owner when I leave. I walk towards it, seeing piles of fabric, kitchen implements and ornaments.

I run my hand over a bundle of bedding. A floral eider-down, sheets and blankets, tied up with ribbon, for just five euros. Far cheaper than paying to stay some-where. There's a chair that's been half upholstered, the fabric cut and in place: it just needs tacking on. I could live without a chair, but at that price, it seems a shame to leave it behind. There are boxes of plates, beautiful cups and saucers and cutlery, all cheaper than I could buy in the supermarket. There are wooden bed heads and stacks of thick mattresses. Then I see a lovely leather-bound book. A work of art in itself. A cookery book of the area, handwritten, and if I'm not mistaken, it's about lavender. I smell the lavender in my hand, as I turn the pages. It could have been written for Le Petit Mas de la Lavande. I try to imagine my home in its heyday as a lavender farm, long gone.

'*Bonjour.*' A polite voice cuts into my thoughts.

An attractive young man is smiling at me. Dark curly hair, dark stubble on his chin. He has big green eyes and is wearing an old leather jacket, despite the sun, and a soft scarf around his neck. For a moment I just stare at him and feel quite hot. I fan myself with the empty pastry bag, scattering crumbs on to the book. 'Oh, sorry – *je m'excuse*,' I say, blushing.

'No problem.' He flicks away the crumbs. 'It's done.'

'*Merci,*' I say, and push the scrunched-up bag into my shoulder bag, on top of the key.

'Are you looking for something?' he says, in stilted English.

'Um, well, yes,' I say, wondering where to start and how to explain my situation. 'I need . . . um . . . everything really! The basics. Cheaply.'

He smiles quizzically, not understanding. 'Let's start at the beginning,' he says. 'Can I get you some coffee?'

My mouth is suddenly dry. 'Coffee would be wonderful, *merci*.'

'*Je m'appelle Fabien,*' he says, and holds out a hand to shake mine.

'Della,' I reply. 'Everyone calls me Del.'

'*Enchanté*,' he says, and something shifts inside me, making me feel young again.

'Let us have coffee and, er, talk about your knees,' he says, leading me into the big warehouse.

'My knees?'

'Yes, are you living here?'

'Oh, I see.' I bite my top lip. 'My needs.'

'Yes. Your knees. Was it wrong? My English is . . .' He puts out a hand and tilts it from side to side.

'No. It's fine. My needs. It's complicated. I was supposed to be living here and now, well . . . I'm staying, just for a bit.' I have no idea what my plans are. 'Until I know where I'm moving on to.'

'So you are here to invade us!' He smiles widely, and I'm wrong-footed.

'What? To invade?' I repeat and he nods. 'No, I was here to live, but now, I'm just staying for a bit, then going back. Definitely not invading!'

He looks confused. 'Sorry, my English, it's not quite . . .' He tips his head from side to side and the smile returns to his face, as it does to mine. 'I mean you are here to live with us.'

'Well, I'm just staying . . . for a bit,' I repeat. I wonder how the locals must feel about so many British people moving here. Do they feel we're invading their towns and villages? Do they resent us coming?

Fabien doesn't seem to resent my being here. But then I remember Ollie and me drinking gin and tonic with the other expats in the 'pub', barely speaking French. I wouldn't blame him, or anyone else in the town, if he did.

He claps his hands together. 'You are staying here so we need to make you as comfortable as possible,' he says, with that killer smile. 'Enough to make you content.'

Comfortable and content would be perfect right now. I can't help but think the people of the town must be laughing at the likes of me and Ollie. Another British couple moving here for the good life, wanting to make a Little Britain beyond the Channel, then packing up and moving back when it all goes wrong. I sigh. I barely speak French. I'd had no idea how I was going to work or where. I can see why people like Fabien might laugh at us. Although, thankfully, he doesn't seem to be. In fact, he's being charming, welcoming and nothing but helpful.

I follow him into the cool warehouse. For the next hour or so, we walk, keeping our conversation to what I'll need for a few days' stay. He grabs suitable pieces and arranges them by the back door to deliver to Le Petit Mas de la Lavande later that afternoon. I think a mattress will do me for a few days, but he insists I need a bed and finds me a big wooden one, with carved acorns on the posts, tells me it's been here for ages and he can offer me a very good price. He sorts out a mattress, and I wonder what on earth I'm going to do with them when I leave the following weekend.

But, right now, the thought of sleeping on a proper bed, with a thick mattress, is worth every euro. And it's still cheaper than a hotel. I take the chair because I like the idea of having a little project to do while I work out where to go next. Fabien insists on four plates and beautiful cutlery, 'because eating correctly is important for the stomach and well-being'. I take some pans from a random box of cooking utensils, which he adds to the pile, with my bundle of bedding. He doesn't ask any more questions about why I'm here on my own, needing 'everything', or why I'm staying just for a bit.

We pass a clothes rail. He picks out a wrap-around dress in a cherry print and holds it against me.

'Oh, I'm not sure I should,' I say, as, with his other hand, he pulls out a kimono top, unlike anything I've ever worn before.

Suddenly a wave of guilt washes over me. I'm not in this warehouse to enjoy myself, just to buy practical necessities. *Enough to make you content . . .* I hear Fabien's words as I look at the dress and the top. I have barely any clothes with me, and the ones I have are for rainy British weather . . .

Next weekend I plan to give the key to the estate agent. I have until then to work out who I am and where I'm going. I can be whoever I want to be. Go where I like. I look at the dress and smile at Fabien so he adds it to the pile with a nod of agreement; it's a good choice.

'*Parfait*,' he says, and holds up another dress, then a silk dressing-gown – 'For the mornings,' he says. I'm blushing a little but I take the gorgeous dressing-gown and he smiles.

Hastily, I tell him I'm done. I have everything I need. I slip the leather-bound recipe book on to the pile. I stare at the bed, the chair – and the small round table, with folding chairs, that Fabien insisted I'd need. I'll leave them in the house when I go so it's dressed for any buyers wanting to view it. It may help to get a sale. He adds up the prices of the items, then deducts some because I'm such a good customer. All of it costs less than the settee Ollie ordered when we moved in.

Quickly, I pull out my purse and my bank card in case he changes his mind about the discount. For someone who feels we're here to invade, he's been very generous.

'Oh.' He looks at the card. 'I'm sorry. My machine . . . *en panne*. Broken. Can you pay cash? I can knock a bit more off if that helps.'

'No, it's fine!' I say. At this rate he'll be paying me to take it away. 'I'll just go to the cashpoint.' I point to the bank. 'I'll be back.' I hurry out into the brilliant sunlight.

I think about Ollie and me as I go, realizing how we stood out in the town. We didn't try to integrate, just arrived and hoped life would be as it was in the UK. I think about Fabien holding the dress against me and wonder if it's obvious that I'm single now. Am I going to be wary of every man I meet, now I'm no longer somebody's other half? I feel as if I have a sign over my head: 'Newly Single Female'. The last thing I want is another partner. I just want to be me. Not a wife, a woman who couldn't have children or who's just lost her mother. I'm just not sure who me is.

I cross the road to the cashpoint and stand in the bank's shade, enjoying the cool and letting the reality of my situation sink in once more. I have somewhere to sleep tonight, and eat. As horrid as it was splitting from Ollie, it's over. We can both get on with our lives now. We need to find new paths away from each other. I have everything I need for the time being. Enough to be content.

I put my card into the machine and type in my PIN. The machine whirs and whirs and then the card slowly disappears inside it. I fumble for it but it's gone. I try to read the screen but the message vanishes before I can. The bank has shut for lunch, and I hear Ollie's voice in my head: 'What kind of country stops for lunch?' But my card is gone.

FIVE

I feel like I've been left alone on an island: the last ferry has just sailed. I now have nothing. I rummage in my bag for my phone to call the bank in the UK. But even if they send me a new card, it'll be days before it arrives. Then I see it: the envelope of cash from the sale of the sit-on lawnmower, which I was supposed to pay into the bank. It had been brand new when we moved here. I got a dog and Ollie got the lawnmower. Once we'd decided to leave, he'd pushed it down to the end of the drive and stuck an '*À vendre*' sign on it. We sold it for half what we paid for it, a quick sale to a couple with a holiday home in a neighbouring village.

I breathe a sigh of relief. But this is all I have until I can get a new bank card. I need to make it last. I return to the *brocante*, this time with only half a smile. I put back the silk dressing-gown and the leather-bound book. And the beautiful vase I had planned to fill with flowers, and tell Fabien a white lie to hide my embarrassment at my new financial situation. I say I'll come back for them when I can get out more cash.

'Of course,' he says, seemingly picking up on my change in mood. (Why was my card eaten?) 'You are welcome to invade any time!' He grins. He's happy to take my money, but perhaps doesn't want me in his country.

I count out the cash for the essentials and hand it to him, glancing at what's left in the envelope.

'You can take the other items. Pay me when you can, if you like?'

Tears fill my eyes but I don't want him to see them.

'I'll come back when I can,' I say, through my tight throat, knowing I won't.

He reverts to slick professional and promises to deliver the goods after lunch. He knows exactly where Le Petit Mas de la Lavande is, he assures me.

'*Merci*,' I say, hurrying out of the cobbled courtyard and through the big iron gates that I know will be locked as soon as I leave: everyone closes for lunch. I hurry past the restaurant on the market square, where many of the stallholders are enjoying lamb ragout, the smell of Provençal herbs in the air, *frites*, salad and steaks, with jugs of rosé in the glorious sunshine. Small dogs sit patiently at their owners' feet, and I wish Ralph was the kind of dog I could take to a restaurant. Cigarette smoke rises with the good-natured chat and I would have loved to have lunch in the restaurant, but I must find out what's going on with our bank account.

I gather a few tomatoes, olives and cheese from the small supermarket as it closes to go with the baguette I bought earlier. I raise a hand to the lavender seller as he packs up for the day. The whole town seems to smell of lavender as I walk through the narrow streets, past the cream- and terracotta-coloured stone walls and shop fronts. The 'pub' in the middle of the square is busy with expats, but I don't stop. I don't want to have to explain why I'm here and Ollie isn't. I hurry towards the road leading out of town and the grassy path along the river, then up the lane towards the house. The water running beside me is clear and calm. The cypresses are set against a bright blue sky. Bluer than I have ever seen before. My spirits begin to lift again as I walk back to Le Petit Mas.

I let myself in with the huge wrought-iron key. It's as if I'm holding the history of the families who lived here before me. Ollie hated the key and wanted to get a locksmith in to replace it.

I push open the door, and Ralph sees me. He launches himself down the corridor at me, once again nearly knocking me off my feet. His welcome, crazy as it is, makes me laugh.

'Okay, Ralph, I'm home,' I say.

I walk into the kitchen where Ralph has knocked over his water bowl and shredded the blanket. My dog comes and stands next to me, panting, wagging his tail, as if relishing the memory of the fun he's had. I rub his head. But I have to make the call to the bank and find out if there's a problem with the account. I go out on to the veranda at the side of the house, Ralph bounding around my feet, and stride to the top corner of the field. I breathe in the scent of rosemary and wild thyme, running my hand along the lavender bushes there. Somehow, I'm filled with courage. I make the call.

'You did what?'

'I reported the cards stolen. If you're serious about this, we need to decide who's getting what,' says Ollie, in work-mode voice.

'Ollie, I need money. That is our joint account.'

'And you are in our joint house,' he replies.

I look back at Le Petit Mas, a shabby stone-built farmhouse, with sagging, peeling shutters. It was supposed to be my new home but now I can imagine a family returning to it from the market or church and sitting round a big table for lunch.

'If you've finally come to your senses, I can talk to the bank, order your new card and organize a flight home.'

I say nothing.

'I've found us a great apartment on Facebook. Friend of a friend is going away for a grown-up gap year. He was looking for someone to house-sit.'

I think of Ralph in an apartment, someone else's apartment.

'I'm sorry, Ollie,' I say, my thoughts as clear as the blue sky I'm looking at. 'But I'm not coming back to you. It's for the best, for both of us.'

'This is madness!' Ollie splutters.

'No, Ollie, it's the most sensible thing we've done in years.'

'What will you do for money? You need money!'

'I don't know . . . yet.' I'll think of something. I hear a car coming up the drive. 'Ollie, keep the money in the joint account and the savings one. And the shares you got with your redundancy package. I'll have the house. I'll sell it, sort out the mortgage on it and keep what's left. Seem fair enough to you?'

'What? You'll keep the house and sell it and I keep the cash in the account, the savings account and the shares?'

'Yes, that should work out fairly, shouldn't it?'

I can hear Ollie doing a mental calculation.

'Fine, but this is madness. You'll change your mind. It's just The Change, you know.'

It is a change, but not the one he means.

'Goodbye, Ollie,' I say softly, as he bangs down the phone. It's as if the door on my past life has slammed shut. I cry out in frustration and pain, then lean against the door frame and cry for the marriage that has died, along with any respect and affection I had for Ollie. It's over. I cry for the family life we never had and the new beginning we tried to start. I cry for my mum. I cry until I can't cry any more.

SIX

Ralph is running around and barking at a car that's pulled up on the drive. I push my phone into my back pocket, sniff away the tears, run my hands over my puffy eyes and walk back around the side of the house. I recognize her as soon as she steps out of the car, pushing up her sunglasses to look at the property. It's the woman from the estate agent's.

'Bonjour, *Madame*,' she calls, and walks towards me.

'Bonjour,' I reply, shaking her hand, then apologizing for Ralph, who is leaping around, barking, delighted to have a new friend to play with.

The estate agent smiles, but keeps her distance from Ralph.

'Are you okay?' she says, staring at my swollen, red eyes.

'Yes, fine! How can I help you?'

'Your husband said you would drop the key to Le

Petit Mas to the shop,' she says, in a strong Provençal accent.

'Ah, yes, the key, *je m'excuse,*' I say, '*mais . . .*'

'It's no problem,' she says. 'I can pick it up from you now. Actually, I have some good news.' She points to the small car as the doors open and a couple just a bit older than myself step out and scan the house. 'Monsieur et Madame Jarvis from England are looking for a holiday home in the area.' Then, more quietly to me, 'Just like this one! And they are cash buyers.'

'Cash buyers.' I nod.

'It's . . . quaint,' says the woman, with a broad south-of-England accent, not taking off her sunglasses. She's wearing white jeans and wedge-heeled open-toed espadrilles. 'Just what we want. Quaint and picture . . . picture . . . Cute-looking. And we have friends in the village, a whole group of friends now, actually. A right laugh that crowd are. It's perfect, innit, Keef? Just out of town, but walkable when you've had a few gins!'

I think of the crowd at the 'pub', drinking their gin and tonic, standing out with their British ways. And then I think of Fabien.

'Yeah, great for walking back from town after the pub,' says her husband, pulling his belt up over his belly. 'I hear quiz night in the pub's a right laugh.' My heart sinks. It's no wonder that local people feel 'invaded'. I don't know why I thought Ollie and I were any different from the rest. We were just like them, moving to France and trying to make it our own, instead of blending in. We went to quiz night in the 'pub'. I shudder.

Just then, a truck comes down the drive, piled with furniture. It's Fabien. I'm embarrassed to be showing another British couple around the house. My stomach tightens.

'*Bon après-midi*,' he says, as he jumps down from the cab. He kisses me three times on the cheeks as if we're the oldest of friends, then turns to the estate agent.

'Carine,' he says, and kisses her three times too. Ralph is barking like crazy as Fabien shakes Carine's clients' hands. Then he steps back and looks at Ralph. '*Oui, et toi. Bon après-midi.*' He laughs.

Ralph stops barking and sits, his tongue lolling out as if he's smiling. Then he raises his right paw in Fabien's direction, and Fabien takes it and says, '*Enchanté.*' I can't help but laugh. I've never seen Ralph like this before. From the cab of the truck, a small, wire-haired Jack Russell pokes her head out to see what she's missing.

'So,' says Carine, regaining control of the situation. 'The house.' She holds out a hand to Le Petit Mas, and I feel strangely protective of it. As if, somehow, I'm letting it down by selling it. Ridiculous, I know.

'Looking forward to seeing it,' says Keef.

'May I?' says Carine to me.

'Go ahead,' I reply, and swallow. Carine leads the way and Ralph barks as the couple follow, making the woman jump and scurry past him.

Fabien starts to unload the furniture. The bed, the mattress and bedclothes, the chair that needs finishing off, the table and the box of plates and cutlery. He doesn't ask why I'm in an empty house, selling it yet buying basic furniture for it. And now I wonder if it would have been far more sensible just to go to a guesthouse. This place could have new owners by the end of the day, if those encouraging voices are anything to go by.

I can hear Carine showing them around the house, 'Its original features . . .'

'Oh. We can get rid of them,' says Keef. 'Gut it and give it a real modern look. I like the view from the kitchen,' I hear.

I *love* the view from the kitchen. Where will I get another view like that?

'I think we could do something with it,' says Keef.

'Knock it down and rebuild it?' says his wife.

Fabien raises his eyebrows as he unloads the last of my things, clearly unable to hide his feelings any longer.

I feel disloyal to the house and to the town, to people like Fabien.

'So, why are they selling?' asks Keef.

'I believe the owners have decided to return to the UK.'

'Couldn't stick it out, eh?' He tuts.

My hackles are up.

'I'll put the bed upstairs, *oui*?' says Fabien, gesturing at the wooden headboard.

'*Merci*,' I say. He takes the pieces up to the bedroom. Soon I can hear him putting the bed together and can picture it looking out over the valley.

'We could put in a hot tub over there, pull out those plants,' says Keef's wife, loudly.

'*La lavande*,' says Carine. 'Fine lavender. It is grown only here in Provence. It is used for healing, for beauty products and in recipes too.'

'Ewwww! Lavender in food?'

'This was a lavender farm at one time. The whole valley was covered with lavender. Like over there.' She points to the other side of the valley. 'The smell was amazing. But every ten years the plants must be uprooted and replanted. Sadly, this hasn't been replanted. The owner died and the family sold the place. Only those plants remain,' she says, with a hint of regret in her voice.

'Well, as I say, we'll uproot them and put the hot tub there,' says Keef's wife.

I can't listen to any more. Ralph barks at me and I take that as agreement in what I'm about to say.

'Hi, Carine,' I say, marching around to the side of the house. 'I wonder if I could—'

'Ah, there you are. We like the house. It'll do,' says Keef.

And suddenly this house, which Ollie chose and I moved into and have resented for the last six weeks, is my house, my space, my home. It kept me safe when my world was falling apart. Suddenly it matters to me.

43

I have nothing but this house and Ralph, a bed, some bedding and a half-finished chair.

'We're cash buyers, so I'm presuming we can come to a deal on the price. There's a lot that needs doing, so we're really just buying the position,' Keef drones on.

Carine looks at me and I look back at her. We may be thinking the same thing. We hold each other's gaze.

'Actually, Carine,' I say slowly.

'*Oui, Madame?*' Her head cocks, her neat bob shifting, and her lips twitch with a smile. The sound of the bed being assembled upstairs has stopped and Fabien is now behind me.

'All done,' he says. 'Where do you want the table?'

I turn to him. 'In the kitchen, please, Fabien, where I can see the view.'

'*Parfait,*' he says.

'Actually, Carine,' I repeat, and Fabien stops in his tracks.

The buyers are staring impatiently at me, keen to agree a deal. He is chewing the arm of his aviator glasses. Her arms are folded over her chest. No one speaks. They are anxious for me to name my price.

'Le Petit Mas de la Lavande is no longer for sale.'

'I see,' says Carine.

'What – has someone else nipped in before us? Okay, okay, I'll give you the asking price if that's what it takes.' He sighs heavily, sweat forming on his brow in the warm June sunshine.

'No. There's been a change in our . . . my situation,' I say, trying to control the waver in my voice.

'You and your husband are staying?' Carine asks.

'I'm staying, Carine. Just me.' I lift my chin, feeling brave, joyous and terrified all at the same time. 'I'm staying at Le Petit Mas de la Lavande. I'm not selling it. I'm not going back to the UK, with or without my husband.'

This time Carine smiles. 'I see. Of course, *et bravo*,' she says, filling me with confidence.

'You mean you're not going to sell?' says Keef.

'Offer her more than the asking price!' hisses his wife. 'I can't be bothered to trail round any more of these old places.'

Keef sighs. 'Go on, then. We'll pay your asking price, and ten per cent. And you've had a lucky day. Make sure it all goes through quick, though. And you can take all that crap away too!' He waves at Fabien and the truck. Fabien says nothing, but I see his fist curl.

'*Le Petit Mas de la Lavande n'est pas à vendre*,' I say, in my pidgin French. 'I'm going to live here. Stay here.' I don't need to look for somewhere else to live. Ollie has agreed that I can have the house. It's mine to do with as I choose, and I'm choosing to stay in it.

'Well, really!' says the woman, and Ralph barks, as if to endorse my decision. I look at Fabien, who is patting Ralph's head, and Carine nods, making me feel I've done the right thing for me.

'We have plenty more houses for you to see,' she tells her clients.

'But I want this one. Offer her more,' says the woman.

'This house is already sold. It has a new life and a new owner,' says Carine, firmly.

That's me!

Ralph barks more as the woman stalks towards the car behind Keef. My dog can contain himself no longer and throws himself at her. She's flapping her hands at him and he's delighted she wants to play: he covers her white jeans with dusty orange paw marks.

'Oh, my God!' she shrieks, and runs to Carine's tiny car, slamming the door as Keef squeezes himself into the front passenger seat.

'Welcome,' says Carine. 'I like your style. You know what you want . . . and what you don't want. A woman after my own heart,' she says, and I explain that that couldn't be further from the truth. I have no idea what I'm doing here. *'Bonne chance,'* she says. 'Maybe we could have coffee when you're in town next.'

'I'd like that,' I say. 'Sorry about the waste of time – and the white trousers.'

Carine waves a hand, dismissing it all. 'It's no problem. I have a feeling, though, that they may be regular customers, the sort that come out here for the good life, then sell up and move home six months later.'

That was exactly who we were. *Were.*

'Only the ones who love it stay.' She smiles. *'Au revoir.*

À *la prochaine,*' she says, folding herself into the car, next to a red-faced Keef. She starts the engine and disappears down the drive. I swear she hits every pothole as she goes.

Fabien is still standing there. His little Jack Russell sticks her head out of the cab's window to see what's going on. Ralph looks up at her. 'If I let her out, she'll disappear,' Fabien says. The Jack Russell barks and again Ralph sits and pants.

'This is for you,' says Fabien, taking something from the front seat of the truck. He holds out the silk dressing-gown to me.

'Oh, no, really. I have to watch my money, now I'm going to be staying.'

'It's for you.'

I take the dressing-gown, but it's heavier than I'm expecting. It's wrapped around something.

'Open it.'

Inside is the leather-bound recipe book with the aged pages. Recipes with lavender.

'Fabien!' I exclaim.

'It is a gift. A moving-in gift!' He laughs. 'I can see you are going to be a very good customer in the future.'

I'm touched by the present, but he's right. He knows a good customer when he sees one. I'm going to need much more now that I'm staying. It's good business sense and tears are in my eyes: tears of relief, of trepidation about how I'm going to make a living, of joy that one part of my life is over and a new one is beginning.

'*Merci beaucoup, Fabien. Très gentil,*' I say. I open the book and a little bunch of dried lavender falls out. Fabien picks it up, sniffs it and hands it to me. I take it, my fingers brushing his. Something like an electric shock passes through me.

'I hope we will be friends.' He smiles, his green eyes alight. My stomach flutters and his charm makes me shy again.

'I hope so too,' I say, and gaze down at the book in my hand, running my fingers over it.

And Ralph barks. I think he's as happy to be at home as I am.

'Yes, and you,' Fabien tells Ralph.

'Thank you for bringing the furniture, Fabien. Would you like something to drink?'

'*Non, merci.* I have to return to the shop.' He gets into the cab where his Jack Russell is waiting patiently. '*Bienvenue!*' But his earlier words echo in my head: *here to invade us.* I'm determined to show him I'm here to be a part of local life, not on the outside looking in.

'I hope you will be very happy.' He raises a hand, and I watch the truck drive away.

I have a feeling that, when the pain stops, I'm going to be just that, I think as I hold the book and the dressing-gown. I look out over the view, trying to imagine it covered with lavender. A happy, healing place indeed. I breathe in the lavender scent and smile.

SEVEN

The following morning I'm up early. After cleaning the house from top to bottom last night, getting rid of the layer of dust the mistral left, I'd made up my bed, just as I do now, with the floral eiderdown I bought from Fabien. I place the dried lavender on the pillow: last night, it gave me the gentlest of dreams. The birds are singing. The cockerel in the distance and the donkey, a little closer, are heralding another new day.

I get dressed and go downstairs to the kitchen, enjoying the feel of the cold tiles under my bare feet. I'm wearing the wrap-around dress I bought at the *brocante* and it feels so different from anything I've worn before. I run my hands over the soft fabric and like the way it makes me feel. I take a deep breath. Right now, I have to think about what I'm going to do with my life. How I'm going to make a living, now that I'm here to stay. The old recipe book is on the table. I find comfort in laying my hand on it, touched, too, by Fabien's kindness. It's been a long time since anyone did something as thoughtful for me. I open the first page. '*Tuiles de lavande*,' I read, running my finger under the words and saying them aloud. Biscuits with lavender. Perfect! I'm going to make a recipe from the book each day. I'll show Fabien how grateful I am for his gift and kindness, that I intend to embrace all things French and lavender. I'll make the biscuits and take them to Fabien as a thank-you present for the book and dressing-gown. My day has a purpose already. It's Monday, market day! Maybe Fabien will know of any jobs going. In fact, he's sure to.

I pick up my basket, slip on my shoes. 'Be good, Ralph!' I say and, putting the book on a shelf so he can't damage it, I leave the house, closing the front door behind me, then walk down the drive to go shopping for the ingredients. The smell of pine is in the air as I stroll into town along the grassy riverbank, past the beautiful blue settee under the tree by the river.

'*Bonjour*,' I say to the two men playing chess, and to another sitting on the settee. I wonder again what this place is. It's like a film set.

'*Bonjour, Madame*,' they reply as I pass, barely looking up. I feel a strange sense of melancholy: perhaps I should ask someone about this place. I'll ask Carine. Maybe we can have that coffee today.

What was the word for 'flour' again? I check Google Translate and run the word, '*farine*', over and over in my head.

At the end of the path I walk down the lane, past olive trees and tall cypresses. Small brown birds flit among them. I can hear voices from open windows, couples in loud discussion, families. An old woman sits outside her front door dressed in an overall, her stockings wrinkling round her ankles, preparing green beans, and a child rides around on a bike. They all greet me with a nod and I head for the market and the shops.

'*Farine*', I remember, and reach for a bag. Now, what sort of sugar? I look at the row in front of me. I don't know any of the brands. Well, perhaps sugar is just sugar. I take the pack with flowers on it. I decide to buy the butter from the cheese stall I passed outside, with what looked like a homemade slab behind the glass.

With my bags full, I walk past the estate agent's and see Carine. She waves, and I can't wave back as my hands are full, but I smile. She comes to the glass door and opens it.

'Del,' she says, and kisses me three times.

'I'm so sorry about yesterday,' I say. 'I hope I didn't make things too difficult for you. Especially with you coming out on a Sunday to show them around.'

'Not at all! It's not a problem. In fact, it has made the job easier. The couple are now so desperate to buy they will take the next house I show them!' She winks at me and I laugh. 'They look heavy,' she says, gesturing at my bags. 'Do you have time for coffee?'

I should get back. I don't want to leave Ralph on his

own for too long, but on the other hand a friendly face and a coffee would be lovely.

Carine locks the shop, having put a sign in the window to say she'll be back in half an hour, and leads me through a stone arch and along a cobbled street to a small café hidden among the shops selling 'Provence' products and a smart guesthouse with lavender lollipops at either side of the light grey front door.

The café has a small covered terrace outside, with a couple of tables and a wisteria, heavy with blooms, trained up along the wall. Inside it's dark, with just a few tables beneath red-and-white-checked cloths, glasses and paper napkins, all ready for lunch. I've never been here before. Ollie preferred the bigger, smarter brasseries and bistros on the main road.

'*Bonjour*, Henri,' says Carine, poking her head into the little restaurant.

'Ah, Carine!' He's an attractive man, silver hair tied back in a ponytail, which suits him. He's in chef's whites and wipes his hands on a tea towel hanging from the apron tied around his waist. He's not fat but is clearly a man who enjoys his food. I'd call it comfortable. He kisses Carine warmly, then looks at me.

'*Mon amie*, Del.' Carine introduces me and tells him I've just moved to the area, into Le Petit Mas de la Lavande.

'*Ah, oui?* It's a beautiful house. I heard some English people had bought it,' he says, in French.

'That's me,' I say quickly. 'But just me.' I make my situation clear.

'Ah,' he says, and waves us to a table. 'Welcome,' he says, and pulls out a chair. I'm grateful he doesn't ask any questions. 'Lunch?' he says to Carine and then to me. 'I have lamb today.' He points to a small chalkboard with today's *plat du jour* on it. 'Or coffee? Maybe an aperitif.'

'Just coffee, please,' I say.

'Sure?' Carine says. 'Henri's *plats du jour* are always delicious.'

'*Merci*.' He nods, his hands behind his back.

'I have cooking to do myself,' I say.

'You are a chef?' he asks.

'No. I used to enjoy cooking. I'm hoping I might again.'

'*Bon*,' Henri says. 'It's an important part of everyday life here in France. Perhaps you will come and try my food another day.'

'I'd love to.' I mean it. 'But right now, coffee would be lovely.'

'Of course.' He goes into the kitchen and soon brings out two coffees with minute croissants on side plates. 'Enjoy,' he says, and retreats inside.

'Henri is always more generous than is good for him,' Carine remarks.

'This place is great. I'm seeing so much more of Ville de Violet than I have in the past six weeks.'

'Well, you live here now. You are not a visitor!' She raises her cup to me.

'Carine, by the river, there's a clearing. It looks like an art project, a blue settee . . .'

Carine laughs. 'It's not an art project.' She dabs her mouth with a paper napkin. 'It's for 'omeless persons.'

My eyebrows shoot up.

'Yes, of course! People give furniture for them to sit on.'

Only in France, I think. A beautiful piece of furniture for people to sit on with some dignity.

Suddenly I see three women I recognize walking towards me down the shaded lane. They are carrying baskets and wearing sunglasses. They are part of the expat community Ollie was so keen for us to join. Will I have to explain my situation? Am I ready to do that? My contentment is replaced with anxiety. I hope they'll just nod and keep walking.

They stop. 'Del? We heard your house had been taken off the market.' Cora, the middle one, pushes her sunglasses up on to her head.

'Um, yes,' I say, not wanting to expand.

'Does that mean Ollie will be available for quiz nights after all?' She beams.

I swallow. 'No, it's just me staying.'

'I can see that must be difficult for you. I can only imagine how it must feel if your partner leaves you. But you seem to be bearing up.' She looks between me and Carine.

I open my mouth to say that I left Ollie, not the other way round, but close it again.

'Well, let's hope you can join us in the pub one night. We'll have a girls' night. Prosecco! Or a couple of gins. You know where we are. We have to stick together and support each other.'

By 'we', I'm assuming she means the British. I look at Carine, who says nothing, staring at the woman from behind her sunglasses.

'And how are you going to make a living?' Cora asks.

'I'm—'

Just at that moment there's a shout and I'm grateful for the distraction. I look to where it came from, as do the three British women and Carine. A young man in a hoodie dodges in and out of the sauntering shoppers, clearly having helped himself to something from the display of bright red strawberries, and disappears. The stallholder throws up his hands, then returns to serving his line of customers, seemingly letting the incident pass.

A man in a suit stops and speaks to him, one hand in his pocket. They shrug and share a good-natured exchange. It's the mayor, I realize. He pulls out a note from his wallet and takes a punnet of strawberries, refusing the change, and the moment has passed. The market crowd goes about its business. Cora, though, is tutting and her friends shake their heads.

The mayor is coming towards us, making for the other part of the market close to the Office du Tourisme. His pace slows. His smile drops, as do his shoulders. He stops in front of the three women. '*Bonjour, Mesdames*,' he says, and greets each one politely.

Then Carine introduces me, and he welcomes me as if I've just arrived. Strangely, that's how it feels. He doesn't ask any questions when Carine explains I've bought Le Petit Mas and am living there on my own. No mention of my husband, my past, just the here and now. It feels as if a weight has been lifted off my shoulders.

'*Monsieur le maire*, you really must do something about that.' Cora points a manicured finger at the sun-drenched square. 'You can't allow that kind of theft to go on without doing something about it.'

The other women all agree. They may have a point, I think. The town feels so safe. It was a surprise to me to see that happen.

'In no time we'll be the crime capital of the south!'

The mayor raises an eyebrow. 'Sometimes,' he says, 'it is better to live and let live. Enjoy the weather, ladies. All is fine here in Ville de Violet. Enjoy what you have. Others are not as fortunate.' He bids everyone good day and sidesteps the women.

'Honestly, you wouldn't get away with it back in the UK,' Cora says. And she's probably right.

'Something has to be done about those people,' she says, then warns me, 'Mind yourself on that riverbank path. You want to stay away from there – anything could happen. The sooner that lot get moved on the better.' She looks at Carine, then at Henri, who is standing in the doorway, neither saying a word. No one seems to be agreeing with her, apart from her friends. Then she turns back to me. 'Let me know if you fancy lunch, or meeting up in the pub,' she says. 'We're here for you, for each other.' She smiles and they leave.

We watch them go.

Henri shakes his head. I wonder if Cora or the shoplifter has worried him.

We finish our coffee and Carine pays.

We begin to walk away. 'So, you are at the start of your new life,' she says, 'here in Ville de Violet.' She links arms with me. 'Let me know if I can help.'

'Actually, Carine, there is something. I need to find work, a job. Do you know of anything?'

'Not at the moment, but I'll keep my ear to the ground. You could always turn your house into a *chambre d'hôte*,' she says. 'Have people pay to stay in a Provençal house, *vraiment charmant*. I'm asked about places to stay all the time. I could send customers looking to live in the area to stay with you, give them a taste of France before they buy.'

We walk slowly back to her shop where a couple are studying the window display. They're clearly British.

'People still want to come to Provence,' she says. 'And who wouldn't? There's sun, wine, herbs, lavender . . .' We laugh.

'I'll think about it,' I say. As we part, I know I've made a good friend in the town already.

I walk back along the riverbank, taking my time, carrying my bags. There are more people under the tree now. A group of younger people, with dogs off leads sniffing around. Some have dreadlocks, wear army surplus clothes, and a few are drinking from cans. Almost all acknowledge me.

I wonder if this was what Cora was worried about when she was telling the mayor that something had to be done. I walk on, catching a whiff of lavender from a garden.

A *chambre d'hôte*, Le Petit Mas de la Lavande? It's a shame there's no lavender now, and that I haven't enough money to get a B-and-B up and running. I'd need to paint and furnish the place, tidy up the shutters and get all the right paperwork. I need to work to earn money straight away, but as I walk home, the idea follows me, and won't leave me alone. If only I could . . . Could I? I stare at the house from the drive, imagining how it could be. I have plenty of room, but no furniture. And, sadly, with no income, and the mortgage repayments, I know it can't happen yet. It may not be a big mortgage, but I have to find that money to stay. Otherwise I'll have to put the house back on the market. There must be a way to make it happen.

EIGHT

I'm the owner of an old Provençal farmhouse, with no money and no way of earning any. To stop myself slipping back into despair at the reality of my situation I throw myself into baking the tuiles. I put the old recipe book on the clean, empty work surface and open it to the first page. 'Okay,' I say to myself. 'Let's try this. If I'm going to live here, I need to do everything in French, including reading a recipe.' I put on the reading glasses that are still relatively new to me, and attempt to interpret the instructions for the *recette*. I run my finger under the words and every now and again reach for Google Translate on my phone.

I turn on the oven. I've hardly used it in the weeks we've been here. Bread, tomatoes and cheese seem to have been our staple diet, when we weren't eating out, Ollie complaining about the prices. We could have eaten in far cheaper places than the brasserie in the middle of town that charged a supplement for its location.

In the box of utensils, for which Fabien charged me next to nothing, I find a chipped old mixing bowl and an electric whisk. I plug it in and switch it on. It works! I start to cream together the butter, sugar and vanilla extract. Then I separate the eggs. The yolks are as orange as the brilliant sun and I whisk each one into the butter mixture. I add the egg whites and when they're incorporated I turn back to the book. I'm pretty sure it's telling me to fold in the flour. If I do a recipe a day, my French is bound to come on. I add the flour – and now for the lavender.

As I focus on what I'm doing I'm thinking less about Ollie and our life together. The memories that have kept me awake at night are of the good times, before we drifted apart. I'm not missing my mum so much as realizing that cooking makes me feel close to her. I can feel her with me, in the kitchen.

I step outside into the sunshine and on to the terrace overlooking the field and pick a few sprigs of lavender. I have no idea how much I'm supposed to use or whether I can use it fresh – but nothing ventured, nothing gained. I go back to the kitchen and run my fingers down the lavender stems and the little flowers fall off. I scoop them up and sprinkle them into the dough, much as I would if I was using rosemary. I'm cautious with the lavender. I have no idea how it will taste.

I roll out the dough with a jam jar full of baking beans that was in the box of utensils and other kitchen bits and pieces, then reach for one of the cups I bought and use it to cut out neat circles. When I try to lift them off the work surface they stick, and I have to start again. *Phfffff!* This time I roll it on the grease-proof paper I bought to line pans. Having cut out the circles, I lift the paper straight on to a baking sheet. Da-nah!

I turn to the rumbling oven and open the stiff door. Inside, it's spotless from when I blitzed the house before we were due to move out just three days ago. It seems a lifetime ago. I slide the baking tray into the oven. Dust off my hands. Put a timer on my phone, then step back on to the terrace and look out over the valley.

I need to work, but what can I do? I'd love to ask around for shop work. But my French isn't good enough. How can I work with the public when I'm still trying to string basic sentences together? Back home I loved my job in the department store. I joined as holiday relief, and stayed. My two best friends moved on. Rhi left to train as a hairdresser so she could set up in business on her own after her husband left her with two young children, and Lou struggled to work again after she lost her husband to a heart attack. We've stayed close, meeting up when we can.

I pick a few more sprigs of lavender from the hedge outside the back door, hold it to my nose and inhale.

It fills my senses. I can smell the tuiles cooking, and imagine Fabien's face when I hand them to him.

Ralph bounds around chasing the little white butterflies that flutter away, leaving him mystified. He turns his attention to the bees buzzing around the lavender, interested but hesitant, eventually backing off and going to search for more butterflies. What would it have been like for Ralph to go to an apartment after this place? It would have been kinder to find him a new home, somewhere like this. A small lump rises in my throat.

I check my timer. All good. Ralph is still being given the run-around by dancing butterflies. In the distance I can see a purple field of lavender. What a sight the deep purple must have been when it grew here at Le Petit Mas. And the smell must have been amazing! Had this still been a lavender farm I could have grown and distilled it, made oil and soap, perfume eventually, then sold it, using my skills from my job in the department store, but one small hedge isn't enough.

I turn to the kitchen, and smell it before I see it. I run to the oven and fling open the door. The smoke makes me cough. Ruined. I could cry! The tuiles are burned in one corner of the baking sheet and over-cooked in another. I toss the tin on to the work surface with a clatter. I look at the flour, the butter and the few eggs I have left. I take a deep breath, the scent of the lavender I picked earlier cleansing the smell of my disaster.

Ralph is standing in the kitchen. 'There's only one thing I can do, boy!' He pants at me. 'Start again!' This time I'd better get it right or my mission to cook my way through the book will be over before it's begun. I have to get it right . . .

By the time I pull the third attempt, perfect golden tuiles this time, from the oven, made with the last of my ingredients, I haven't taken my eye off them for a second. I'm hot and tired. But I've made biscuits with lavender. Tuiles! I lift one from the baking sheet and snap it in half. And then I can smell the lavender. I bite into it. It melts in my mouth and the lavender is floral, subtle. But the little I used was just right. I'm quite proud of them – no, I'm really proud.

I put them on a plate, one of the patterned ones I bought from Fabien at the *brocante*. Then I split them between two plates to show off the lovely pattern and even put a sprig of lavender across them for decoration. Now I need to deliver them.

NINE

I call Ralph into the shade of the kitchen and close the doors, telling him to be good. Then, in the afternoon sunshine, the plates in my hands, I walk towards the riverbank and the path into town. It's so important that I do this: I need to feel I'm living here, not just existing.

As I walk towards the clearing with the beautiful settee I remember Carine telling me it was a place for the homeless and suddenly understand how lucky I am. I have a roof over my head. The rug can be pulled out from under any of us at any time. I think of Lou and Rhi, having to rebuild their lives when they were left on their own. As for me, well, I've chosen to be here. But I couldn't have stayed with Ollie, not when I was so unhappy.

I hear a commotion at the clearing before I get to it. Two men and a young woman are standing in the river, trousers rolled up to their knees. The dogs, off the lead, are barking, and just for a moment I feel a spike of panic.

A small group on the side of the river is calling to someone and I'm trying to make out what they're saying. Is someone in trouble? Instead of turning back, which might have been advisable, I quicken my pace. I have first-aid training from working at the store: maybe I can help. As I near the group they're lifting something out of the water. My heart lurches. It's the blue settee with the gold legs. It's dripping wet and heavy by the look of it. Between them, they move it out of the river and across the path, where it sits, sodden. Then they help each other on to dry land. There is laughter and the dogs settle as their owners return to them.

I skirt around the settee and the group standing around it. '*Pardon, Madame*,' says a long-haired older man with a beard. And the others join in, making room for me to pass. I thank them and glance at the two plates of biscuits I'm carrying. Far too many for one person. I turn to the older man and offer him the plate. He looks at me, then at the tuiles with the sprig of lavender.

'*Merci*,' he says, and takes one.

'*Non*,' I say. '*Pour tout le monde.*'

He's surprised, and thanks me again. Then he hands the plate around to the small community.

'*Merci*,' he says again, the group echoing him.

*

65

I find Fabien on his knees in the *brocante*, cleaning an old bed frame.

'It's beautiful,' I say. Even the furniture in this place gets a second chance at life.

'It will be,' he says, standing up, and suddenly I'm feeling ridiculous, coming here with a plate of biscuits.

He kisses me on both cheeks, then a third kiss on the first cheek. My stomach flutters, as if the butterflies Ralph was chasing have flown right through me. 'How are you?' he asks, wiping his hands.

'*Très bien*,' I say, and he smiles. '*Et vous?*'

'*Tu*. We are friends, *non?*'

'*Oui*,' I say, suddenly infuriatingly shy. He looks at the plate and I realize I'm going to have to explain myself. 'Um, I made you these.' I hold out the plate, anxious now. I've made biscuits for a Frenchman: he may think they're awful. 'I wanted to thank you for bringing the furniture and the book,' I say quickly. I don't want him to think I make a habit of turning up with baked goods. But I do want to prove to him I'm here to stay, not another blow-in, in today and out tomorrow.

He pushes back the hair from his face. 'It was my pleasure. But so are these.' He takes the plate. 'I will make some coffee,' he says.

I love it here. There are so many things I'd love to buy that would look beautiful in the house.

Outside, in the courtyard, he puts down the biscuits

on a tarnished old wrought-iron table, but no coffee. 'I thought maybe an aperitif instead,' he says, and produces a bottle of rosé wine, the sun shining through it as it lowers in the sky. 'To my new friend from Britain!' he says, and I hope he means it.

'Lovely,' I say, a little confused. On the one hand he's being friendly, but on the other he's highlighting the differences between us.

'Fabien, how does it feel, having people move into the town, buying up the old houses? Do the local people resent it?'

He shrugs, holding two glasses. 'It depends. Some people come here to be part of our community. Others, well, they don't want that. Here we welcome everybody who wants to live as part of our town and community.' He smiles and I smile back, because that's exactly what I want to do.

He puts down two elegant glasses and invites me to sit on a chair that matches the table. 'Op,' he says, raising a finger. He goes back inside for a third glass and puts it on the table. Then he takes a corkscrew from the back pocket of his jeans and pulls the cork, which releases with a pleasurable pop. As he pours the cold pink liquid into the glasses, the glugs seem such a joyous sound. He hands me a glass, then holds out the plate of biscuits to me. I take one, as does he. He raises his glass to me, then takes a bite of the biscuit and a sip of wine. I hold my breath. I liked my lavender tuiles, but that was the first time I'd ever eaten them.

He looks at me, his eyes teasing, then breaks into a smile. I breathe a huge sigh of relief. 'These are really good.' He has another bite. 'You have used just the right amount of lavender. Too much and it overpowers. Lavender was used as a herb, like rosemary, a flavouring in food for a long time, but sadly seems to be dying out. Maybe people used too much and went off it. They see it as a flower nowadays, not as a herb. These are perfect.'

I'm feeling happier than I have in a long time. I'm sitting here in the sunshine, enjoying a glass of rosé, and have taken a tiny step to show I want to be part of this community. I look at Fabien, and feel a tiny fizz of excitement about my new life in France and what the future may hold.

Just then Fabien calls to someone and raises a hand. It's Carine. I wave too. She crosses the road and comes into the courtyard and the shade of the olive tree where we're sitting.

'Well, this looks wonderful,' she says. '*Bonjour*, Del.' She kisses me, then turns to Fabien. '*Bonjour, chéri.*' She kisses his cheeks with her bright red lipstick. He slips his arm around her waist and kisses her back.

'Here, I got a glass ready,' he says as she sits down, and I realize Carine and Fabien must be an item. Which is fine! They're the right age for each other. They make a lovely couple. Of course they do. Someone in their late twenties or even early thirties isn't going to look twice at me, ten years older. I hope she doesn't think

I'm some desperate, newly single, practically middle-aged woman preying on her man. He's handsome, with those amazing green eyes, and he has a way of making you feel good about yourself. He's a lovely man, and Carine is a lucky lady. Thank goodness love and happiness are still out there for some, even if it's not what I want right now. In fact, a man is the very last thing I want in my life. Now I can relax, knowing that Fabien is with Carine and we can be friends.

Carine lights a cigarette and blows the smoke into the sky. Fabien tuts.

'I know, I know,' she says, wafting away the smoke. 'I keep promising him I'll give up!' she tells me. Then, with her free hand, she reaches for a tuile. 'What are these?'

'Oh, just something I made . . . I haven't cooked in years . . .' I hope she won't think I was making a play for her boyfriend with them.

'A thank-you present to me, for a book I gave her and for helping her settle in,' Fabien fills in.

'To prove,' I say boldly, 'that I'm here to live and be part of life here.'

'Of course!' He grins.

'And to say thank you for driving my furniture to the house.' I put the situation on a firm business footing and feel much better.

'Fabien is very kind,' she says, and takes a bite of the biscuit. 'Hmm, these are good,' she says. 'Just the right balance of lavender.' She confirms what Fabien said.

'You should have a stall at the market. Sell lavender bakes, biscuits, *macarons*. They even make nougat with lavender.' Fabien tops up our glasses. 'Use recipes from the book!'

'Yes!' Carine exclaims. 'That's a brilliant idea! Biscuits and sweet treats from Le Petit Mas de la Lavande!'

My heart is pounding with excitement. 'Really? Do you think I could?'

'Of course!' they say.

'Do you have any experience?' Carine asks.

'Well, I used to work in a shop. A big shop.' My confidence is about to leave me. I may know about shops, but a market stall, selling bakes I've made? 'I'm not sure . . .' I'm worried that my French isn't good enough – or my baking for that matter.

Carine claps her hands gleefully. 'I will speak to *Monsieur le maire* for you. His office will deal with everything. I will tell him you are a friend of mine! It won't be a problem. I will organize a stall for you for next Monday,' she says. 'It is sorted!'

Fabien looks at Carine with a raised eyebrow. I'm not sure what his expression means.

'But . . . why would you do that for me?' She barely knows me.

She seems to understand. 'I like you. I like your . . .' she searches for the word '. . . your bravery. You are making a life for yourself. Everyone needs a helping hand. I think you will take it,' she says. 'Not everyone wants to come here and make a life. They want a life without change.' I wonder if she's referring to the people she showed around Le Petit Mas. 'I see it all the time. And when it's not how they want it, they leave. You want to stay,' she blows smoke into the air, 'and I'm happy to help.'

'And I will find you a stall,' says Fabien.

Carine and Fabien are looking at me. I'm not sure if it's the wine, or the sunshine, or just that I have no other ideas as to how I'm going to make a living. Or maybe I feel I still have something to prove to Fabien that makes me say, 'In that case, I'd love to! If you think I can.'

'I think you can,' says Fabien. I feel he's challenging me, and I'm determined to show him I can do it. It will bring me in a bit of cash each week to live on and I can use the rest of the lawnmower money for the first mortgage repayment next month. In the meantime, I'll work out how to turn my house into a *chambre d'hôte*.

'The place by the river for the homeless people . . .' I say.

'The art installation?' Carine laughs, then explains to Fabien that that was what I'd thought it was.

'What about it?' Fabien takes another tuile.

'Is there ever any trouble there?' I ask carefully.

Fabien shakes his head. 'Only the trouble others make for those who live there.'

'How do you mean?'

'Some people don't want them there. But they do no

71

harm to anyone. They don't have a place to call their own, and they need somewhere to rest and sit. It's a human right.'

'The blue settee had been pushed into the river this afternoon when I walked past. They were fishing it out.'

'The settee? Tsk!' He shakes his head. 'I will find a replacement.'

'You gave them the settee?'

He nods. 'I find pieces and take them over. It's a small help. But others don't like it and try to put a stop to it.'

'It is a small gesture to help keep everyone in our town happy. We all live together happily . . . well, most of us,' says Carine.

'I'll find something and take it over to the river in a bit. The blue one will take ages to dry.'

'Who would have done that?' I ask.

Fabien shrugs. 'People who don't want homelessness on their doorstep. People who think life here in Provence is . . . photo-perfect.'

'Picture-perfect?'

'Yes!' He smiles. 'It may be beautiful here, but life is just like it is anywhere else. You can't run from the problems. They are all around.'

'Everywhere,' I gently correct him.

'*Exactement!*' he says.

After I've said goodbye to Carine and Fabien, I stroll back towards the slowly setting orange sun and the riverbank. The blue settee is there, but no one is around. There on the verge is my plate, clean, washed in the river, and a note on a roughly torn piece of paper, held down by a stone: *Merci*.

I pick up the plate and head for my home, where I belong. Now all I have to do is bake the tuiles again for my stall next Monday. I'm in business! How hard can it be? I used to run a department in a big shop. Selling my own bakes is a long way from where I used to be. Is any French person going to buy lavender biscuits from an Englishwoman?

TEN

I spend the next week trying to decipher the recipes in the book and testing them, a new one every day. Each morning I get up and turn the next page in the book, as if I'm opening a window in an advent calendar. It's the reason I need to get out of bed, and with every recipe I feel as if Mum is in the kitchen with me.

On Tuesday I make shortbread. It's crumbly and buttery, just as it should be, and I think I've conquered the oven. On Wednesday, I attempt *macarons*, which come out of the oven a bit wonky. Thursday is a chocolate gateau with lavender, and on Friday, I make apricot jam, with apricots from the greengrocer in town and lavender from the hedge in the garden, and use some to fill a sponge cake. Each day I walk down the river path with my bake and deliver it to Fabien at the *brocante*, where Carine joins us for coffee. We all agree the *macarons* need more practice. The chocolate gateau is delicious, rich, moist and floral, but too crisp on one edge: I may need to turn the next around during cooking. The brilliant orange jam could be sold in jars to display its bright colour, like the sun, with the flecks of lavender . . . Provence in a jar.

'It reminds me of my *grand-mère*,' says Fabien.

'She was orange?' Carine says, and we both laugh. Her English is much better than Fabien's.

He looks momentarily confused, then shakes his head. 'No! In the garden. The apricot trees. My brothers and I would play there. Pick apricots. She made jam with lavender, just like this. We had it on bread, with thick butter, in the mornings, with *chocolat chaud* from big bowls.' His eyes seem to mist.

'I remember that too!' says Carine. 'I was in the house next door. I loved stealing the apricots from the trees.'

Then Fabien says, 'She's dead now, of course.'

'Oh, I'm sorry,' I say.

'The house was sold to a British family, for holidays. A Provençal farmhouse.'

'They cut down the apricot trees for a pool,' says Carine.

'They are practically never there,' Fabien finishes.

I feel sad and want to hug him. 'Are the rest of your family still here?' I ask.

'My parents moved to be closer to my brothers. They live north of here. This is a very expensive place to buy houses and they all have families and need room for them,' he says.

Like they would have in my *mas*, I think. I'm one of the people to blame for French families moving away. I have a big family home with just me in it. I feel a stab of guilt and can see why he would resent people like me living here.

'The estate agents must be very rich,' he says. He's looking at Carine and making a joke. She sticks out her tongue at him.

I can't believe how much I enjoy cooking again. I haven't baked in years. Not since Ollie decided we needed a fitness regime to improve our chances of getting pregnant. 'No takeaways, no alcohol, no cakes' became no carbs, protein shakes and nights at the gym for him. I used to love cooking for him. On the first occasion I made a Portuguese pork and clams dish, followed by pineapple upside-down sponge with custard. He told me there and then he loved me and planned to marry me. I laughed. I laughed a lot in those days, and I loved to make others smile. Mostly that was through cooking. I liked nothing more than having friends round on a Saturday night after work for a pot of chilli and chocolate pudding, or for Sunday lunch, beef with all the trimmings, and Yorkshire puddings that got a gasp when I brought them to the table. One day, I thought, I'd be feeding our own family around the table. But when that didn't happen, the meals around the table stopped. Even eating together became a chore as Ollie would insist on tiny portions, saying he wasn't hungry. It was as if I'd cooked a meal just to annoy him.

Ollie has sent several sharp text messages this week, which I've received intermittently when I've walked to town for provisions. In the last one he said he's given up trying to 'talk sense into me'. I haven't felt so happy or excited in a long time. Or maybe excited and nervous. I have a market stall to prepare for: I'll be back behind a counter, selling to people, where I'm happy. And I'll turn my home into a *chambre d'hôte*, just as soon as I can afford paint and furniture. I have a plan. I'm just not sure it's going to work. But it has to. I have to make a living. If I can't, my new life will be over when it's barely begun. Tomorrow, market day, I'll find out.

ELEVEN

I breathe in deeply as the early-morning mist rolls around the valley and up the hill towards the house. I'm taking a moment to settle my nerves. It's barely light. I have been up baking from, well, the middle of the night. I have packed all the biscuits and shortbread into boxes Fabien got for me from the greengrocer on the main street, and I make a note to shop there by way of saying thank you and to take her some apricot jam. And I think of Fabien's grandmother, with a sunny orange face and her apricot trees.

I finish my coffee and look out on the mist again, rolling up the valley, burning off the morning dew, promising a glorious day, and try to calm myself. I have to make this work. It's my only chance of earning some money and staying on here.

I walk over to the lavender hedge. There is a smell in the air, the same smell I noticed on the morning after the mistral, when I hadn't returned to the UK and had decided instead to stay. It is the scent of a new dawn and a new day. The cobwebs on the lavender are covered with dew, which sparkles like diamonds. I pick some of the lavender and hold it to my nose. It seems to calm me. What's the worst that can happen? I ask myself. That I don't sell anything. Panic grips me again.

As if on cue, I hear a friendly toot and the crunch of tyres on the stony ground at the front of the house. My stomach flick-flacks. This is it! I'm going to make it work. I want to be a part of this community, at the heart of it, and I want it to be my home.

Ralph practically falls over himself, trying to co-ordinate his legs in his excitement at greeting a visitor. He barks, then catapults to the front of the house, banking round the corner, probably taking out Fabien's legs from under him as he bowls into him with sheer joy.

'Whoa!' I hear Fabien laugh. He could charm anyone with that laugh. If he can get Ralph to do as he's told, I'm sure he has women falling at his feet all the time. But he and Carine are a solid couple.

'Ralph! Ralph!' I call, and follow him to the front of the house. 'Ralph!' The morning peace is shattered.

I round the corner, slow to a standstill and catch my breath. Ralph is sitting obediently, his tongue hanging out, panting, raising his paw to Fabien for him to shake. Fabien, wearing his battered leather jacket and a bandanna around his neck, smells delicious, I realize, as I move closer.

'*Bonjour*, Del. All ready?' He steps away from Ralph and kisses my cheeks, the delicious scent wrapping itself around me, like a hug. Ralph barks at him impatiently, but Fabien ignores him.

'*Bonjour*, Fabien.' I felt his breath on my lips as he kissed me. Dawn is breaking on the skyline and the cockerel down the road crows. Night turns to day in what feels like an instant. As light begins to seep through the trees, there's a spring in my step.

'*Oui!*' I smile.

'Have you slept?'

'Not a wink!' I laugh. 'I'm too excited. And I've been up baking!'

'It smells delicious,' he says, and follows me into the kitchen to pick up the boxes. I lay a tablecloth on top of one. I found it in the bundle I bought from Fabien. A beautiful Provençal print, slightly faded but still full of colour and life.

'I have a table for you in the back of the truck and Carine has organized your pitch with the mayor and his office. It is a little out of the way,' he shrugs, 'but they don't know you yet. You are from out of town. It is a start, though.'

'*Merci*,' I say, as I follow him out to the truck where his little dog is waiting patiently in the cab. Ralph seems to be doing the same beside it, as if he's expecting to come too. 'I'm so lucky to have met you and

Carine,' I say, as we put the boxes into the truck and he climbs in to tie them in securely.

'The feeling is very mutual,' he says, his green eyes twinkling at me. As he pulls the ties tightly into place, a shiver runs up and around me. I rub my arms.

'Do you have everything?' he asks, climbing down.

'Yes. I'll just put Ralph inside.' I call him, but Ralph doesn't move. He just stares at the cab in contained anticipation.

'He can come with you? *Non?*' says Fabien. 'Keep him on a lead.'

'Oh, I don't know . . .' I say. Then I think about the shredded blanket and the upturned water bowl. And now I have furniture in place, maybe it would make more sense to have him where I can keep an eye on him.

'Okay, come on, then, Ralph. But you have to promise to behave!'

'Move over, Mimi,' Ralph tells the Jack Russell, as he gets into the driver's seat.

I open the cab door and Ralph jumps straight in, much to Mimi's chagrin. She resettles herself and stares out of the window, ignoring Ralph. He tries to copy her but can't stop panting, filling the cab with his hot breath. Fabien and I sit at either side of him and laugh. That's certainly put paid to any attraction I might have felt, had I been riding next to Fabien in the truck. He is a friend and the last thing I want is to find him attractive. Thank God for Ralph, I think, as I wind down the window and breathe in the warm, pine-scented Provence air as Fabien sets off down the drive.

It's not even 7 a.m., but the town is alive with chatter and the clatter of stalls being erected, shouts of directions as vans are parked, goods unloaded and displayed. It feels like the opening night of a big musical and we all have our own part to play in it. Fabien talks briefly to the woman from the mayor's office who points to my pitch. It's down the alleyway, between the square and the main road leading to the car park. A bit off the beaten track maybe . . .

Fabien seems to read my mind. 'So it's not the best pitch . . . but it's a start.'

'It's great,' I try to enthuse, but it really is out of the way and I'm terrified that all our efforts will have been for nothing.

'They don't know you. You're from out of town – out of the country! You'll have to work for your custom. If you want it, you'll have to go and get it,' he says. Again, I feel he's challenging me. What he means is, I have to prove to the mayor and the locals that I'm really here to stay.

'But at least it'll be out of the sun.' Fabien smiles one of his killer smiles.

'And right next to Henri's bistro,' I add, thinking how much I'd love a coffee right now. Just then, Henri comes out to greet Fabien and me.

'Welcome! And *bonne chance*!' he says. Ralph is

darting this way and that, taking in all the smells, and cocks his leg on an olive tree in a pot outside the smart *chambre d'hôte* next door. Fabien and Henri laugh. I tie him to the table once Fabien has set it up and thrown the cloth over it.

'Wait!' says Fabien, going back to the truck. 'A chair, for quieter times,' he says. I decide to tie Ralph to that, rather than the table.

'*Merci*, Fabien, for everything. You have been a good friend. You and Carine,' I emphasize.

He smiles. My stomach flick-flacks.

'Perhaps you would like to join me for lunch after the market?' He tilts his head to one side.

Is he asking what I think he is? I bite my lip.

'And Carine?' I ask tentatively. 'You and Carine?'

'Carine is . . . She has an appointment,' he says. A flash of irritation crosses his face.

I'm uncomfortable. I'm not sure how Carine would feel if I was to have lunch with Fabien on my own. I wouldn't have liked Ollie to have lunch on his own with female friends.

'I'm sorry, Fabien. I can't.'

He frowns. 'I thought . . . we could get to know each other . . . understand each other better, *non*? Lunch. It's what we do here in France.'

'Well, I may have only just moved here, and I want to be part of things, but where I come from . . .' I stop and think to myself. 'Where I come from we do not go out with our friends' partners for lunch to "understand each other". 'That was where it went wrong for Ollie. 'I'm really grateful to you and Carine for everything. But I can't meet you for lunch. Perhaps we can meet with Carine, soon.'

He nods slowly, as if not quite understanding. I thank him again. He wishes me luck as he turns to go and open the *brocante*, hands shoved into jeans pockets. He is in a relationship with a friend. It was the right thing to do. And then, as I watch him go, I wonder why I feel so disappointed that I had to say no. Just for a moment I wonder what it would have been like if Ollie had stayed, if we'd tried to be part of the community instead of just hanging out with the expats. Life might have been very different. I feel lonely again. Just like I did when I told Ollie I wasn't going back with him. I take a deep, restorative breath. Right now, I need to be me, on my own.

I start to lay out my tuiles and shortbread with shaking hands. I'm not sure if it's nerves about showing the world my cookery or that Fabien has put his cards on the table and so have I. I lay out some *macarons* too, hiding the wonky ones under the better ones. I drop sprigs of lavender across them, and sprinkle over some of the flowers. Then I put a bunch in a jar on the table. Other stallholders and some shopkeepers are in the main square opening up, or pass me on the way to the car park and wish me a good morning, eyeing me and my products with interest. Will anyone buy anything? Or will they just walk past?

Henri comes out with a coffee for me, and a mini croissant. 'A welcome gift,' he says, refusing any money.

'*Merci*, Henri.' I smile gratefully.

I sip my coffee as the market in the main square begins to fill with people. Even Ralph settles down to watch them passing without expecting to greet everyone.

'You need to let them try your goods,' Henri tells me. 'They need to know the story of the food and where it came from, from the hills around here.' He squeezes my shoulder and returns to the bistro. 'Tell them your story,' he calls back to me, 'why you fell in love with the place. Why this food matters.'

A few people pass my stall on their way between the two market squares – the main square and the car park. They're walking past and looking but no one is stopping to buy. Henri's right, I think. I should know this from working in the department store. You have to draw people in. You have to get them interested in what you're selling. You have to let them try. I put down my coffee and, with shaking hands, break up some shortbread and toss a piece to Ralph for behaving so well. I put the fragments on a plate, then take a huge breath, walk out from behind my stall and offer them to passers-by, hands still shaking. The French-women, smart, with sunglasses on their heads, no doubt on their way to work, raise a hand, decline politely, smile and walk on. It's going to be a complete disaster! But as the morning warms up, the tourists start to trickle by. They're happy to try and, to my relief, I start to sell. The more I tell people about what I'm making, the more interested they become in the lavender. I offer them lavender-infused biscuits and explain where I live, that it used to be the biggest lavender farm of the area. I turn to see Henri watching me with a smile. He was right. They seem to like the story, and the fact that I've left the UK to live on a lavender farm here. The more I tell the story, the more it seems to grow. The tourists reach into their pockets and purses and buy. It's the story of a woman turned lavender cook that they buy as much as the biscuits.

'Well, this looks lovely!' Cora and her friends have appeared and I feel bad that I haven't taken them up on their suggestion of a drink at the 'pub'.

'Hello, Cora,' I say, and she makes a big event of kissing me loudly. The French don't make a sound but Cora does it with a 'mwah' each time, making her stand out from the crowd.

'How very brave of you,' she says. 'I mean, living here is one thing, but trying to get the French to accept us, then beating them at their own game, that's brave!'

'I'm not trying to beat anyone, Cora. I'm just trying to be a part of things.' I smile, unsure of what she means. My confidence dips.

'Well done you. I'd invite you to join us for coffee, but you seem tied up. If you get fed up, you know where to find us.'

'I do. Thank you,' I say, knowing exactly where to find them. They'll be in the 'pub', more British than French now, with seating in the middle of the square under the plane trees by the church. A glorious setting with prices to reflect it. It was Ollie's favourite, too. 'But I think I'll be here until we pack up at midday,' I say.

'Hope you smash it!' she says, and wishes me good luck. *'Au revoir,'* she adds, and walks on without buying anything. Henri is standing in his doorway, wiping his hands on the tea towel tucked into his white apron, which is tied around his gently rounded middle. He smiles, then urges me to get back out there and start selling again. So I do.

The morning passes quietly and I sell about half of my stock, in little clear freezer bags. I pop a sprig of lavender into each one. I plan to get paper bags soon and some stickers made with 'Le Petit Mas de la Lavande' on them to underline that my bakes are from a lavender farm. I'm not making a fortune today, but at least I have some money to live off and next week I'll try to extend my range.

The church clock chimes, signalling midday. The stallholders start to pack up, giving last-minute reductions and making end-of-the-day sales, then head for the café off the car park, which will be full of people greeting each other, shaking hands, kissing, chattering, the smell of cooking, and jugs of wine. Even Henri's little bistro has filled up and he is taking orders and serving customers with his dish of the day. Every now and again he looks over to see how I'm doing. I give him a nod and a smile.

'You're selling?' he asks, as he brings me another coffee. 'Did it go like hot cakes?'

I thank him profusely for the coffee, and when he won't take any money, I offer him a biscuit instead. Suddenly I'm nervous again. What was I thinking, offering a French chef one of my home-baked biscuits? The tray I'm holding wobbles as my hands shake. From the main square I hear the shouts of stallholders as they manoeuvre their vans.

With one hand, Henri pushes back his silver-grey hair, which has come loose from its ponytail, and lifts the biscuit to his nose with the other. He smells it. I watch his face. The little silver beard beneath his lower lip twitches. Then he breaks it in two and nods, clearly impressed. Now all he has to do is taste it. I watch as he lifts one half of the biscuit towards his mouth. I hope I'm not making a complete fool of myself here. Maybe I am. Maybe he's laughing at me. 'Brave', Cora had said. Did she really mean 'stupid'? Maybe she was right. Henri opens his mouth, and I have an overwhelming urge to grab the biscuit from him and say, 'Don't bother,' but I watch and cringe.

At a shout from behind me, then another and a bark, I swing round. Henri spins round to look in the direction of a commotion.

TWELVE

A boy in a hoodie has grabbed a handful of biscuits from my stall while my back was turned. He dodges nimbly in and out of the people there. Someone is shouting, 'Stop him!'

'Hey!' I yell. Ralph jumps up, thrilled with the new game, and leaps after the boy. The chair he's tied to catches around the leg of the table, then table and chair shift across the cobbled street as Ralph chases his new playmate. *Macarons* fly from the table, like marbles bouncing over the cobbles, rolling under people's feet. Ralph leaps for the lad, who jumps, dropping something from his pocket, then swiftly sidesteps my dog and is gone through the square and into the shadows of the dark little streets beyond.

A leg of the table is broken, the *macarons* strewn everywhere. Ralph is panting and smiling. Cora and her two friends, no doubt on their way back from coffee, are aghast.

'Terrible! Someone needs to do something about that,' says Cora. 'It's affecting the whole town. Are you okay?' she asks.

I put my hand to the money belt Fabien lent me before he left me this morning. The money I made is still safe. I peer at the debris on the ground. I still have a box of shortbread in my hand. It's just the *macarons* that bit the dust and Ralph is busy hoovering them up. A passing chihuahua attempts to join in but is persuaded away by its owner tutting. I nod to her and smile.

'I saw exactly where he went. Got a look at his face too!' says Cora, pointing a painted nail. 'I'll watch the dog while you go after him!' She tries to grab Ralph's lead, still attached to the chair and the broken table leg, then reels backwards when Ralph leaps up in excitement.

There's a hand on my shoulder. I turn to see Henri beside me.

'Maybe we should just pack these things now,' he says calmly, seeing me caught between giving chase at Cora's command and common sense. 'It's not worth getting too stressed about,' he says. 'It's the end of market.'

'Not worth getting stressed about? It's the thin end of the wedge! No wonder we have problems round here with that attitude.' Cora marches off, skidding on a *macaron*. Her friends follow her, frowning in Henri's direction.

'Come,' Henri says, leading me back to his bistro. 'Let me help you clear up.'

'Shouldn't I tell someone what just happened?' I ask, thinking maybe I should at least report it to the woman from the mayor's office.

'Sometimes people do things because they have to. They don't mean to hurt anyone. That young person didn't mean any harm,' he says, with real kindness. 'Here, let me give you lunch by way of making it up to you.' He holds up a hand at my hesitation. 'I insist,' he says, and I can't help but smile at his kind offer.

I fold the tablecloth and stack the table and chair ready to go back to Fabien. I tie Ralph to another chair, this time outside Henri's bistro, and give him a bone Henri has found for him to chew. Then, I pick up all the runaway *macarons* from the doorways of the shops opposite and sweep up those crushed underfoot with a broom borrowed from Henri. As I sweep, I spot something out of the corner of my eye. It must be what fell out of the shoplifter's pocket, I think, as I reach down and pick it up. I stare at it and shove it into my own pocket. I have no idea what to do with it, but it must mean something to someone.

THIRTEEN

I sit outside Henri's, at a table for two, next to the wooden railing with rectangular window boxes along the edge, filled with red geraniums, that denotes his terrace. As lovely as it looks, I'm feeling a little uncomfortable. This is a first for me. I have never eaten in a restaurant on my own before. I look around. Plenty of others are alone. Men and women. Not on their phones, they're focusing on their food and taking in the passing world in front of them. I sit back and try to relax, letting the sun massage my face. Henri puts a small jug of rosé in front of me, then pours me a glass and tells me, 'Enjoy!'

'Are you going to join me?' I ask, then realize I may be giving out the wrong signals.

He shakes his head and I feel a little relieved. 'I still have a few customers to see to. Have an aperitif.' He puts down a small plate of thinly sliced toast with terrine spread on the top and a sliced cornichon to the side. 'I will bring you your lunch in a moment.'

I look down at Ralph and do exactly as I'm told. I attempt to enjoy it. But I can't stop thinking about the young lad who stole from my stall. It didn't seem like a prank or a dare. There were no other youngsters around. Why was Cora so wound up? And who owns the thing he dropped? The questions scratch at my brain.

I finish the morsels of toast and my first glass of wine without really noticing. Henri arrives and breaks into my thoughts. *'Boeuf bourguignon,'* he says, and puts down a round white bowl, with a basket of sliced bread. Soft flaking beef, orange carrots, a deep rich brown gravy and herbs that remind me of my walk into town, *herbes de Provence*. My mouth waters. Then he pours me another glass of wine and I feel quite light-headed, as if my worries are drifting away. I may not have made a fortune today, but enough to pay Fabien back a little of what I owe him on account. And, once again, I feel honoured that he's put his trust in me. I have been welcomed far enough into the community to be running a tab. He trusts me enough to believe that I can get this business up and running. I have somewhere to live and plans for the future. That can't be a bad place to be. The sun, the food and, of course, the second glass of wine have lifted my spirits. I wonder what my friends would say if they could see me now, having lunch on my own, planning the next phase of my life. I wonder what Mum would have said.

She loved Ollie. He and I first met when he came into my department store one Christmas Eve, looking for a very late Christmas present for his girlfriend. He bought her eau de parfum, which I wrapped, then I wished him a merry Christmas. He told me he liked my smile, that I made him laugh, and he hoped my boyfriend knew what a lucky chap he was. I told him I'd been single for three months and was spending Christmas with my friends, Lou and Rhi. A week later, Christmas over, Ollie came back into the shop to tell me he was now single. His girlfriend had not appreciated the last-minute expensive perfume gift, especially as she'd sent him precise details of the shoes and handbag she wanted, and hinted that she'd been expecting a diamond ring and to announce their engagement. Instead she had announced the end of their relationship. He joked that he'd like a refund on the perfume, and asked if he could take me to dinner. I was twenty-nine, heading towards the big three-oh. Everything about Ollie just seemed right. It was like he'd been sent to me by Cupid. Here is Mr Right: ticks every box! We dated. Everyone thought we were the ideal couple. Mum was delighted. He seemed to fit right into her idea of the perfect husband for me, so that I would not make the mistakes she had made. I was never a mistake, she hastened to add. She always let me know that I was the best thing that had happened in her life, and I was determined to make her proud of me, to become a career woman, a family woman, everything that could make her proud. Not that she ever asked for those things. But the day I was promoted to department manager she was proud, as she was when Ollie and I stood at the altar, making our vows. Now, that seems so wrong.

My phone buzzes into life. It's Rhi, asking what's going on. She's seen Ollie. Am I back? I feel guilty that I haven't told her and Lou. But I'm not ready to explain that Ollie and I have come to the end of the road and I'm attempting to set up on my own. Then I do something else I've never done before. I lift my phone and take a photo of myself in the sunshine. I'll send it to Rhi and Lou, telling them I'm taking a little break and will be in touch soon. But I'm fine! And send the picture.

I put away my phone and dive back into the *boeuf bourguignon*, smelling of the herbs that fill the hillsides around here. There is something so comforting about it, as if Mum had served it to me, made with love. We didn't have much money when I was growing up, but Mum always cooked for the two of us, and nothing was ever wasted. She could make a chicken last a week. Although I tell myself I won't, I wipe up every bit of the juice with the bread. I can't think when I last enjoyed a meal out so much. I don't have to worry about Ollie and his frustration, our dwindling finances, or watch his fingers twitch, desperate to get back on his phone as soon as the meal has ended.

Henri is taking payments and, as he passes my table,

he tips the last of the wine in the little jug into my glass. I almost protest but then think, Why not?

'Take your time,' he says. 'Now, for dessert.' He pulls a face. 'I'm afraid I only have ice lollies left. Actually, it's all I had . . . *vanille, fraise, chocolat.*' He goes to the chest freezer and pulls out ice lollies on sticks.

'I couldn't eat another thing, but *merci.*'

He puts the lollies away and shuts the door. Then he reappears outside. '*Café,*' he says. He puts down a cup and saucer in front of me and another next to it. 'May I?'

'Of course.' The little restaurant is practically empty now. He can't make much of a living with such a small place. Small but perfect. I think of the bistros on the main road, fancy and expensive, especially the one with the terrace in front of the church that Ollie insisted on frequenting . . . mostly because it had a good Wi-Fi connection.

Henri bends down and rubs Ralph's head affectionately, then sits in the cool of the awning and sips his coffee.

'That was delicious, Henri. Are you sure I can't pay you?' I reach for my bag but he holds up a hand.

'My pleasure,' he says. 'Like I say, it makes up for some of your lost stock.' He nods to the boxes of biscuits.

'I lost more to Ralph's antics than I did to the shoplifter.' He only took a couple of biscuits. Ralph scattered most of the *macarons* over the ground.

'Perhaps I should take the rest to give as dessert to my customers. They're really very good.'

'Really?'

'Yes, of course. I didn't get the chance to tell you when we had the problem here.' He points out into the road. 'But it was very, very tasty.'

'Here. Take them,' I say, handing him the box. 'I can't use them for anything. And it's only me in the house.'

'You live alone?' he asks softly.

I swallow. 'I do now. Just me and Ralph,' I say. Another first! I managed to say it. I live alone. 'I've split from my husband. But it was the right thing for both of us.'

'I split from my wife after the children left home. We had nothing in common. I had work and spent more and more time there. We became strangers. And the children are now adults and live their own lives. I sometimes think they only get in touch when they want something.' He laughs gently, one hand on his stomach. I wonder if that would have happened to me and Ollie if we had had children. When we discovered we couldn't, there was nothing left. I had a dog that I wasn't sure I wanted, and he hatched the idea of France. It had felt like something to put on the Facebook page.

'Here, take the biscuits, Henri,' I say. 'Really. They're yours.'

'I will pay you for them,' he says. I start to argue but

he won't hear of me refusing. Then we eat a plate of tuiles with our coffee.

'These really are good. I cannot bake or make desserts. And I don't have the time or patience to learn. Hence the ice creams. I have ice creams in tubs, but when they're gone, it's lollies.' He takes another bite. 'Do you have other recipes?'

I nod. 'A whole book of lavender recipes Fabien gave to me as a moving-in present. I'm working my way through it.'

'Ah, from the heart of Provence! Then why not bring to me what you make? I will buy them from you. A daily dessert!'

My mouth hangs open. I can continue through the book. Another day, another recipe. 'Really?'

'Of course!' He gives a belly laugh, a big hearty one. 'Desserts were never my thing. Too much sugar isn't good for me.' He pats his stomach. 'I'd be delighted if you made them. And, as I say, I can pay you.'

'That would be wonderful, Henri! You have no idea how much that will help!' I want to throw my arms around him in gratitude. Instead, buoyed by the wine and his offer, I kiss his cheek and thank him again. Life is finally coming together. He laughs again, the sound as warm as the sunshine on my face.

'Ah, Fabien,' says Henri, and my cheeks burn as I see him walking towards the small terrace. As he approaches, he looks at me and then at Henri, raising an eyebrow. With a tiny tilt of the head he seems to be questioning what's going on. I can see how it might look. I open my mouth to explain.

'So, a good lunch?' he asks, looking at our coffee cups.

'Delicious,' I say, not knowing whether to reply in English or French, my tongue tying itself in knots. I wonder if he's annoyed that I turned down lunch with him and now am here, clearly having had lunch with Henri. Would he care?

Before I can explain what's happened, Henri replies, 'Great dessert,' and pats me on the back. I accept his compliment gratefully as it hides my blushes.

'I will take the table and chair back,' says Fabien.

'You can always leave them here, in the restaurant, if need be,' says Henri to me.

Ralph barks from under the table but doesn't move.

'It looks as if you had a good day,' Fabien says.

'Not bad. But Henri here has just made my day better,' I say.

'I'm glad to hear it,' he says softly and, once again, I feel I should explain it's not the kind of offer his tone implied.

'She is going to make my desserts daily.' Henri cuts across me as I gather my thoughts. I nod. 'We're in business!'

Now Fabien smiles too. 'Perfect! Looks like your business is up and running!'

My heart tap, tap, taps and my stomach fizzes. I'm in business!

'Yes,' I say. 'Looks like I'm here to stay.'

Fabien holds my gaze for a second and my stomach fizzes again. 'I'll get the table,' he says, breaking away, and I wonder if Henri noticed.

'There was a problem with one of the legs. Let me help you,' I say.

'No problem, I'll fix it before next week and bring it back to Henri's. Stay. Enjoy your coffee,' he says. 'Enjoy the sunshine . . . and your new life.'

'Are you sure you won't join us, Fabien? A beer, perhaps?' asks Henri, but Fabien declines, picking up the table.

'*À bientôt*,' he calls over his shoulder, and waves.

'*À bientôt*,' I reply, watching him walk away and wishing he'd stayed. But now, I have something else to worry about.

'Henri?'

'*Oui?*' he says, standing and clearing away his coffee cup. 'More coffee?'

'*Non, merci*. Henri, you said you knew the young person who took the biscuits.'

He nods.

'I think I should pay him a visit, return something he dropped.'

Henri looks at me and then puts down the coffee cup. 'Okay, I'll write down the address for you, but, Del . . .'

I take the piece of paper from his order pad on which he has noted the address.

'Not all parts are as . . . relaxed as this bit of the town,' he says. 'Just be aware. On the outskirts, sometimes, it's not always picture-perfect, even in France.'

I take the paper and promise I'll be careful. My heart beats a little faster. But something in me needs to return the boy's property to him and see for myself where he lives. I hurry from the restaurant, across the square, following Henri's instructions, feeling him watch me as I go. I walk down into the dark streets on the other side of town beyond the square, suddenly very pleased to have Ralph by my side.

FOURTEEN

'You're a girl!' I say, standing in the dark room, only a piece of thin material as a curtain covering the door from the hallway where people are coming and going, up and down the stairs, shouting to one another.

'*Putain!*' she swears, clearly taken by surprise.

'I tried to knock. Someone let me in. I asked for Steph.'

There is another piece of fabric over the window, pinned in place to attempt to mute the light, but so thin it's of little use. She is standing over a mattress on the floor, presumably her bed. There is an unpleasant smell about the place, could be the drains, and an atmosphere that matches it.

The whole area couldn't be more different from the one I've just left, tucked away beyond the town, right on the outskirts, over the river. Walls are graffitied, there is shouting and a sense of aggression about it. A small, sad estate of forgotten flats, a far cry from the beautiful buildings in the town and up in the hills where Le Petit Mas is.

The girl eyes Ralph warily, standing with her back and arms across the corner of the room, protecting or hiding something. 'How did you find me?' Her hair is plaited, her hoodie top down now.

'Henri told me where to come.' I look around the little room. The area is squalid, but the room is clean and tidy, if sparse. There's nothing here. The remnants of my biscuits lie on a small table. She follows my gaze.

'I only took a few!' She lifts her chin defensively. 'You can have them back if that's why you're here!' she says, with a thick, gravelly accent.

Distantly, I'm amazed by the fluency of her English. Her honesty catches me off my guard. I'd been ready to give a young boy a talking-to about stealing from people who are trying to make a living.

'It was the end of the market. I just took what was going to be thrown away,' she says.

'Your English is amazing,' I can't help saying.

'I went to school. I took myself when there was no one else to do it.' Again jutting her chin at me.

Ralph barks. She drops her head, looks at him, then back at me. Suddenly I hear a small giggle.

'The dog's friendly,' I say quickly, then look down to her knee, and up again at the girl, who is suddenly unsure, watching my face. 'You have a child,' I say quietly. The little one giggles again, Ralph barks playfully – and everything drops into place. She was taking fruit the other day from the strawberry stall, and now the biscuits, not for her but for the little boy, who is holding a tuile in one hand and pointing at Ralph with the other. She picks him up and holds him to her on her hip. Something in me twists at the sight of him smiling, crumbs around his mouth and over his hands, holding the girl's plait and covering that with crumbs too.

'*Maman*,' he says, and tries to poke the biscuit into her mouth, clearly used to sharing food, but she moves her mouth away.

'*Non, mange!*' she tells him. Eat. She is doing what anyone would, feeding her child first. But how old can she be? Sixteen, seventeen? Certainly no more than eighteen. A child herself.

'Is . . .' I say tentatively, '. . . is he yours?' I smile at him. He points at Ralph, who pants, his tongue hanging out of his grinning mouth. And right now, I think Ralph is the best dog in the world. We may not have got off to a great start, but I couldn't love him more for being Ralph.

'Yes! He's mine,' she snaps back. 'I am a good mother!'

'Yes, yes! I'm sure you are.' Outside the room people are still going up and down the stairs, men's voices shouting, and I wonder how on earth she can live like this. I feel sick, realizing how full of pity I was for myself the night Ollie left. But I have a house and it feels safe. Not like this place. The little boy points to me and smiles.

I have no idea how to talk to children – I'm not used to being around them. I don't have nephews or nieces, and I'd kept my distance from friends who were having babies and then second babies. It was like a world I wasn't a part of. Some tried to include me, asking me to be godmother, but I declined. I always felt on the back foot when I saw them, trying to work out how to speak to the children or hold them. It just made me more awkward. In the end, I turned down the invitations to birthday parties and days out. I felt I was on show, having to play a part. I couldn't have kids so I was labelled the 'fun aunt'. But it wasn't fun: it was strained. And the hole inside my heart got bigger. But I smile back at this little boy and reach out a hand to touch his.

'May I?' I ask the girl, who is scowling at me. She thinks about it, then gives a curt nod. I take his crumby one.

'*Bonjour*,' I say. I waggle his chubby fingers and, again, can't help smiling. 'What's his name?'

'Tomas,' she replies.

'*Bonjour*, Tomas,' I say. 'I think I have something that belongs to you.' I reach into my pocket and pull out the item that's brought me here and hold it up, by the chewed ears. A soft, worn, light blue-and-white toy rabbit.

'*Monsieur Lapin!*' The girl's face softens and she nearly smiles, but not quite. Tomas's face erupts into joy and he kicks his legs happily into his mother's side and reaches for his rabbit.

'You dropped it, when you . . .' I search for the right words. 'When you left the market.'

'When I stole from you. I'm sorry. I just wanted . . . It was for Tomas. There is not much money left after I pay for this place,' she says. I wonder how anyone can charge money for this sweltering hell-hole. 'He was sleeping, and I wanted to find something for him. Sometimes the stallholders are throwing things away. Sometimes . . . I . . . take.' She lifts her chin again. 'I'm not proud of it. I don't take what I think the stallholders will mind losing. And your biscuits looked so good.'

I feel a ridiculous sense of pride.

'And, let's be honest, you had a lot left!'

She's teasing me.

Suddenly I laugh. 'I did!'

'But they tasted really good,' she says. 'Tomas loves them.'

'Well, Tomas, come by next week and I'll give some to you,' I say, holding his little hand, and he points again at Ralph, who gives a little bark of agreement. Tomas giggles into his mother's neck and, once again, the sound echoes round the hole in my heart where I wish my own child had been.

'Is it just you?' I ask, in awe of how she's managing to bring up a child in this place.

She nods. 'Just me and Tomas.' She's letting me know that she and Tomas are just fine.

'Okay,' I say. There's nothing more to be said or done here. I've returned the soft toy to its grateful owner and there is no way I'm going to reprimand her for the few biscuits she took. Next week, I'd love her and Tomas to come by so that I can give him some. I turn to go.

'*Merci*. Thank you,' says the girl, quickly and quietly. 'And, again, I'm sorry I stole from you.'

'I'll see you next week at the market. And you, Tomas,' I say, touching his little hand once more, for the first time in ages not feeling that anyone is judging or pitying me. I turn with Ralph and push back the curtain. An argument is taking place on the floor above. A woman is berating someone loudly. A man is arguing back. Now, two men are arguing with the woman. I shudder. What a place! I can't wait to get back to Le Petit Mas. I hurry towards the door, holding Ralph tightly. As I reach it, the two men are tumbling towards the landing at the top of the stone stairs, obviously exchanging blows. Ralph barks loudly, lurching towards them. This is not Ralph who wants to play but Ralph on the defensive, a Ralph I haven't seen before. The two men are still in dispute at the top of the stairs but turn to stare at me. I hold on to Ralph's lead even tighter, taking hold of his collar too. He growls and I've never heard him like this before, clearly unhappy. The two men are glaring at me and I swallow hard. I reach for the front door, open it, pull Ralph outside and slam it shut behind me.

Then I stand against the wall to the side of it, finally letting myself breathe again. The sooner I get out of here the better. On the waste ground in front of me a group of young boys are playing football. That will be

Tomas in a few years. A couple of bigger lads walk through the middle of them, sending them on their way, and sit on a graffitied wall. If I'm not mistaken they're doing business, exchanging a small package for euro notes. The two older boys shake hands and go in opposite directions.

The front door to the flats opens and one of the men involved in the scuffle emerges. Ralph barks at him loudly. He swears at me, wiping his hand across his mouth, and storms off, shouting at the teenager on the wall as he goes.

I take my opportunity to get out of here, and hopefully not come back. Just like every town, life isn't all roses around the front door, but I'd quite like to get back to the lavender by mine. My house, I think, where I intend to stay. Something about it makes me feel that life is going to be okay. I'm happy there. That house has given me a second chance at life and I'm grateful.

I march determinedly back towards the bridge and the alleyways that led me here. With each step I take, I can hear the arguing on the landing above the little back room where Steph and Tomas are living. I can feel Ralph's nervousness. My steps slow. What am I doing? Ralph is looking at me as if he's asking the same question. I slow to a standstill.

'What am I doing, Ralph?'

'Woof!'

'I have no idea,' I say to myself . . . but I know I have to do something.

FIFTEEN

'Why would you do that?' says the young woman. Tomas is on the floor now, running his hands through Ralph's thick coat, both enjoying it.

'Because . . .' I try to come up with a suitable reply. I think of Carine, a new friend in the town inviting me out for coffee. I think of Fabien putting my furniture together, giving me the book. I think of Le Petit Mas and the second chance it's given me.

'I stole from you!' she persists.

'You said yourself I had a lot left over. It was only going to waste.' I don't tell her that I gave the rest to Henri: lovely, kind Henri who treated me to lunch and put in an order for daily desserts. 'From the heart of Provence,' I hear him say. The three who have helped me get started here.

'Why?' She narrows her eyes. Then we both look at Ralph and Tomas.

'Because everyone deserves a second chance,' I say. I think of the failure I felt at being unable to have children. But it's not failure if we grow and learn along the way and take life's chances, a chance at happiness. I hope I can learn to live with not having children. I hope the pain will start to fade. I hope I can learn to live a life here, happily too. Right now, I just know I can't walk away.

'Come and see what you think. If you don't like it, I'll bring you, Tomas and your belongings back here. I promise.'

She frowns.

'I'm just offering you a chance. I have a house, plenty of room, and I need someone to work with me. Help me develop my . . . business.' I'm thinking on my feet. I'm inviting a young woman and her child into my home, to live with me, I have no idea how long for, but all my instincts tell me I can't walk away from a girl trying to do her best for her baby in a place like this. 'I'm turning my home into a *chambre d'hôte*. You work for me in return for accommodation and food. If and when . . .' am I really saying this? '. . . I get the business going, and if we get on okay, I can begin to pay you too. It's a fresh start for your son.'

'I don't need charity! I'm doing fine!'

'I'm not offering charity. I'm offering you a job and somewhere to live,' I say firmly, sounding much more professional than I feel. I've done one day on a market stall and I'm going to make daily desserts for Henri.

I've barely started and have no idea how I'm going to support another two people. But I have a house, a safe one, which is more than this is. I shudder. The front door slams and the shouting starts upstairs again. We look towards the curtain-for-a-door and the stairwell.

'I'm offering you a job, a place to live, and food,' I repeat.

She stares at me defiantly, wanting to turn down my offer, but eventually she says, 'I will think about it,' as if she has lots of options right now.

'But one thing, Steph—'

'Stephanie. You can call me Stephanie,' she says, rolling out the name with beautiful vowel sounds. 'I prefer Stephanie.'

'Stephanie,' I say. 'Just one thing. We all need a second chance in life but there won't be a third. If you steal from me, you will have to leave. Understood?' I am shaking inside but I can hear my mother's voice speaking kindly but firmly to me as a teenager. The boundaries need to be put in place for this arrangement to work. Mum would probably have done the same as I'm doing now. My friends were always coming to her when they'd fallen out with their parents. She'd put food on the table and make up a bed, let their parents know they were safe and send them home in the morning. This is me, learning from my mum.

There is more shouting outside. This time Tomas cries and Ralph starts barking. There is louder shouting. Tomas cries harder. Stephanie gazes at her son. 'Okay,

I will come and look.' Within minutes their belongings have been shoved into blue carrier-bags that look as if they've done many moves before. Tomas is clutching *Monsieur Lapin* as we pull back the curtain and it falls, listlessly, open.

The man stops shouting mid-flow and turns his attention to Stephanie, clutching Tomas and her blue bags.

'Hey!' he shouts, and talks quickly at her, his arms flying. Clearly he's the landlord, or the tenant who's letting the rooms. He wants to know what she's doing. She can't just run out on the room. She has to pay rent. She stands there and, for a moment, she looks like a young child herself. An older woman, possibly his wife, the one shouting, wearing a faded dirty dressing-gown, follows him down the stairs. My hackles rise.

'Stephanie, keep walking,' I instruct, and point to the door. My heart is banging, but I can't back down now. I can't leave this girl and her little boy here. I just can't. I hear my mother's voice again, calm but firm. Stephanie looks at me for reassurance. 'Keep going,' I say. The man turns to me angrily. Stephanie moves towards the door. The man takes two steps down the concrete stairs after Stephanie, who opens the door wide and walks out. He tries to push past me after her, shouting. But Ralph is having none of it. He launches himself towards the man, barking loudly, and the man retreats back up the stairs, fear in his eyes.

Neither moves. Ralph continues to bark at the man

on the stairs in his stained vest, with his unshaven face and the cigarette hanging from his mouth, the woman behind.

Ralph doesn't let them move.

I glare at the pair. No one moves, until I turn and see that Stephanie is safely outside and walking in the direction of town. I give the man one last scowl, then turn and run out as quickly as I can to catch up to Stephanie. The man and the woman follow, shouting. But neither can run fast and no one else takes any notice as we race across the bridge to the alleyway leading into town. And when we stop running, we pause to catch our breath and stare at each other. Then a laugh of relief escapes us, and Stephanie lets Tomas slide from her hip to the ground, where he pats Ralph's head, and we walk up the pretty path along the river, taking us home. As the sun softens in the sky, I have no idea what is likely to happen in the future, but right now I just want to go home to Le Petit Mas.

SIXTEEN

What have I done? We stand and look at the bare room. What on earth was I thinking? I've invited a complete stranger and her child to stay in a house with no furniture and offered her a job in my barely off-the-ground business. The cold reality of the situation is sinking in.

The walk from town along the riverbank took us about twenty minutes, what with carrying Stephanie's bags, Tomas stopping to examine irises and draping wisteria, chasing butterflies and the gently flowing river without toppling in. We passed the clearing where a few people were gathered, a couple playing chess, and I saw that a new settee had been installed under the wide-reaching arms of the big pine tree. They acknowledged us with 'Bon après-midi.' Stephanie, I noticed, put her head down and speeded up, almost embarrassed, slowing once we'd passed and letting Tomas

114

walk on his own. I let Ralph off the lead too. The two sniffed flowers and chased each other, Ralph always on the side of the water, not letting Tomas near it. And, just for a while, I thought I was doing the right thing.

'*Maman!*' Tomas shouted, pointing at a fast-moving lizard, and I watched Stephanie enjoy his delight as she seemed to relax. We reached the end of the riverbank and headed up the hill to the entrance of Le Petit Mas de la Lavande.

Stephanie looked at the house in what seemed like awe as we walked up the drive, Ralph leading the way. Tomas followed him, tottering, tumbling, giggling, getting up and doing it all again, not letting the bumps in the road put him off the joy to be had in being there.

I led them up the few stone steps to the front of the house, where I'd stood on the day of the mistral and decided not to leave. I pulled out the big key and put it into the lock.

'Wait!' said Stephanie, and I turned back to her.

'I don't understand. Why am I here?' Suddenly she looked like a terrified child again and I wanted to give her a hug, but I knew she'd never allow that.

'You're only here if you want to be, Stephanie. I have the house, the room. I now have work, too. I need help baking and getting this house fixed. In return you and Tomas can live here, for as long as you want, and help me.'

'But I cannot cook!' she said, dismayed.

'You're French – of course you can cook!' I said lightly.

She was suddenly defensive again, shattering our new-found trust. I could have kicked myself. 'We didn't all have the perfect French upbringing, you know! We didn't all go out and buy bread every day, sit around the table with grandparents, learn to cook at our mother's knee!' she snarled angrily. 'You' – and by 'you', I'm presuming she means we Brits – 'you think life over here in France is so perfect, but not for all of us! Some of us had to learn to bring ourselves up. Some of us don't have family homes to go to. Some of us are still fighting to feed ourselves and our loved ones in any way we can.' She stopped, angry tears in her eyes. I thought of the homeless by the river. She was right. I'm the lucky one.

'Don't worry,' I said, trying to soothe her. 'I don't need you to cook, just to help me.'

'If you tell me what to do, I can do it.' She lifted her chin again. 'I work hard!'

'Then we'll be fine. We'll help each other.' I smiled, the storm seeming to have passed. I turned back and opened the big wooden front door to the tiled hall.

Now we're standing in the empty bedroom, with windows looking out over the trees and the field sloping away.

'You said you had room!' says Stephanie, flatly.

'I do!' I stutter. 'I just don't have . . .' How could I

have been so stupid? A spur-of-the-moment decision, thinking I could make a difference, giving her false hope.

'You have room,' she agrees, 'but no furniture. Not even a mattress!' She looks around the big room, taking in the view, imagining, perhaps, what it could have been like. The sun is setting and the sky is turning pink and baby blue. What on earth can I do? I can't let her go back! If the landlord would even have her! She's in an even worse position than she was before. At least there she had a mattress to sleep on.

'I'll sort something,' I say. I wonder if this is how parenting feels: you have to do something, but you've no idea what.

Stephanie gives the room a final look as if glimpsing a life that might have been, then having the door shut in her face.

I brought her here. I'm responsible for this mess. But I remember that room she lived in and know I did the right thing. I just have to think of another right thing.

She turns and walks downstairs to where Tomas is sitting at the little table, with a glass of milk, eating biscuits. Well, he's feeding biscuits to a well-behaved Ralph, delighting in his barking, and rewarding him with more. Stephanie marches over, scoops Tomas up from the chair and puts him on her hip. He begins to cry, reaching for Ralph, who is still sitting obediently, giving the occasional bark, hoping to be rewarded.

'Wait, Stephanie!' I say, as she scoops up her plastic bags with one hand.

'It would seem, *Madame*,' she says pointedly, but I know she's hurt and disappointed, 'that you do not have room for us after all. I cannot ask my son to sleep on the bare floor. We would have been better to stay where we were.' She walks towards the front door. 'I'm sure you thought you were doing a good thing.'

She stops and looks at me. 'Do you have children?'

'No.'

'Well, you can't have mine!' Her words sting me, like a slap in the face.

'I don't want your child. I wanted to help you. Like I say, we all deserve a second chance. You're practically a child yourself,' I say.

'I am a mother. A good one! Better than mine was! I didn't have family to eat with or cook with. I am surviving the only way I know how. But I must put my child first.'

The slap in the face still stings. She's right. I thought I should be helping her and the child. But I have no idea what a child needs. I'm out of my depth. Instead of helping, I've just made things a hundred times worse.

I watch as she walks towards the drive. Where on earth will she go?

'Where will you go?' I call after her.

'Back to the river clearing. I have friends there,' she

says, over her shoulder. 'Everyone will be gathering about now.'

She carries on walking, Tomas reaching out his arms to Ralph.

My eyes fill with tears and I look away, trying to stop them falling. And then I see the solution! Why didn't I think of it before? Why hadn't I remembered it?

'Stephanie, *wait*!'

SEVENTEEN

I run back inside, grab the key from the kitchen drawer and run back out, beaming. Stephanie has stopped and put Tomas down. I don't know if it's because he's heavy or she's prepared to hear what I've got to say or show her. But I'm taking my chance.

'Follow me.' I wave my arm in a big circle and hold up a key with the other.

For a moment she stares at me, but then, making my heart skip, she follows me.

'Okay, it'll need some work,' I'm talking nineteen to the dozen, 'and I'm not even sure we remembered to clear it when we were moving out. Ollie used it as storage space.'

'Ollie?'

'My husband.'

'Your husband?'

'He's gone. Back to the UK. It's just me now.'

'Ah,' she says. 'With your furniture?'

'Yes, with . . . everything.'

'Ah.' Things seem to be making sense to her.

'Here.' I bend down through the pine trees and go into a small clearing. I wait for Stephanie to reach me. She straightens and stands next to me.

'Look, it might not be what you were expecting, but I'm pretty sure it's got everything. As soon as I can get more furniture, you can move into the house, if you want to.'

She says nothing. Is she going to swear, turn and walk away? 'Do you want to see inside?'

Slowly she nods and, if I'm not mistaken, her stare doesn't convey disbelief and horror: it's the look of someone falling in love.

'It's a gypsy caravan,' she says slowly.

'It was here when we bought the house, hidden away. I thought it might be nice for guests. But we were here for such a short time that I didn't get around to doing anything with it. Well, actually, after my first look inside it, I forgot about it. Life's been a bit . . . hectic,' I say. 'But I wish I'd remembered it on my first night here alone. At least there's a bed in it, from what I remember.'

'You stayed here alone, with no furniture, nothing?' she asks.

'Yes.' I stop on the wooden steps I'm climbing. 'I just knew I couldn't go back.'

'Same,' says Stephanie, and I don't know if she's

talking about going back to where she's just come from, or to where she was before she ended up in that awful room.

I don't ask. If she wants to tell me she will. Right now, I have to fulfil my promise and find her somewhere of her own to stay. I push the key into the old padlock and turn it. Then I open the half-door, jump down from the steps and let Stephanie up them.

'There's a lot of stuff inside that Ollie left behind.' His golf clubs, the exercise bike and the small electric lawnmower we had before he upsized to the big sit-on one. 'But there's a bed and a stove, and we can tidy it up.' I look at the peeling lavender woodwork. Stephanie is inside it now. Ralph and Tomas have joined us. Tomas is climbing the wooden steps and sits at the top. A red squirrel darts across the grass to a neighbouring tree, to his excitement.

Stephanie comes out and stands on the platform outside the caravan. I hold my breath. She looks at me.

'It's . . . it's not right, is it?' I stammer. 'It's not suitable for Tomas. I'm sorry. Like I say, I don't have children. I wasn't thinking. I just wanted to do something. That place was so horrid. I'm sorry,' I gabble. 'I'll help you back with your stuff,' I say, and look up at her.

Her face breaks into a huge smile. 'It's perfect! Thank you! Tomas seems to love it! It will be an adventure! He's safe here. We will sleep well.' She gazes at the pine trees and breathes in deeply.

'Right!' I say. 'Let's clear this rubbish out, get it aired and the bed made. Tomorrow we'll start fixing it up.'

'And I can really stay here?'

'For as long as you want,' I confirm. 'Or move into the house when I get some more furniture.' And we laugh.

'I have always dreamed of my own little place for me and Tomas. My own front door. This is perfect. Thank you,' she says, with what I think might be a sparkle of tears in her eyes.

'You're welcome,' I say.

And that evening as the big sky turns from baby pink to red, we clear it out, clean it and make up the bunk bed with the remainder of the bedding I had. Then we eat omelettes cooked outside, over a fire in an old bin lid, and sit by it until the sky is dark and the stars are shining.

Tomas is curled up asleep in one corner of the bed as I wish Stephanie a good night. 'Up early tomorrow. We have desserts to make!' I say, and call Ralph to my side, reluctant to leave his new playmate. I walk back to the house, feeling content. I glance up at the big sky over the empty valley and wonder if Mum is looking down on me. Whether she is or she isn't, I can feel her with me, telling me I did just fine today.

'Thank you, Mum, for everything. For giving me the strength to do this.' I think of Stephanie and Tomas tucked up in bed, safe and sound. I did some good today. I open the front door and wind my way to bed with Ralph by my side. And as I walk up the stairs I remember Fabien's words: 'Enough to be content.'

Fabien! Why do my thoughts always come back to him? Carine has been so kind to me and I hope we will be good friends. So I must stop thinking about Fabien. I can't let thoughts about him get in the way of my friendship with Carine.

EIGHTEEN

The next morning Stephanie is up early with Tomas, appearing from the woodland clearing. Tomas is as pleased to see Ralph as my dog is to see him when I let him out. Stephanie and I stand on the terrace, the early-morning sun reaching through the trees, as dog and boy run about on the dewy grass, its scent fresh and new.

'Where do you want me to start?' says Stephanie. 'Tell me what I should do.'

'Whoa! Let's have some breakfast.' Just as I wonder how long it will take me to walk into town for bread, there is a parp, parp at the end of the drive: the bakery van.

'Tell her to wait! I'll get my purse!' I say to Stephanie. She, Tomas and Ralph run down the stony drive to the road.

When I join them, I'm slightly out of breath.

'*Bonjour*,' says the young woman from behind the counter in the Citroën van. 'I heard there were new people here,' she says, 'so I thought I'd stop by. *Bienvenue*,' she says.

'*Merci*,' I reply.

'The last people who were here were very strange. The owner told me not to come because he didn't eat bread.' She laughs. 'Who moves to France and doesn't eat bread? Bread is our life blood, like wine!'

I'm smiling to myself, the pain of Ollie's and my split easing a little. I wish he could have seen this place as I'm beginning to see it, from the inside out. Maybe that was the problem: we saw each other's worlds so differently.

'Well, we'd like you to stop by every morning,' I say warmly, as warm as the smell of the freshly baked bread. I look at the array of baguettes, the baskets of croissants and *pains au chocolat* and my mouth waters.

We carry the table and chairs from the kitchen out to the terrace where Stephanie and I drink coffee and eat bread and croissants. Tomas has warm milk and a *pain au chocolat*, swinging his legs contentedly. Ralph never leaves his side. After breakfast, we move back into the kitchen and wash our hands. Tomas wants to help us work.

'I have an order to make for Henri at the bistro,' I tell her. 'He wants desserts every day, bakes, like tuiles or shortbread, to go with his ice cream.'

Stephanie looks worried. 'But you know I can't cook. I didn't have that kind of home life growing up.'

'Don't worry.' I pick up the old recipe book, feeling a flicker of excitement just from holding it. I put it in front of Stephanie on the work surface. 'You teach me how to read this book and speak French, and I'll teach you to cook!' A smile creeps across her face. 'Deal?'

'Deal,' she agrees.

'Deal!' repeats Tomas, and we all laugh, Tomas the loudest. I can see happiness returning slowly to Stephanie. This place has a knack of putting people back together. Thank you, Petit Mas, I think, as we flip through the pages of the book.

Tomas starts to drag a chair over towards the work surface. Stephanie stops him.

'No,' she says, putting the chair back.

His face crumples and he starts to cry.

'Oh, it's fine,' I say. I used to stand on a chair beside my mother in the kitchen. He looks at me hopefully, the tears stopping. But maybe it wouldn't be safe to have him there.

'Sorry, it's not my place,' I say. 'I . . .' I don't know how to get out of the hole I'm digging for myself as Tomas's cries start up again. He tugs at the chair, which Stephanie is holding.

'Whatever you think best,' I say.

She gives it a moment's thought. 'Okay – *mais fais attention*,' she tells Tomas and helps him pull the chair to the counter. She and I stand at either side of him to stop him falling off. I pull the book towards us and turn the page. Tomas points to a picture and shouts,

127

'*Ça! Ça!*' I prop the book up, hoping we can make a dessert that will suit Henri and please Tomas, our chief taster.

'Right.' I take a deep breath. I look at the recipe. 'Looks like we're making chocolate and lavender cake. We'll need flour, eggs and the big mixing bowl.' Stephanie, keen to please, dives for the box of cookery stuff and so do I. We collide.

'*Désolée.*'

'Sorry,' we say at the same time.

'I tell you what,' I say. 'You read out the recipe and hold on to Tomas. I'll get the ingredients.' After that, things go a little more smoothly, although when it comes to the flour, Tomas ends up covered with it from head to toe as he tosses handfuls in the direction of the bowl, himself and the floor.

Eventually, we're proudly pulling our cakes from the oven. 'It's such a big order,' I say, as we dust icing sugar over the chocolate and lavender cakes, with lavender sprigs and flowers stripped from the stems, just as the recipe told us when Stephanie read it aloud. 'I'm sure he won't sell it all.'

'Henri always makes plenty.' Stephanie smiles. 'Enough for everyone.'

'How do you know him?' I ask, as we put the cakes out of Ralph's reach on the work surface.

There is a moment of silence. Then she says, 'Henri was there when I needed him most. It's what Henri does. He catches people before they fall.'

Lovely kind Henri. Isn't that exactly what he's done for me?

We walk into town, past the clearing by the river, carrying the cakes carefully between us. Just a few people are there, a couple playing chess, all sitting in the shade of the big pine tree.

'*Bonjour,*' they greet us.

'*Bonjour,*' I say. This time Stephanie doesn't hurry past but greets the group with a small smile. The smile of someone who has found a little bit of contentment.

After dropping off the desserts and drinking a coffee with Henri, we head back to Le Petit Mas. Stephanie spends the afternoon cleaning the gypsy caravan and there are moments when I think I hear her singing. I sit in the shade outside and wonder what else I'm going to do. I'm making desserts and biscuits for Henri and the stall, but will it be enough? I look at Le Petit Mas. Could I make a go of this place as a *chambre d'hôte*? A place for people to stay and benefit in the way Stephanie, Tomas and I have?

I sit down with a pen and some paper, looking out over the bare field that undulates away from the farmhouse to the river that is the boundary to our land. Across the valley, sunflowers nod, and the field of lavender is so purple it seems unreal.

As I'm sitting there, notebook in hand, I hear a car pull into the drive and Ralph's enthusiastic greeting. Who's he knocked over now?

I stand and walk quickly around the corner. To my annoyance my stomach flick-flacks when I see Fabien's truck and Ralph sitting up smartly as Fabien pats him.

Carine slides out of the cab, dusting herself down with a glance of disgust at her mode of transport. She comes over to me and kisses me. I look at Fabien, just behind her, and he leans towards me to greet me. I haven't seen him since he found me yesterday with Henri, having lunch, and it feels weird that I haven't explained why it happened. But I'm pleased Carine's there as Fabien leans in to kiss me, without touching me. My skin leaps at the smell of his.

'I brought the table back. All fixed,' he says.

'That's so kind of you. Henri says I can leave it in the restaurant from now on,' I say. 'Save you bringing it to and fro.'

'Henri?' Fabien raises his eyebrows and I think he's going to follow it up with 'Again?' But he doesn't. I have to explain that Henri is just a friend. I'm not looking for a partner. But now isn't the time. 'I'll drop the table there, then,' he says.

'And I just came for the ride to see how you were settling in and if you'd thought any more about my idea of the *chambre d'hôte*,' says Carine.

'Come in, sit down,' I say quickly, and guide them to the side of the house and the terrace. Just at that point Tomas comes running out of the clearing, pretending to be a dog, barking.

Carine and Fabien stop and stare. Fabien bursts out laughing. Carine looks as if she's waiting for a wasp to fly away.

Stephanie follows Tomas from the clearing, calling him. She pauses and, for a moment, they all stare at each other, then Stephanie's head drops. I can see she recognizes Fabien and Carine from the town. I step in to break the silence.

'This is Stephanie. Stephanie is my new assistant. Chambermaid and kitchen assistant,' I say, thinking on my feet, wishing I could come up with a really good title. Clearly Stephanie has been transported back to her reputation as the young single mum who sometimes steals.

Fabien moves forward and puts out his hand. '*Bonjour*, Stephanie,' he says. '*Bienvenue.*' He speaks as if she's new to the area and starting a whole new life, just like me.

'*Bonjour.*' Carine is keeping a wary eye on Tomas, who is running around a little too quickly for her liking by the look of it.

'Let's have coffee,' I say. 'Stephanie, come and help me.' She looks at me gratefully, clearly glad not to have to explain how she ended up at Le Petit Mas.

'I have something for you,' says Fabien, going back to the truck. 'I'll get it while you make coffee.'

As we bring out the tray with some of the chocolate cake, I spot a box by the table. I put down the coffee and cut the cake.

'*Le cadeau!*' Carine scolds Fabien good-naturedly.

'Ah, yes,' he says, pulling himself away from Tomas and Ralph. 'It was Carine's idea.'

'This is my way of making sure you stay!' She smiles.

Fabien hands me the big wooden box. 'Fine lavender plants,' he says, and as he hands me the box, our fingertips touch, jolting me. 'A friend of mine has a farm over there.' He points to the lavender field across the valley. 'But he's getting on and finding it hard to manage, these days. He sells in the market.' I remember the old man who gave me the lavender at the antiques market. 'He sent these, wished you luck and tells you to keep smiling!' I look down into the box at the six plants.

'It's a start!' says Carine. 'You'll bring Le Petit Mas de la Lavande back to life.'

I'm thrilled. What a thoughtful gift.

'You'll need more lavender if you're going to continue to cook with it for the stall,' Fabien says.

'And for Henri,' says Carine.

'And Henri,' Fabien says quietly.

'Thank you so much! I can't think of anything I wanted more!' And then a thought strikes me. 'May I meet your friend? I'd like to ask him how to plant and care for them.'

'His name's Serge. Of course I'll take you to see him,' says Fabien.

Our friendship may be getting back on its feet. This was Fabien's idea. He wants to help me stay. He wants to help me work with Henri. I feel a huge wave of relief wash over me. I smile at him, and he smiles back.

'*De rien,*' he says, with a hint of regret. It's clearly his way of saying sorry. I'm so grateful for it. I hated the thought of having to avoid him, knowing he was in town, looking out for him. It's going to be fine, I think.

Tomas tugs at his hand and pulls him away to play on the grass in front of the field. Stephanie lingers in the background. 'Come and join us!' I say.

'I will just make more coffee,' she says, and I feel a little bubble of pride at how quickly she's learning.

Carine and I watch Fabien as he plays tag with Tomas – and Ralph, who is running around barking.

'How long have you and Fabien been together?' I ask.

Carine lets out a long laugh, and blows cigarette smoke into the blue sky.

'Me and Fabien? We're not together. We're just friends.' She takes another drag. 'We were together as teenagers but it didn't last. We have very different ideas about what we want from a relationship, from the future. We are much better suited as good friends,' she tells me.

I let the information sink in. They're not together. I cringe as I think about him asking me to lunch and me turning him down. He was just being friendly. And then he thought I'd agreed to lunch with Henri. No wonder he gave me that look. A look that said, 'You turned me down but then went to lunch with Henri.'

No wonder he thinks Henri and I may have something between us.

At that moment he catches my eye. My stomach does a full somersault. I look down at the lavender and breathe it in, distracting myself from his look. I focus on the lavender and the calm it brings, imagining its taste on my tongue.

'I prefer to be organized. Everything in its place. Enjoying the moment. We were looking for different things, and Fabien is still looking.'

NINETEEN

The following day, Stephanie, Tomas and I slip quickly into our routine. He pulls over his chair, then she holds him on it and reads out the recipe. I get out the ingredients and Stephanie insists that I attempt to read the recipe aloud in French while she weighs everything. We give Tomas a little bowl of flour to play with. After making much-improved *macarons* – bite-size swirls of soft-centred crunchy white meringue, with the floral hit of lavender – we deliver them to Henri for lunchtime. I watch his delight at hearing Stephanie explain how we made them and seeing Tomas choose a lolly from the freezer. I may not be used to children, but I do remember the joy of ice lollies when I was a child. And I promise to attempt homemade sorbet and ice cream for Henri soon.

We return home, along the river path, Tomas's ice lolly dripping on to his hands, him licking the dribbles.

A truck is waiting on the drive. My stomach flips and I feel flustered.

'*Bonjour*,' he says, as he climbs out of the cab. Mimi peers out of the window at Ralph. He kisses Stephanie and Tomas first. I watch, nerves jangling. Then he kisses my cheeks, taking his time, just as he did with Stephanie. The soft bristles of his stubble touch me, sending shock waves through my body. I can feel his breath on my face and smell his aftershave, spicy and woody. With the morning greetings over, I step back and let myself settle. Stephanie is so pretty when she smiles.

'I have something for you,' he says.

'Oh?' I reply, wishing it hadn't come out as high-pitched as it has.

'An invitation to visit my friend Serge.' He points to the other side of the valley. 'He invites you to visit his lavender farm, see how it is grown.'

'Great!' I say. It really is. I'd love to know more about the plant. 'When?'

'Now, if you are available?'

'*Available?*'

'He means if you are free.' Stephanie laughs.

'Free, yes.' Fabien nods earnestly. 'Sorry for my English.'

'No, no, not at all,' I stutter.

'No, you're not free?'

'Yes, I mean no.' I stop. Grow up, Del! I tell myself. 'I meant your English is fine. And, um . . .'

'Yes, she is free,' says Stephanie.

I'm suddenly torn. Do I want to go with Fabien to the lavender farm? On my own? I need to keep a distance. He has this ridiculous effect on me every time he's near and I can't let myself get involved, I just can't. Everyone I've loved has gone. Mum, the man I married – that Ollie is long gone – and the child I never had, will never have. I need to move on alone. Just me. I can't let myself fall for anyone. Any happiness that comes my way is given with one hand and taken away with the other. I'm not going to let that happen again. I just want enough to be content ... I look at him looking at me.

'Why don't Stephanie and Tomas come with us? She's as much a part of the business as I am now.'

Fabien misses only the slightest of beats before he says, 'Bien sûr! Of course!' And Stephanie's smile is back on her face.

Only I noticed the missed beat. This is for the best. I need to keep my distance. It's for the best, I repeat to myself.

We all pile in to the van's cab, Tomas and Stephanie next to Fabien, with Mimi, disgruntled, on her lap and me last, beside the door. Ralph has to stay at home. There's no room for him. Next time, I tell him. But I know there won't be a next time.

'On y va!' Fabien says, turning the truck in the drive and snatching a glance at me. Stephanie is stroking Mimi and I distract myself by pointing things out to Tomas.

'Dragonfly,' I say, and he laughs as we head down the drive and across the river to the other side of the valley.

The smell hits me before Fabien has even stopped the van. We bounce around in the cab as we go down the rough drive and, instinctively, I find myself reaching out to hold Tomas steady, but Stephanie is there before me and Fabien reaches over too so I withdraw my hand. She smiles at me. His mum has him. I'm still not sure when I should help with him. Stephanie and Fabien seem so natural around Tomas, unlike me. Perhaps I never had the maternal instinct.

Two old dogs are barking and sniffing around the van as we pull up, and the small bent man from the market is there, dressed in blue working trousers and jacket, wearing a black hat, just like he was in the market, waving to us. We climb out of the cab and Serge shakes hands with Fabien, then kisses Stephanie and me. His hands are tanned but gnarled by arthritis. He grins, showing the gap where his tooth once was, and comments again on my 'lovely smile'.

I blush and turn my attention to the farmyard, the dogs, the blue work trousers and jacket drying on the line. A large cockerel struts around the yard, and Serge beckons us forward.

'Please, follow,' Fabien says. 'Serge will show you the lavender fields.'

As we walk around the back of the small, single-storey stone cottage, the sight takes my breath away.

The fields around us are full of straight rows of glorious, deep purple lavender in dark red soil, speckled with white stones. I breathe in, finding strength and calm in its glorious smell. I can see my own farmhouse from here, the fields where once there would have been lavender like this. Serge holds out his arm for me to walk through the lavender. Tomas is ahead, running through the flowers, Stephanie not far behind him. Serge bends and picks two stems of lavender.

Fabien takes them, gives one to me and keeps the other for himself. 'Smell it,' he says. 'He wants you to breathe it.' Stephanie returns, following Tomas, who is giggling as he runs unsteadily up the row.

'This farm has been in his family for four generations.' Stephanie stops between Serge and Fabien, who is trying to translate as Serge talks in his deep, thick accent. I don't understand a word he's saying.

'He says the fine lavender grows up here, enjoying the cool mountain air. Not like lavandin, which is taken from a different, cultivated plant and used in washing powders,' says Stephanie. Serge wags a finger. 'This is the lavender that can be used for medicinal purposes and for cooking,' she goes on. Serge holds up a sprig. 'It is part of the mint family, use it like rosemary,' she says.

I'm so impressed with her English.

'It used to grow wild up here on the mountainside,' Stephanie translates, and I can feel Fabien watching me. 'It was harvested and distilled here, in the fields.

A still would be brought to the field on a cart, a horse pulling. That's why farms were set up near the river, so they could use the water to distil the lavender into oil in the field.' She points to the river. My land is on the other side.

Serge indicates his barn and beckons us to follow him. When he pulls back the doors, the scent is even stronger, wrapping around me and drawing me in. Dried bunches of lavender hang from ladders, held up by the beams overhead. I think of the recipe book that has mapped out my days since I've been on my own here: lavender has already become part of my life.

Serge goes to a box and hands me a little bottle of oil. '*Un cadeau.*'

'*Merci!*' I open it and am assailed by its restorative scent. He is watching Tomas chasing chickens in the yard, but turns away, takes down a bunch of dried lavender and hands it to me.

'With hot water,' Stephanie says. 'Like tea.'

Suddenly Tomas shrieks and we whirl round. He's tripped and fallen. Fabien is closest and goes to scoop him up, then carries him back to Stephanie, saying soothing words, Tomas's sobs settling to a sniffle.

'You have a way with children,' I say, focusing on Tomas, not the image of Fabien holding him.

'I have many nephews and nieces,' he says, and my heart squeezes at the sight of him comforting the little boy. 'But I don't see much of them. They live further north. Families are more separated than they used to be,' he says, and repeats it in French for Serge, who nods in agreement. 'Serge grew up with my grandfather. Schoolboys together. My grandfather had the *brocante* from his own father. I joined after school but lots of our families moved away to find cheaper houses.' Serge is talking and pointing around the farm and the fields. He holds Tomas's hand and talks to him like a grandfather would, making him smile. Perhaps it's only me who doesn't know how to comfort or speak to a child. Tomas has been living with me, but I've had little to do with him. I'm not a natural, like Fabien, Serge and Stephanie.

Serge tells Fabien his family, too, are living elsewhere. He'd like to see more of them now his wife has passed away. He has no one to take on the lavender farm after him.

'Would you like some plants to take with you?' Stephanie translates for me.

'Me?' I say, surprised.

'*Oui.*' Serge gestures to an area where some pots are sitting in a damp patch, having been recently watered.

'I wouldn't have a clue what to do with them. I'm not really a gardener . . .'

He picks up one of the plants, then leads us to the field where Tomas is soon helping him to plant the lavender. When they have finished, Serge sits up on his haunches. '*Très simple!*' he says. 'Like falling in love.'

'Simple, like—'

'Falling in love,' I cut Fabien off. 'If only love were

that simple. Falling in love is simple. It's staying in love that's the hard part.'

'Finding it and recognizing it can often be pretty hard too!' Fabien laughs, and my stomach flutters.

'You will know it,' says Serge, and Stephanie translates. I'm presuming he's thinking about his wife and missing her. 'You feel it in here.' He bangs his chest. 'Love is like the lavender when you have it in your life. It brings peace when you have it.'

He struggles to his feet, his hips clearly painful. He walks stiffly towards the plants and picks a couple up. '*Et maintenant . . .*'

'And now,' Fabien translates, 'you have it in *your* life.' Serge proffers the lavender and Fabien holds my gaze. It takes all my effort to pull it away from him and direct it to Serge.

I thank Serge and kiss him on both cheeks, then a third time, as he reminds me with a laugh. He instructs Fabien to take all of the plants by the back door and load them on to the truck for me. As I'm thanking him again, Stephanie and Tomas are helping Fabien. From a distance the three look like a family.

Serge tells me to take care of the plants and to come and find him if I need any help or advice. He's happy to see lavender returning to Le Petit Mas. He'll be watching, he says, pointing over the valley to my house opposite. Just for a moment, I stand in the lunchtime sunshine and imagine the whole valley covered with lines of purple.

We leave Serge and jolt down the bumpy drive. I've had a whole education in lavender and what it means to the area, and am determined to nurture my few plants. I feel I have my part to play and, somehow, that these plants are weaving me into the fabric of the place.

Fabien drops us off and I thank him again.

'I shall return to check on the lavender plants,' he says from the cab, his arm out of the window, Mimi by his side.

As the sun sets on another day, Stephanie, Tomas and I set to work, digging over the ground at the top of the field, planting and watering our lavender. When we've finished, we go back to the house and toast the new plants, with rosé from the bottle Serge also gave me. Lavender has returned to Le Petit Mas and I hope I will keep it blooming here. We sit and watch as the swifts fly overhead and the woodpecker rat-a-tat-tats in the woods.

As evening sets in, the bats swoop to and fro, and Tomas dozes in Stephanie's arms. I remember the love and safety I felt in my mother's arms when I was young and feel I've found some peace at last. I wonder what tomorrow's recipe will be, knowing for sure that it will include lavender. I am beginning to feel content just being me, being here. Enough to be content.

TWENTY

I'm standing at the top of my field, which rolls away from the house, wandering through the lavender plants, watering them, using the bottle from the wine Serge gave me, now filled with water. I keep having to go back to the house to refill it.

It's been a few days since we visited Serge and we seem to have found a rhythm to our working day. Stephanie is taking the desserts into town to deliver to Henri, and picks up payment. Delighted to be trusted, she gives me the money in full. After lunch, we turn the page in the old book and study the next recipe. I read it aloud in French and she translates, if necessary. Then I work out what we need to buy and how we'll make whatever it is, adjusting our techniques to fit with the quirks of the oven. She and Tomas go back into town and pick up the ingredients, ready for baking the following morning. She brings me the change, showing me the receipt, making sure every cent is accounted for.

Fabien seems to find more and more reasons to come to the house. He likes to check on the lavender, he tells me. Every time he arrives, my stomach flips, hard though I try to stop it.

'Fabien!' Tomas greets him like an old friend, as Fabien scoops him up and kisses him on each cheek, as I imagine he does with his nephews and nieces. Ralph sits obediently, at Fabien's word, when he puts Tomas down.

'*Bonjour*, Fabien. How's the *brocante*?' I make polite conversation.

'It's busy,' he says. 'How are the plants?'

We all walk to the field, which is filling gradually with purple flowers, Tomas never leaving Fabien's side and Stephanie close behind. We talk about the plants and the cakes Stephanie and I have made. It's the only way I can distract myself and stop myself falling for him. He's so good with Tomas, and Stephanie seems to adore him for that. I'm beginning to wonder exactly how she is feeling about Fabien and it's starting to worry me. I think she may have a crush on him, and I don't want to see her hurt. He's too young for me, but too old for Stephanie. Perhaps I should warn him about how she may be feeling.

Monday's market is much better than it was last week. We set up our stall and watch people pass between the two marketplaces, barely seeing us in the shadows. Again I offer samples, but the French, out early, aren't interested. Seeing this, Stephanie pulls back the hoodie she hides behind in public and talks to people as they pass, telling them about the farmhouse, how we're growing lavender again, and they turn to welcome me. Some even stop and buy from me.

Stephanie is glowing. Her hair is clean, brushed and not tied back, and I wonder for whose benefit that is. I think of Fabien, and worry again. I look at Henri, standing in the doorway of the bistro, watching Stephanie at work, like a proud uncle, and then me. He's been a good friend to me. With the money I make from the desserts and the stall, I'm earning enough to feed us and put some away for next month's mortgage payment. But it's tight. And with Ollie still sending me regular messages from the UK, asking if I'm sure about my decision, no matter how many times I tell him I am, I can't help wondering if I've done the right thing. But even if I wanted to, I couldn't go back now: Stephanie and Tomas are relying on me.

TWENTY-ONE

After a good day on the stall, I wander round the market, thinking I might be up for a couple more lavender plants. I see Serge, who greets me like an old friend. I tell him I've come to buy two more plants and he puts them into a box for me.

'You've given me too many!' I tell him.

'*Un cadeau*, because of your beautiful smile,' he says. 'I am happy that the valley is coming back to life.' I understand his words, and smile all the way home to plant them.

This morning, we finish baking in good time: soft, moist sponge, with sticky lemon drizzle and floral lavender.

We seem to have developed a good system for baking some of the favourites and introducing something new every day. The woman in the bakery van has offered to take some of my lavender tuiles and short-bread to sell on her rounds. I've accepted happily. The *macarons* still need to improve, but all the packages now have little stickers, saying the contents are from 'Le Petit Mas de la Lavande, la Coeur de Provence', with a little purple heart. It was Stephanie's idea, and when we told the printer in town what we wanted, he gave me a very good deal and wished me luck. Later we took him some biscuits to thank him.

Stephanie has gone into town with Tomas to deliver today's desserts to Henri. The woodpecker is hard at work in the copse of oak and pine trees where Stephanie's caravan is now cleaned and polished to within an inch of its life. She even has plans to redo the paintwork in the same colours as our little stickers. A washing line is hanging between the trees, and though I've said that, now money is coming in, we can get some furniture and she can move into the house, she says she'd like to stay in the caravan. Finally, she has a home of her own.

Cyril, the red squirrel, is popping in and out of the bushes around where I'm working, teasing Ralph in a fruitless game of tag. Eventually he loses interest and goes back to chasing little white butterflies. The smell of lavender fills the air. Big fat bumblebees move throughout the original hedge, from bloom to bloom, and I'm hoping they'll get to work on the new plants too.

In the distance the cockerel is still letting us know

it's another new day, even though it's mid-morning. I'm stretching out my back, trowel in hand, when I hear the familiar sound of a vehicle coming up the drive and Ralph's ecstatic welcoming barks.

I hear the door slam. It's a sound I know well now: Fabien's van door. My heart skips, even though I know it shouldn't. But he is my friend, a good friend, and I'm pleased he's here, but I know I have to speak to him about Stephanie: she blossoms every time he comes here, which he does a lot. Either with something that's arrived at the *brocante* he thinks might suit the house, or something for Tomas, like the small truck he found in a house clearance and some cars, which Tomas adores. And Stephanie adores him for it, I can see.

'Hey.' I hear his voice and my heart leaps into my mouth.

'Hey,' I say, pulling off my gardening gloves.

He steps forward and kisses me on both cheeks. I hold my breath so that I can't breathe in his deliciously spicy aftershave.

'They're looking good,' he says.

'Yes, I'm really pleased,' I say, looking at the few plants, then the rest of the empty red earth, peppered with white stones, like confetti. 'I just wish I could see this whole field covered.' I glance at Serge's.

'Actually . . .' says Fabien.

'Were you looking for Stephanie?' I say quickly, realizing he's not here to chat with me. 'She's in town, delivering to Henri, with Tomas.' I'm falling over my words and cringing at my clumsiness.

'Actually,' he repeats slowly, 'it's you I've come to see,' and a large lump rises in my throat. Fabien is ten years younger than me. Of course there will never be anything between us. I just wish . . . What? That I was ten years younger? That I could have a child like Tomas? But I'm not, and I can't.

'Come,' he tips his head towards the front of the house, 'I have something for you.' He smiles and my insides melt. I'm hot, very hot, and I put it down to hormones, and my premature change that has meant I can't conceive. The hormones that Ollie blames for my defection and attempt at a new life. I grab a bottle of water off the terrace table and follow Fabien to the van. He walks around to the rear.

'Here,' he says. 'These might help fill the field.' He drops the back of the van and I see rows and rows of tiny lavender plants.

'Uh . . .' I catch my breath. 'How . . . where?'

'With Serge. We did a deal.'

'But . . .' I'm lost for words and all I can say is, 'I need to pay you.'

He laughs. 'Serge had lots of plants. He told you. He's finding it harder and harder to manage his farm and he wanted you to have them. He's delighted to have found them a home.'

'This is amazing!' I say. 'The lavender farm here is coming back to life. *Merci*, Fabien.'

'I'm glad you're pleased,' he says. 'And life as a lavender farmer seems to suit you!' His green eyes are
dancing, fixed on me. My nerves are buzzing.

'You are . . .' I struggle to find the words '. . . such a
good friend,' I say, unable now to meet his eyes. 'It
wouldn't have happened without you.'

'A friend?' I look up and he's raising an eyebrow,
making my heart squeeze. I look away and then I have
to look back at him, something drawing me that I can't
resist.

'You know, Del . . .' he says quietly.

'About Stephanie!' I blurt, and he's taken aback.
'When you come here to visit and check the plants . . .'

He stares at me, his face moving closer to mine and
I can't move or pull my eyes away.

'But it is not the plants I come to see . . .' He smiles
and my heart starts to pound.

'No?' I manage, my mouth dry.

'No,' he says, shaking his head, moving closer to
me. 'It's you, Del. It's you I come to see.'

'Me?'

He nods.

'But I'm . . .' What? Older? Still married? Overweight?
Desperate to be loved?

'Beautiful,' he says, and I can hardly believe I'm
hearing the word. 'You are beautiful.' He takes my face
in his hands. I want to argue, but can't think what to
say. Instead my heart is floating high above us, soaring
and swooping. I feel as if I'm living in a dream. This

gorgeous man, who makes my heart skip every time I see him, is telling me I'm beautiful.

'But I thought you . . . I mean, I'm ten years older than you. I'm . . .'

'Beautiful,' he repeats, his eyes scanning my face. I don't know whether to laugh or cry as he moves his lips towards mine. And although everything is telling me I shouldn't be doing this, I can't stop myself.

And just as his lips touch mine, they are gone. '*Oooffff!*' He reels away and the dream is shattered.

'Fabien!' Tomas has launched himself at Fabien's legs, taking him by surprise. We laugh, and I see Stephanie, back from her visit to town, her face as thunderous as it was the first time I met her. Cold and closed against the hurt in her heart.

'Stephanie!' I call, hoping she didn't see what I think she might have seen. But she doesn't answer and runs to the caravan. I hear the door slam. Fabien and I gaze at each other, worried.

'I'll go after her, explain,' I say.

'Explain what?'

'That it was nothing . . .' I wave a hand, trying to think on my feet '. . . just a silly kiss.'

'Just a silly kiss?' he says, his face darkening too.

'Yes, I mean, no . . .' That's not what I meant!! 'I mean . . .' I have no idea what I mean or what it was. I just know how I feel and how I've made Stephanie feel.

'I think I'd better go,' says Fabien, closing the van on the lavender plants. And I'm flustered. I take hold of

Tomas's hand as he waves to Fabien, begging him to stay and play.

'Fabien!' I don't want him to go like this. I need to explain. But 'The plants!' is all I can think of saying.

'I'll bring them back later,' he says, gets into the cab and turns the van in the drive, accelerating at speed in a cloud of dust. Suddenly there's the blast of a horn and he swerves to avoid another car coming up the drive. I look in the direction of the caravan, then at Tomas, still waving, and then at the car.

Ralph appears from the back of the house, barking with delight.

Who can this be?

TWENTY-TWO

'So, this is where you've been hiding?'

'Lou!' I say in disbelief, as she emerges from the back of the car, then throw myself forward and hug my friend, hoping the tears won't spill: I've upset the two people closest to me.

'And me!' The other door of the taxi opens and out steps Rhi. 'Surprise!'

I run around the car and hug her too. The taxi driver fetches their cases from the boot, then climbs back in and, with a friendly toot, disappears down the drive. I'm left staring at my two best friends and wondering what they're doing here.

'Ollie sent us,' says Lou, answering the question before I've even asked it. 'Wants us to see if you're okay and when you're coming back.'

'Wanted us to check you were okay,' says Rhi, more diplomatically.

'I am, I am.' I wipe away a stray tear from the corner of my eye and glance in the direction of the caravan. Now they register the little boy clinging to my leg, and stare.

'This is Tomas,' I say, picking him up and setting him on my hip, as if it's the most natural thing in the world. He buries his head in my neck. My two friends stare at him, then at me and then at each other. Ralph runs around barking, and Tomas looks up, giggling.

'So, Tomas,' says Lou, tall, bottle blonde, her fake tan just a tad too orange. 'Are you childminding him?'

She reaches forward but he buries his head in my neck again.

'No, Tomas lives here,' I say, glancing again in the direction of the clearing and the gypsy caravan. When I turn back, Lou and Rhi are looking at each other. Where Lou is tall and dressed to kill, Rhi is shorter than me, in a sunhat and sensible shoes. She's usually bubbly, but right now, they both look worried.

'Oh.' Then I explain, 'No, I mean he lives here, but with his mum.'

'*Maman*,' says Tomas.

'That's right, Tomas.' I give him a watery smile. His mum is probably feeling that yet another person has let her down. I must go to her and put things right. Both my friends are still looking worried. 'Um, I just have to go and speak to Tomas's mum. Tomas, would you like some milk and biscuits?' I ask, then again in French, and my two friends raise their eyebrows, impressed.

I lead them all to the kitchen, grab milk, a plate of biscuits and a bottle of rosé, then take them outside to the table where I pour drinks. When everyone is happy, I leave Tomas with them while I run to check on Stephanie.

I knock at the caravan door tentatively. 'Stephanie?' I call, but she doesn't reply.

I open the door gently and see she has packed most of her belongings back into their blue bags. She is lying on the bed, her face in the pillow. The little caravan is wonderfully clean and welcoming. A small vase of lavender sits on the side, filling the air with its scent. She sits bolt upright, her eyes as dark and defensive as they were on that first day.

'Oh, Stephanie.' I reach out to hug her but she backs away from me.

'I didn't know there was something going on with you and Fabien,' she says, jutting out her chin.

'There isn't.' I'm desperate for her to believe me, and to convince myself. 'I promise. We were just . . .'

'Just what?'

I sigh.

'He's just a friend. There's nothing between us,' I lie, not proud of myself but sometimes there's a place for a small lie, if it stops someone else being hurt.

She sniffs. 'He would have made a good father for Tomas,' she says. 'He's really good with children. I think he misses his family. He would make a good father and husband.'

'He's much older than you, Stephanie.'

'Age doesn't matter,' she says. 'Age is about how old you feel. Some of us have lived a lifetime already. Becoming a parent makes you grow up.'

I wonder if it was a dig, but let it go. She's upset. I remember being a teenager and wish I'd told Mum how sorry I was for all the hurtful things I said in the heat of the moment, that I didn't mean any of them. But I think she knew that. Just like I get the feeling that Stephanie doesn't mean to hurt me now.

'Love is love,' she says.

'And do you love him?' I ask.

She pushes out her lips as only the French seem able to do, telling me all I need to know. I look around at the bags. 'Please don't do anything you'll regret. Don't go anywhere. This is your home. Yours and Tomas's.'

She suddenly looks horrified.

'Tomas! Where is Tomas?' She leaps to her feet.

'He's with some friends of mine who have just arrived. He's introducing them to Ralph.'

A smile tugs at the corners of her mouth. I would love to hug her and tell her everything will be fine, but I know she's not ready for me to do that. So, I do the only thing I know that will make this better right now: 'I promise, Stephanie, that there is nothing between Fabien and me. Nor will there be.' I lift my chin. 'Now, wash your face, unpack these clothes and come and say hello to our guests.' I speak gently but firmly, hoping I've got the tone just right. And, by the look of it,

I have. She nods and starts to unpack the blue plastic bags. This time she hasn't run. She's stayed put, and I feel proud of her for that.

'This is Stephanie,' I say to Lou and Rhi, who are sitting at the table on the terrace, watching Tomas chasing Ralph chasing butterflies and smiling. They're still clearly bewildered, the wine giving their cheeks a hint of a glow.

'Tomas's *maman*,' I explain.

'*Maman!*' he shouts, runs to her and clutches her leg.

'*Bonjour*,' says Stephanie, shaking hands with Lou and Rhi in turn.

'Stephanie is my chambermaid and kitchen assistant here at Le Petit Mas,' I say, and Stephanie's smile is back. Now it says she has a place in the world that is all hers.

'Chambermaid?' says Lou.

'Kitchen assistant?' says Rhi.

'Yes, for my business. Lavender bakes from the heart of Provence.' I look at Stephanie proudly, throw my arm around her shoulders and pull her to me.

Lou and Rhi are still confused.

'You sound as if you're staying here,' Lou says, and Rhi laughs. 'Ollie told me to help you pack up and get you home. He said you were . . . unwell.'

'I've never felt better.' I look out over the lavender fields. 'And I'm not going anywhere. This is my home. Mine, Stephanie's and Tomas's.' And I pour myself a glass of wine and a small one for Stephanie, who has to look after Tomas and says she doesn't want much. 'To Le Petit Mas de la Lavande.' I raise my glass.

Lou and Rhi raise theirs too, clearly wondering if I'm insane or the happiest they've ever seen me.

'So, you're running this as a hotel?' Lou asks.

'A *chambre d'hôte*,' I tell them, offering them the biscuits Tomas has left. 'A B-and-B. Well, that's the plan. When we've done the work.'

'Great! So you're okay for us to stay, then?' says Rhi.

'Of course!' I reply. 'Plenty of room. And you can help with the painting while you're here. Just out of interest, how long are you here for?'

'A few days, a week maybe,' says Lou.

'Just as long as you need us!' Rhi says.

'Rhi, you left the salon!'

'Ah, but I have this,' she says, fishes out her iPad and opens it. 'I've had CCTV fitted all over the salon and I can watch everything that's going on from here.' She beams, looking at the screen.

'Oo, internet's not great!' and she peers at the screen.

'I've managed to reschedule my nail appointment for next week, although, they may need doing while I'm out here,' says Lou, flourishing her perfectly manicured talons.

'So, we're all sorted.' Rhi claps her hands together.

'There's only one problem,' I say. 'We just have to find you something to sleep on.' And there's only one place to go for that. I swallow hard.

TWENTY-THREE

We walk along the river path into town, past the clearing where the homeless people greet me as I pass, and one praises my '*macarons délicieux*'. Again Lou and Rhi are bemused. And I have no idea how he knows about the *macarons*: I've only left biscuits here, and only once.

Stephanie stays at home to start cleaning the rooms. I hope we've moved on from the flare-up. I know now that Fabien has no intentions towards her and I think the situation will pass. All she really cares about is that she can trust me, which means I must keep my promise to her. Nothing can happen between Fabien and me. A knot twists in my stomach and in my heart. But that's how it has to be. Right now, Stephanie's faith in human nature must be restored, for Tomas's sake as well as hers. It's his future too. And that's why I have to do what I'm about to do.

We walk through the backstreets, the way Stephanie

has shown me, a short-cut after the riverside clearing, making the journey much quicker to the *brocante*. With every step my heart is beating harder, and I wonder if Lou and Rhi can hear it. It would appear not, as they exclaim at the cream and peach walls, the red and orange terracotta roofs.

I slow as we head towards the *brocante*. I have no idea what to say to Fabien. We both know it was far from 'a silly kiss', but I have made a promise and I need to stick to it.

We walk into the courtyard through the big wrought-iron gates. I see him straight away and he rushes towards me.

'Del,' he says, then stops, seeing Lou and Rhi right behind me.

'Fabien,' I say, my voice cracking. 'These are friends of mine from back home.'

'Friends of Ollie and Del,' says Rhi, pushing past me eagerly to shake Fabien's hand.

'Ollie,' Fabien repeats.

'Her husband,' confirms Rhi, not letting go of Fabien's hand, until Lou elbows her out of the way.

'Out of the three of us, she's the only one who's married and she seems to have forgotten where she left him!' She laughs, a little too high-pitched.

'Her husband,' Fabien repeats, and my cheeks burn. He knows Ollie and I have split up. What he doesn't know is that I can't look at him without wanting to wrap my body around his.

'Mine left me, with two small children, twenty years ago,' says Rhi, who was a teenage mum, a bit like Stephanie.

'Mine died at the gym, trying to get fitter,' says Lou, drily.

For a moment there is silence and I feel guilty. I had a husband, a life, and walked out on both. Not for anyone else, but because I was unhappy. Was I just feeling raw after losing Mum, after the failed IVF? Would we have found our way back into each other's hearts if I'd stayed with him? Is Ollie showing he still loves me by sending Rhi and Lou over? My head starts to hurt. Just when I thought everything was clear in my mind. I look at Fabien. Did I feel like this when I first met Ollie?

'Welcome, and how can I help today?' He is nearly his usual cheery self and I almost can't bear to hear it. 'You have come for souvenirs to take home?'

'Erm, no.' I clear my throat. 'Actually, Fabien, I need bedroom furniture, for my guests.'

'I see.' He nods. 'You are staying, ladies? A holiday?'

'Yes.' They seem as unsure about why they're here as I am. 'Just until everything here is sorted.'

'Sorted?' says Fabien.

'Just until . . .' Rhi trails off. What was she going to say? Until they've persuaded me to go home? To go back to Ollie? Because he still loves me and this is just a blip?

'Just for a while,' I finish the conversation.

'Then I look forward to seeing you around, ladies,

both of you.' He grins, and Lou smiles warmly while Rhi practically faints at his feet.

'You look around and I will find what you need,' he says. 'Del? Would you like to join me?' He gestures for me to follow. And I do.

He starts climbing over some furniture at the back of the barn-like building.

'I have some more beds back here,' he says loudly, for Lou and Rhi's benefit, and then, in hushed tones, 'How is Stephanie?'

'She's fine. Just a bit . . . upset. She thought . . . She likes you.'

He shrugs kindly. 'It's my fault. I should have realized. She is hurting.' He looks at me and my heart flips over and back again. I turn my head away quickly, unable to find the words or the strength to keep my promise if I'm looking at him.

'And all because of "a silly kiss",' he whispers. And I feel like I've been slapped across the face. I look up at him as his chin lifts, his eyes narrow. 'I got carried away, I'm sorry.'

'Look at these lamps! Only ten euro!' Rhi is exclaiming. 'We'll take them.'

'And this,' says Lou, of a bundle of bedding.

Fabien is still gazing at me, the warmth gone from his eyes. I have no idea what to say.

'You . . . agree?'

'Of course,' he says, and jumps down from where he's standing on a chest of drawers. He switches the charm back on. Did he charm me? So nothing he said meant anything? It really was 'just a silly kiss'. Then why had it felt like so much more? Is he already looking elsewhere? Or have I really hurt him with what I said, in the heat of the moment? I feel so stupid! The way I felt when I looked at him, the way I thought he looked at me, it felt so real at the time. And now he's acting like we're strangers. He's making Lou smile and Rhi laugh as he shows them more of the gems he has in his warehouse.

'Put it all together. Shall I put it on account, Del?' he calls, as friendly as if nothing has passed between us.

'Oh, I'll pay,' says Lou, reaching into her tasselled shoulder bag.

Fabien waves her away. 'It's fine. Del and I understand each other,' he says.

I wish there was something I could say to make him understand why I had to say what I did. Anyway, even if I didn't mean it, to him it was just a silly kiss. My eyes sting with tears I blink away.

'*Oui, merci.* I'll pay you soon,' I say quietly, through my tight throat.

'And I have some big pots of paint that might be useful. I can lend you brushes, if you like. Just drop them back when you've finished.' I'm not sure if he's talking to me or Rhi and Lou, but I thank him and wish I could wind the clock back to when we were standing by the truck with the smell of the lavender and his eyes only on me. 'I'll bring it all up later, and the lavender plants, if you'd still like them?' he asks, making a note of all the items I have and rounding off the numbers to a very acceptable figure.

We leave the *brocante*. Fabien kisses Lou and Rhi on the cheeks and, very briefly, me. I yearn to feel his cheek against mine.

'Well,' says Rhi. 'Whoever he goes home to at night is a very lucky person indeed.'

Yes, I think, very lucky. But it won't be me, and my heart shatters all over again.

TWENTY-FOUR

Rhi and Lou insist on taking me for lunch. I'm not sure if it's to make up for their sudden arrival or they want to see if what Ollie has said is true and I really have lost the plot. I take them to Henri's, through the ancient archway, down the cobbled street to the little bistro, where the awning is out, and the tables are laid outside.

Henri greets me, Rhi and Lou warmly, and tells me he is so proud to see Stephanie working with me. 'She is blooming, like the *lavande*!' he says, then adds, 'And you too! Le Petit Mas is good for both of you!' Rhi and Lou are looking at me with interest.

We order the wine and water and Lou gets straight to the point. 'So, what's going on here?' she says. 'Ollie said you'd lost the plot and refused to come home.'

Rhi kicks her under the table.

'What?' Lou flicks her straight blonde hair. 'He says

you keep saying you're not going back and now you've stopped messaging him. Look, if it's the baby thing . . .'

'The baby thing?' I ask.

'What Lou means is . . .'

'I know what she meant,' I say to Rhi, with a sigh, and the ache in my heart has suddenly returned.

'Look, I know you both mean well, and you're my dearest friends,' I lean over and put my hands over theirs, 'but, really, this is for the best. Ollie and I, we'd come to the end of the road. We wanted different things. We're not the same people we once were, and separating, before we could make each other thoroughly miserable, was the right thing to do. It was just the end of the journey for us. No blame. Just the end.'

They stare at me, clearly hearing what I'm saying and that I'm not talking gibberish. 'It's sad, really sad, but we both deserve the chance to be happy again, away from each other.' And there is a pain in my heart that will leave a deep scar because we couldn't make the distance together. 'I can't go back to our old life, the same things. This is about moving forward, wherever it takes me. And I have no idea how things are going to turn out. But I need to try.' I look at them both. 'I'm not going back. I'm here to stay. So, if you've come to persuade me otherwise, you're wasting your time. But if you've come to stay here as my friends, I'm delighted to have you. As long as you don't mind doing a bit of painting!' I suddenly laugh. I have never felt clearer about anything in my life. I lift my glass.

After a moment of stunned silence, Rhi says, 'I better get that brush out, then!' She picks up her wine and smiles.

'Best we order another bottle first!' says Lou. The three of us clink glasses.

'To new beginnings,' I say. 'What is it Dr Seuss said? "Don't cry because it's over, smile because it happened."'

'I'll let Ollie know,' says Lou, grappling for her rhinestone-decorated phone, and we smile. They understand. This is me. This is now and I'm not going back.

'I've told Ollie. He knows. He just has to accept it,' I say sadly.

'To new beginnings,' they both say, and Henri smiles from the kitchen door. The smell of bouillabaisse, the rich tomatoey fish stew with thyme, fennel and garlic, reaches us and tells us lunch is on its way. Henri places a big basket of crusty bread on the table that I know we'll be using to mop up the juices at the bottom of our bowls. I'm happy. And I can't help but think Le Petit Mas has had a lot to do with it. Henri was right: it seems to have healing powers for those who stay there.

Carine passes us as we're finishing our meal and I introduce Rhi and Lou to her.

'*Enchantée,*' she says, shaking their hands.

'Will you stay and have a drink with us, Carine?' I ask, pointing to a chair.

'I'd love to, but I have an appointment. A date!' She grins naughtily. 'But I will see you all soon!' She swishes her smart dark bob and carries on through the town in the direction of *le mairie*.

After lunch, we walk back unsteadily along the river-bank after our second bottle of rosé, and an extra glass each on Henri, then up the hill towards Le Petit Mas. Ralph bounds up to us, jumping at Lou and leaving his pawprints on her white trousers. But even she sees the funny side. At the side of the house the lavender plants, in the shade, are waiting to be dug into the ground. Tomas runs to us and Stephanie is behind him, wiping her hands on a tea towel, looking very much at home.

'All okay?' I ask Stephanie, hoping that a little time on her own has helped her.

She nods. 'Fabien came. He put together the beds, left the paint in the hall and the other stuff in the kitchen. And the lavender.'

'Thank you,' I say.

'And I made a quiche, for *le diner*, with *salade*,' she says. I think it might be her way of saying sorry. Whatever it is, it fills my heart.

'Wonderful!' I say. We made a quiche together one evening – to produce one on her own is a big step forward. I put my arm around her and she gives a huge smile.

'And Fabien?' I ask.

'He had to get back,' she says.

It's for the best, I think. No complications, but my heart is still saying otherwise.

That evening we sit outside, listening to the birds and the chorus coming from the river at the bottom of my field.

'What's that noise?' says Rhi, who, having said she'd never be able to eat anything after all that lunch, has tucked into Stephanie's quiche and salad, then had seconds.

'Frogs,' I say.

'Frogs?'

'Yes, frogs,' I repeat. 'Down by the river.'

'*La grenouille,*' says Stephanie to me, and I repeat it back to her.

Tomas jumps down from his seat and hops about. 'Ribbit, ribbit!' We all laugh.

'So, what happened to his father?' Lou asks, in her usual direct way.

Rhi gives her a nudge and I turn to Stephanie.

'Did he leave you? Mine did,' says Rhi, trying to smooth over any awkwardness. 'But my kids are doing great. One's in college and the other's working. It's getting better. If you think these years are hard, wait till he's a teenager! Sorry . . .'

'Nothing to be sorry for,' I tell her. 'I was a teenager too once! I remember how awful I was. I just wish I could have said sorry to my mum.'

'Mums know you don't really mean it,' says Rhi.

'I'm just glad we didn't have children. I wouldn't have had a clue what to do,' says Lou. 'Patrick was enough for me at the time. We were completely in love.

We didn't need anyone else,' she adds, in a rare moment of letting down her guard.

'Having JB was enough, too,' Stephanie says quietly, and we all turn to look at her. Her head is lowered, and I can feel her pain.

'You don't have to say if you don't want to.' I put a hand on hers.

'It's okay,' she says. 'He was the good bit in my life.' She looks at Tomas. 'I didn't have the best start. My mother was not a good mother. She drank and smoked and eventually drank herself to death.'

My heart twists.

'But I got myself to school when I wasn't looking after her. After she died, I got a little lost. I knew JB from school. He and I got together, but the other boys teased him, saying I was the scruffy kid, from no home. But I always kept our little flat nice. When I got pregnant, I ran. I didn't want to ruin his life. He didn't need a child and to have the other lads tease him. I didn't want to tie him down.' She pauses. 'I came here with no plans. If it wasn't for the support of the others by the riverside clearing, and people like Henri, I don't know what would have happened to me.'

I hear a sniff from Rhi, and Lou has something in her eye too.

'And now you,' she says quietly, and I squeeze her hand.

No one speaks. We all watch Tomas being a frog as

the sky turns to an amazing shade of light purple, of lavender.

'I don't think Tomas could ruin anyone's life,' I say. 'And I think he is very lucky to have someone like you to love him.'

'We should find this JB!' says Rhi, banging the table, making the empty bottles rattle. 'Let him know he has responsibilities!' And I get the feeling she's referring to her own experience as a young single mother, and Michael, who walked out on her and the kids. She ended up working at the department store with Lou and me one Christmas to afford presents for the kids, but later, when they were at school, she went back to college to retrain. 'I'll give you a good haircut too! It can really change how you feel about yourself,' she says. I'm hoping she means in the morning, not now.

'She's right,' says Lou. 'JB might be delighted to find out he has a Tomas in his life. And a good haircut really does make you feel great!' She holds up a finger shakily. 'Nails too!'

My mind is whirring about what to do for the best.

'It's up to you, Stephanie,' I say, clearly not having drunk quite as much as my friends. 'If you want to find JB, we can . . .'

Suddenly I find myself wondering what Fabien would think of this idea and wishing I could ask his advice. But maybe Henri is the person to speak to. He has much more experience and has brought up daughters. Am I saying the right things? I think of Mum and what she might do. I can only do what I feel might be right for Stephanie and Tomas.

'Really? You think he'd like to know?'

'Look, there are no certainties, but maybe he deserves a chance to get to know his child.'

She looks at me. 'Then I'd like Tomas to meet his father. I always wanted a father. Sadly, it was never meant to be.'

'I never met mine either,' I tell her quietly. 'He and my mother broke up before I was born. My mum brought me up. I never felt the need to track him down. I was happy with Mum. We were a family.'

'Didn't you want to know? I did,' she says. 'I always hoped there was someone out there who'd love me like I wanted to be loved.'

I shake my head. 'As long as you feel loved, that's all you need.'

'I didn't,' she says, with a flash of anger in her eyes. 'My mother loved drink and drugs far more than she loved me, or she wouldn't have left me to bring myself up, would she?'

We all fall silent.

'It's up to you, Stephanie. It's your choice,' I finally say.

'I'd like Tomas to know his father, to know there was someone else he could turn to if anything happened to me.'

'Then it's a plan!' says Rhi, banging the table, her enthusiasm fuelled by wine. 'Tomorrow!'

Tomas falls over and cries. Stephanie jumps up and goes to pick him up, as does Rhi.

'Ah, he's tired,' says Rhi, and Stephanie stares at her. 'Sorry, sorry,' says Rhi. 'I have to remember I'm not a mum any more. Well, not one that's needed. At least the salon still needs me. Must check the iPad!'

'But you're a good friend,' I say, stopping her getting it out again, as she's been doing at every opportunity. 'And I'm so glad you came.'

'And tomorrow we'll find Tomas's father,' she says.

'Hmm, but now we have to make up your beds,' I say, and can see that my two wobbly friends are going to be of no use whatsoever. I look at all the lavender plants I have to deal with. There's a lot to do. I just hope I'm doing the right thing in helping Stephanie find Tomas's father. But I know we have to try. I've never felt such responsibility for someone else's happiness before, and it's terrifying.

TWENTY-FIVE

'How was Henri?' I ask Stephanie, when she returns from delivering the desserts the next day.

'A little tired. I told him he should rest but he said he's fine. He has too much to do to put his feet up. Too many people relying on him.'

'Surely he could close the bistro for a week or two. Go on holiday.'

'Henri would never close.' She puts the money on the table, with the shopping, then hands me the receipt.

The swallows circle high in the clear blue sky, and the crickets chirp among the grassy clumps in the big empty field under the hot July sun.

'I should plough this if I'm going to put in these plants, or weed it at least,' I say, looking out through the French windows at the field, then across the valley to the purple patchwork quilt of Serge's land. I look at all the lavender plants I watered early that morning in

175

the sunlight as it reached through the tall oak trees, hanging with balls of mistletoe, like great Christmas baubles. The air was full of the smell of pine, rosemary and lavender, and I want to start digging over the soil for the new plants. But we have other things to do today, ghosts to lay to rest. I take a deep, reviving breath, feeling the calm and strength the air here gives me. I must get them planted soon and send a gift to Serge to thank him. I'll take him some biscuits on market day, I think.

'So, are we going? Did you mean it?' Stephanie asks nervously, having helped me put away the shopping. The kitchen has become much more like home than the empty shell it was the day Ollie left.

'If you want to,' I say cautiously. It must be her decision. I don't know JB so I can't know if this is a good or bad thing. I can only be there for her.

'I've decided. I want to find JB. I want him to meet his son,' she says. 'He may not want me, but I hope he'll want Tomas. I think that's why I like Fabien so much, because he likes Tomas. I want the best for my boy.'

My heart and stomach lurch at the sound of his name. 'I know you do. Come on, then. Let's find JB and see if we can introduce him to Tomas. Do you know where we're going and how to get there?'

She nods, with an excited smile on her face.

Soon the five of us, including Tomas, are on the bus. Once Rhi and Lou emerged from their long, peaceful night's sleep, we went into town and we're on our way. It's hot outside but the bus is cool. Rhi is checking the salon on her iPad, using the free Wi-Fi, checking bookings and giving clear instructions to her staff about clients she would usually handle and how they like their hair. I know what a sacrifice she has made to come out here. Lou is checking her reflection in the tinted window, thinking I can't see her doing it but I can.

We travel to a smart, plane-tree-lined neighbouring town. We get off the bus.

'This is lovely,' says Rhi. 'We could have lunch?' she suggests, and we all frown at her. 'After we've found JB, of course,' she adds hastily.

'Why didn't we just find him on Facebook, like everyone else?' asks Lou.

'Stephanie felt, and I agree, that Facebook isn't the place for this kind of conversation. She'd rather meet him face to face.' And I'm nervous for her.

It's a much newer town than Ville de Violet. Small and neat. Everything in its place. There aren't the older properties of our town, or its quaint cobbled streets, characterful archways and alleys. There is a cream-coloured town hall, and a sparkling fountain in the middle of the main square, a big new chemist, next to a huge supermarket, and floral decorations on the roundabout.

'This way,' says Stephanie, holding Tomas close to her.

We follow her off the main street into an estate of

small, neat houses. I can tell we're getting close when her footsteps slow. She seems to be making a different journey of her own.

'Is this where you grew up, Stephanie?'

She shrugs in the way she does when she wants to keep life at arm's length. 'Not here, but near. That way,' she jerks a thumb, 'keep going out of town, past the skatepark, following the graffiti trail. Before that, we were in Marseille. Mostly Marseille,' she says. 'We tried living here when she wanted to get clean, but it didn't last. She ended up spending more and more time back in Marseille.'

'Is this . . . ?' I start.

'She died in Marseille. The *gendarmes* came to tell me,' she says. There's a hollowness in her eyes I haven't seen before. A deep well where the love is missing.

'*Maman*,' says Tomas, too tired to walk now. Maybe we should get a pushchair for him.

Stephanie scoops him into her arms. Then she looks at me. 'Here, take him,' she says, and hands him to me. 'I'll go there alone and see if JB's in. If he is, I'll speak to him first. Then I'll come back to you if he wants to meet Tomas.' The hand-over happens without me thinking about it.

'You sure you don't want me to come with you? Rhi or Lou could look after Tomas.'

She shakes her head. 'You look after him, please.'

She's entrusting me with everything that means anything to her in the world.

'We'll take a little walk over to that bit of greenery,' I point, 'and look at the flowers, *les fleurs*, eh, Tomas?'

She drops her head and walks away just as she did when she arrived, like a whirlwind, in my life just a few weeks ago. Both our lives have changed since our worlds literally collided. Ralph pulls at his lead, wanting to sniff and explore. What an unusual bunch we must seem: Lou, with her Dolly Parton looks, Rhi on her phone, ringing the salon back home, me, Tomas and Stephanie, all of us here for each other. All of us with a past that's left its footprints in the landscape of our lives.

I put Tomas down and he runs around chasing bees and butterflies in the unrelenting July sunshine, while Rhi and Lou head for the shade of a big tree. I can just see Stephanie from where I am. She's standing on a doorstep talking to someone. She isn't invited in, and I'm indignant on her behalf. I can just see the person pulling the door closed behind them and joining her on the front doorstep. It must be JB. My heart lifts for her and Tomas. They're talking. That's good, I think. I watch intently, hoping that, any minute now, they'll walk this way together for Tomas to meet his father. I check his face and give it a quick polish with a wet wipe, then turn back. They're not standing on the doorstep any longer. The front door is shut and I have butterflies. Then I see Stephanie appearing from behind a large yellow flowering bush. I can't see JB. Is he following her? Or is she walking back to us on her own?

TWENTY-SIX

Her head is held high. She says nothing. Scoops Tomas up and holds him close to her, despite his protests. She looks at me with angry tears in her eyes, and I feel their fury burrowing into mine. She turns and walks, without a word, towards the bus stop. We follow her silently, and return to Ville de Violet and Le Petit Mas. None of us speaks because there is nothing you can say when the father of your child has just refused to see him or have anything to do with you. I feel wretched, and angry, and I want to go back and tell JB what a mistake he's making, what a wonderful mum Stephanie is, what a precious little boy Tomas is. I want to tell Stephanie how brave she is. But, right now, I think she blames me for the pain she's feeling.

TWENTY-SEVEN

Next morning, after a sombre night, I walk downstairs, wondering how to make things right with Stephanie. I need to tell her how brave she is, and what a great job she's doing with Tomas. As I come downstairs, I hear the front door click shut. Strange. Stephanie must still be avoiding me. Or maybe it's the wind whipping up outside again. The mistral is back. The shutters are rattling on their hinges. I walk into the kitchen. Tomas is sitting at the table, Ralph at his feet.

'Stephanie,' I call. Maybe she's nipped back to the caravan, knowing I was here to keep an eye on Tomas when she heard me coming downstairs.

'Would you like some *chocolat chaud*, Tomas?' I ask. Usually Stephanie has started to get out the ingredients for the next recipe in the book and decide what she needs to buy when she walks into town to deliver that day's desserts. Today the work surface is empty and she hasn't turned on the oven to warm up.

'Stephanie,' I call again, looking outside towards the caravan. There's the *toot-toot* of the bakery van, and Tomas jumps down from his chair, clutching *Monsieur Lapin*, which he never goes anywhere without, and the two of us run down the drive to buy bread and croissants for everyone's breakfast. I hand over a box of biscuits to Simone, the baker, and receive our baguettes, croissants and Tomas's *pain au chocolat*. He insists on carrying the baguettes, which are far too long for him and almost topple out of his arms. It makes me smile, until I remember Stephanie's tears when she walked away from JB's home. Today we will throw ourselves into our work and hope that it helps to mend her broken heart.

We walk into the house as Rhi and Lou are coming downstairs.

'Coffee? Tea? Breakfast?' I ask. 'Stephanie!'

'*Maman!*' Tomas shouts, carrying his bread with pride into the kitchen.

It's only then I see a note on the table.

TWENTY-EIGHT

I snatch it up and read it, the blood draining from my face. Suddenly I'm freezing cold despite the sun warming the day outside. My phone rings. I spin to left and right, looking for where I've left it. Rhi and Lou join in. Rhi sees it in the fruit bowl and hands it to Lou, who tries to pass it to me but it slips through my hands on to the floor with a clatter, making Tomas jump. He drops the baguettes and bursts into tears as Ralph snatches one and runs off with it.

'*Allô!* Stephanie!' I shout, into the phone. I scoop Tomas on to my hip and sway gently to soothe him.

'Del? It's me!'

My heart plummets.

'Ollie,' I say flatly, disappointed. 'Look, I'm really sorry but I can't talk right now.'

'Del, I really need a conversation with you.'

'Ollie, there's something I really need to do.'

'Del, after ten years of marriage, it's the least you can do. Just hear me out!'

I take a deep breath. Tomas has settled and Rhi has handed him a *pain au chocolat*, which he is eating, scattering crumbs over my right shoulder. I try to put him on a chair, but he starts to cry again so I stand up and hold him.

'What's that noise?' asks Ollie.

'Oh, nothing, just a chair, squeaking.' I look at Rhi and Lou.

'So, Rhi and Lou are there. I asked them . . . I wanted to be sure, Del. Is this what you really want?'

'Is what what I really want, Ollie?' I snap.

'Is it really over for you? Is there no way we can get over this?'

'No, Ollie, it's really over.'

'You're sure? I want to be clear that this is what you want.'

'I'm sure.' I sigh, needing to get off the phone. 'We agreed. You get the money in the account and I get the house.'

'And that's okay with you, is it?'

'Yes. If you need me to sign something, just send it on. Now, I've really got to go, Ollie.'

'And you're staying in France for good,' he says.

I sigh again. 'If I can, yes, I'm staying right here in Le Petit Mas.' My home, I think.

Suddenly there is silence and I wonder if he's going

to say something else. But I really don't have time. 'Okay, Ollie? I have to go.'

'Right, but, Del?'

'Yes?' I'm about to press 'end call'.

'I'm sorry, okay?'

'Really, nothing to be sorry about. We just have to be happy in our new lives,' I say, and mean it. 'But I have to go.'

'I feel I should explain,' Ollie says.

My heart sinks. We're about to go over old ground. 'Ollie, I'm sorry. We've been over this. No need for any explanations. We're living our own lives now. I have to go.'

'Goodbye, Del.'

'Goodbye, Ollie,' I say quickly. I throw the phone on to the table and pick up the note again.

'What's up?' says Rhi.

'Is Ollie okay?' asks Lou. 'Did he talk to you? He said he was going to phone. Explain.'

'It's not Ollie that's the problem.' I look at the two of them, who glance at each other. 'It's Stephanie!' My mouth goes dry. 'She's gone!'

TWENTY-NINE

'Gone?' they say at the same time.

'She can't have gone! Not with Tomas here!' says Rhi. If they're looking as devastated as I feel, this must be happening.

'Look.' I hold out the note and slowly lower Tomas on to the chair, his ever-faithful companion Ralph by his side. He reaches out and puts one hand on top of his head.

Rhi takes the note and passes it to Lou.

We all look at it, written on a paper bag from the greengrocer.

Dear Del, Thank you for giving me and Tomas a home.
Tomas has been so happy since he moved here. This is
the kind of life I dreamed of for him. I cannot give it to
him. But you can. And so I have decided to leave and
let him have a life with someone who can do better

than me. Please tell him I love him and have done this because I love him and want the best for him. Do not try to find me. This is for the best. Stephanie. x

'She's gone!' Rhi looks at Tomas. 'Without Tomas!' He smiles a crumby smile and my heart cracks wide open. 'Because she thinks you can give him a better life. She thinks she has nothing to offer.'

'There's a girl whose confidence is at rock bottom,' says Lou, shaking her head. 'You can't rely on a man to fill the hole in your life.'

'You can't rely on a man full stop!' says Rhi.

'I don't think that's necessarily true,' I say. 'You've never trusted a man since Michael left you, and you don't let anyone close enough so you can't get hurt,' I say.

They start to argue, but we all know now is not the time. Maybe I shouldn't have said that, but it's true. None of us has got it right.

'You were the only one with a man and you dumped him,' says Lou.

'Not now,' says Rhi, sensibly, and we all bite our tongues.

'But I do know that I'm to blame for her feeling like this. She looked to me for advice. And after the business with Fabien . . .'

'What business with Fabien?' asks Lou, straight to the point again.

'Nothing,' I say. 'She asked my advice about JB and

I told her to go for it. I thought she was being so strong and brave when actually she was cracking under the strain. We have to find her.' I shove the note into my back pocket. 'I may not be a mum, but one thing I do know,' I say, gesturing at Tomas, 'is that everyone needs their mum.' Mine had probably given me the strength to do what I've done here. She always made me feel that everything would turn out okay in the end. And if it wasn't okay, it wasn't the end, she used to say. Stephanie doesn't have that person. She needs to know it will all be okay in the end. She needs to be with Tomas. And I need to swallow my pride. I need to talk to Fabien.

THIRTY

The three of us and Tomas hurry into town, Rhi, Lou and I taking turns to carry him. Tomas refused to leave Ralph behind, so he's come too, bounding along the riverside path, darting this way and that, each of us taking turns to hold the lead and be towed along. I have no doubt where I need to go first. All my instincts lead me there, despite my promise to keep my distance. There is only one person I need to get to right now.

'Fabien!' I call, as I hurry up the road to the *brocante*, hot, out of breath and terrified something dreadful has happened to Stephanie, a young woman who thinks she has failed at everything in life, and who has been rejected by everyone she ever cared about, her mother, Fabien and now JB. I try to think back to when I was that age. Seventeen and foolish. I can't say I'm particularly sensible now. I've separated from my husband to live in an empty house and am scraping a living selling lavender bakes and desserts. Plus I've taken in a vulnerable girl with her child because I couldn't leave her where she was. Now I've made her life a thousand times worse. However, although I may not be any more sensible now than I was at seventeen, I have learned to take account of my gut feelings. And right now they're telling me to find Stephanie – fast.

Fabien is with a young woman, about his age, who is looking at a damaged but beautiful dappled-grey rocking horse. He turns to me, his eyebrows raised in surprise. Tomas cheers, delighted to see him.

'Fabien! I need your help,' I say quickly. 'It's Stephanie!'

He excuses himself from the customer, who looks miffed, and hurries over to us. He grasps Tomas's outstretched hand, and kisses it. My heart somersaults and breaks a little more. Why couldn't JB have felt like this? If he had, maybe Stephanie wouldn't have run away and Tomas would still be with his mum. She is all he needs. One good parent is better than no parent, as I know.

'She's disappeared,' I say quickly.

'*Disparu.*' Lou finds some school French and clearly thinks I need help explaining.

'Leaving Tomas!' Rhi joins in.

'I'm really worried about her,' I tell Fabien, gazing into his green eyes and knowing he understands without my having to say any more.

'She left a note,' Rhi is still explaining.

'She thinks she can't offer Tomas anything, that he's better off without her.'

I am racked with guilt. I only wanted to help – and now I've forced a young mum to do the worst imaginable thing and walk away from her son, because she thinks she's worthless. Tears slide down my cheeks. I heard somewhere you cry different tears for different types of sadness. These aren't the same as the ones I wept on the night I spent in the house after Ollie left: they were for my failure, as a wife and mother. These tears are of sadness, loss and grief, like the ones I cried when Mum died, just months ago. I feel helpless, lost and utterly wretched.

'I have to find her, Fabien. I have to put this right,' I say. I wipe my face with my forearm. Tomas hands me *Monsieur Lapin*, which makes me cry and smile at the same time.

'Okay, don't worry.' Fabien reaches out a hand and hesitates – I think he's going to wipe the tears and my insides thunder with excitement. Instead, he lays it on my shoulder in a friendly, reassuring way. It's not half as intimate as touching my face, and my heart starts to slow. Now he ruffles Tomas's hair gently and speaks quietly to him, telling him that everything will be okay. Tomas holds *Monsieur Lapin* to my cheeks. The stuffed rabbit smells of lavender. It smells of home. Like a hug from my mum. Now I need to find Tomas's mum so he can have one of those hugs too.

'I'll message Carine. If Stephanie is hiding in any of

the empty houses, or holiday rentals, Carine will know. She can put out feelers. She has many . . . contacts,' he says. I think he's referring to her lovers. 'She is even . . . close friends with the mayor. They will all look out for Stephanie and contact Carine if they see her.' He finishes sending the message. 'In the meantime, we will go and see Henri. He'll be able to tell us more. He knows most of the stallholders in the market, the shop owners and—'

'Henri! Good idea! He might have seen her.' I spin round and head out of the courtyard, as Fabien apologizes to his customer, who tuts and flounces out. He pulls the gates to the courtyard shut behind him and locks them.

I head across the road and through the worn stone arch, then down the narrow street, as fast as the shiny warm cobbles will let me, towards Henri's bistro where the awnings are out and tables laid, the paper cloths flapping in the constant breeze.

I hurry to the restaurant, still carrying Tomas, my arms aching. I don't want to pass him to Rhi or Lou – I can't let him down. I say hello to Henri, accept his kisses and explain what's happened. Henri nods and listens.

'I'll speak to people. Put the word out. She won't have gone far,' he says reassuringly. 'Give me your mobile number. I'll text if there's any news.'

'What should I do? Where can I start looking?'

'Remember what it was like to be seventeen,' he tells

me. 'She's hurt. She's angry, with you, with the world. Give her time. She'll come round.' He looks at me kindly, then wraps his arms around me and Tomas, and I let him, taking strength from him. 'And she may be seventeen and angry, but she's also a mother and she loves this one. She won't stay away for long. She won't leave him, no matter what she's saying. Don't worry. We'll make sure she's safe.'

I don't ask who he means by 'we', but I trust what he's said. I study his face. Stephanie was right: he looks tired. There are dark circles around his lined eyes.

He pushes his white hair off his forehead. 'Go back to Le Petit Mas, in case she comes home and wants to see Tomas,' he tells me.

'If you see her, tell her I'm sorry,' I say. 'Tell her to come home.' This is home. He nods, understanding, and briefly hugs me again. I turn to see Fabien looking straight at me, making me blush.

We walk back to the main road. Fabien says goodbye and starts to cross the street to the *brocante*, pulling out his keys to unlock the doors.

'Thank you, Fabien,' I say.

'She'll turn up. Try not to worry. Henri knows,' he says, and unlocks the gates. Suddenly I feel a huge distance between us and it's not just the road.

We turn silently towards the river. There, outside the swanky bar that Ollie loved, are Cora and her friends.

'Cora! I'm looking for the young woman, Stephanie,

who's staying with me,' I say quickly, before they can kiss us all. I need to spread the word, and fast.

'Oh, yes.' She nods politely, clearly snubbed by my having cut out the formalities.

'Have you seen her? She has blonde hair, and is very slight,' I blurt.

'Ah,' says Cora, slowly and deliberately, infuriating me. 'I heard you had one of those homeless people staying with you.' She smiles but it doesn't reach her eyes.

'Um, Stephanie isn't homeless. She lives with me and works for me.'

Her eyebrows shoot up. 'Lives with you? I assumed she was doing some kind of community service, pay-back for what she did to you.'

My hackles rise and I bite my lip.

'And who's this little chap?' she asks, reaching for Tomas, who pulls away and nestles into my neck.

'This is Tomas,' I say impatiently.

'Oh, and is he visiting too?' She looks at Rhi and Lou.

'No,' says Lou. 'He lives at Le Petit Mas.'

'Sounds like quite a commune you've got there!' Cora smiles again. 'Just, well, you don't need me to tell you to be careful.'

She sips her *café au lait*.

'What exactly do you mean by that?'

'Well, a leopard can't change its spots, dear. Once a thief, always a thief. Whatever you might think. Whatever your good intentions . . .'

I am now fully fuelled on rage. 'Stephanie is not a user or a thief. She's a hard worker and a great mother.'

'Really?' says Cora. 'Then where is she now and why are you out looking for her? What kind of a mother leaves their little boy? I'm just looking out for you, Del. We have to stick together out here.'

I won't listen to this woman. Stephanie is a good mother. It's me that's in the wrong. 'I am sticking together, Cora, with my community. We're all living in the same town. We're all residents here.'

'Of course, of course. Stay, have a drink with us,' she says, pulling out a chair. 'I can see you're upset.'

I shake my head. 'Sorry, I have to go. Sorry to have interrupted your coffee.'

'Call me if you want a get-together,' she calls after me, and I find myself rolling my eyes.

We pass the clearing where the few people there raise a hand and wish me a good day.

'How come they all know you?' Rhi asks.

'Um, I'm not really sure,' I say. 'I did leave them a plate of biscuits once . . . Come, let's go home. We'll wait for *Maman* there,' I say to Tomas.

'*Maman?*' he says. His mouth turns down and tears fall. I hope Henri is right and she comes home soon.

THIRTY-ONE

That night, I lie awake, Ralph at my feet, listening to Tomas sleeping and calling for *Maman*. I have no idea what to do when he wakes, other than sing him the song my mum used to sing to me. I'm just winging it, like the rest of my life right now. And when I'm not soothing Tomas or worrying about where Stephanie might be and how she must be missing her little one, my thoughts flick to Fabien. I remember how he looked at me when I was hugging Henri. What was the expression in his eyes? I felt as if he was on one side of the river and I was on the other, and although he was trying to tell me something, I couldn't hear him because of the distance between us. Was it just a silly kiss? I don't want to be his fling with an older woman . . .

Stephanie, where are you? I get up and walk to the window, looking for signs of light in the gypsy caravan. But there are none. I gaze up at the dark sky, scattered with stars, and hope she's safe. I even find myself asking Mum to keep an eye on her, and trying to explain how Stephanie came into my life, how I feel responsible for the chaos I've caused but also how much I've come to care for her and Tomas.

Morning comes, and Tomas is up early, with the birds and the cockerel. I had just dropped off to sleep. He runs down to the kitchen, with Ralph protecting him on the stairs, then he's out of the door and staring at the gypsy caravan, wanting to find *Maman* and tell her about his sleepover with Ralph. My heart plummets. Just for a moment, like Tomas, I'd hoped she would be back.

The bakery van turns up and I tell Simone that Stephanie is missing. She's already heard and is keeping an eye open. She hands Tomas a *pain au chocolat* and refuses any money, wishes me luck and hopes Stephanie will be home soon.

We spend the day at Le Petit Mas, waiting. Rhi decides that she and Lou should start painting the bedrooms. I'm not sure that Lou has ever held a paintbrush. Only the ones she uses to put on her makeup.

I am going to put in the lavender plants, once I've made Henri's desserts for the day. I get Tomas to stand on a chair next to me and throw the flour on to the work surface. I miss Stephanie being here, making me read out the recipe in French and correcting my pronunciation.

'*Non, répétez,*' she would say, sounding like a French

schoolteacher. In return, I made her cook, like Mum used to do with me, showing her and overseeing her as she broke eggs into a bowl, missed and scooped up the egg as it ran over the work surface.

'*Merde!*' she would say, and I'd raise a disapproving eyebrow, telling her to relax when she cooks instead of worrying, and watching the pride on her face when she pulled out a tray from the oven. Biscuits and pastries made with lavender . . . and love.

Tomas and I make basic shortbread for Henri. I can't be more adventurous, not with Stephanie missing. Looks like we're back where we started, only worse off, with both of us more miserable than we were before we met, both wishing for things in our hearts and losing them. What will happen if Stephanie, God forbid, doesn't come back? What will happen to Tomas? I scoop him up and hurry into town, leaving Ralph behind. He flumps, dejected, on to the cool tiled floor.

'Henri?' The bistro is still closed when I get there. I knock on the glass of the door, with its dark-wood surround, and try to look in through the window, which is half obscured with French lace. 'Henri?' I shout up at the windows above the bistro, the shutters still closed. 'Henri?' I call again, sliding the box of biscuits on to an outside table that, unusually, wasn't put away when he closed last night.

The shutters open. '*Oui, j'arrive!*' he calls.

I breathe a sigh of relief.

'Sorry, I slept over,' he says, rubbing his hair and his unshaven face.

'Overslept!' I manage to smile.

'Yes, yes!'

'I brought the biscuits. I hope they're okay. Is there any news?'

'The customers love the biscuits, with *café* and ice cream. Do you think you could try lavender ice cream?' he asks.

'Of course,' I say, not thinking about ice cream at all. Within no time he's dressed and opening the front door.

'I've seen Stephanie,' he says.

'Oh, thank God!' My body feels as if all the air has been let out of it and wants to collapse in a heap on the floor. 'Where is she? Is she coming home?'

He holds up a hand. 'Give her time. She's angry and hurt, but she's safe,' he says. 'She'll be missing the comfort of her own bed and this little one very soon.' He kisses Tomas's hand.

'Thank you, Henri,' I say. 'Please tell her I'm sorry. And tell her how much Tomas is missing his *maman*. He needs her. Please tell her to come home.'

He puts a hand on my shoulder. 'Go home. Wait for her,' he says, and coughs. 'Summer cold!' he mutters, then turns into the restaurant and opens the blinds, ready for business.

I walk back up the cobbled street and find myself heading in the direction of the *brocante*, wondering whether to pop in on Fabien, share the news that Stephanie is alive, but not home yet. I look at the open gates – but what can I say? She's still gone. And whatever happened between me and him had a part in making her leave. I have to stay away and, with all my strength, I turn, catching a glimpse of him as I do, and walk towards the river, feeling the divide between us growing wider.

The sun is hot now. I'm desperate to get back to the cool of the house. I walk along the shade of the riverbank, past the clearing, but there's only one person there, sitting under the tree. I recognize him. He's here more often than not. He has the long beard and long hair. He nods as I pass, watching me go. Tomas is chasing butterflies.

Back at Le Petit Mas, Rhi and Lou are sitting outside the kitchen, with glasses of rosé in their hands, which are covered with white paint.

'To be honest, we weren't as good at painting as we thought we might be!' says Rhi, after I've told them the news about Stephanie. They lead me upstairs like guilty children.

'I don't know how all these TV programmes make it look so easy!' says Lou. 'You'd think anyone could buy a château and pick up a paintbrush . . .'

We stand in the doorway of the room Lou has been sleeping in and they've been painting. To be honest . . .

'It looks dreadful!' I say. We wince, then start to laugh, a release, and find we can't stop. Tomas joins in, then stands on the paint tin's lid and walks white footprints across the floor.

'You can see all the cracks still!' says Rhi.

'I like the cracks,' I say. 'They add character.'

'Isn't that where the light comes in?' asks Lou.

She's probably right. It's going to be a while before this place could ever be ready for B & B guests. Anyway, right now, I like it being just us. 'It makes it what it is, cracks and all.'

'Just like us!' says Rhi. I walk across the room, drawn to look out of the window at the sun-drenched valley. Once more, I wonder where Stephanie is and when – if – she'll be back.

'Oh, no! No, no, no, no, no!' I run to the stairs, the others in hot pursuit behind me.

THIRTY-TWO

Ralph is panting proudly, his fur stained red from the freshly dug red soil he's standing in. There is soil everywhere and lavender too, from the new plants Carine and Fabien gave me. I put them in and have been diligently watering them every day. I could cry. In fact, I hold my hands over my face and let the tears come in sobbing gulps for the mess I've made of things. Everything. The house, Stephanie and Tomas, Fabien . . .

Rhi and Lou wrap their arms around me. Tomas hugs my knees. Ralph barks, not wanting to be left out.

The sobbing eases, and I say what I know everyone is thinking.

'What if I've made a mistake? What if I shouldn't have stayed? What if it was just an impetuous hormonal moment of madness? Maybe I should have gone home and made it work with Ollie.'

My friends look at me and for once Lou doesn't speak first.

'What if you're just tired and worried?' says Rhi. 'Only you can know if this is what you really want, or if you'd rather have your old life with Ollie. No one's going to judge you.'

'You've always been there for us, Del, and we're here for you, whatever you want to do,' says Lou. I straighten and look at the dug-up plants with despair.

Rhi looks at me, then at the plants, picks one up, digs a hole with her hands and puts the plant back. 'Am I doing it right?'

I smile and nod. Lou, in her painting clothes, takes a plant and does the same. I sniff. 'How about it, Tomas? Shall we plant the lavender too? Start again?'

And he nods. I just wish Stephanie was here with us.

We spend the afternoon replanting the lavender, in the heat. When we've finished those, we plant the ones Fabien brought from Serge. We're much better at planting lavender than we are at painting and house renovation. We wear big straw hats against the afternoon sun, and the repetitive nature of the work seems to bring us comfort as we wait for news. In the middle of the afternoon, I hear a car pull up the drive. Fabien's truck. I'm hot, dirty, and my face is still puffy from all the crying I did earlier.

Rhi takes one look at me and says, 'I'll go.' Before I can say anything she's run round to the front of the house, while I dust myself down. Tomas follows her, with Ralph.

I take a deep breath, lift my head and walk round the side of the house, in time to see Fabien's truck disappearing down the drive in a cloud of dust.

Rhi turns to me and shrugs. 'He wanted to know if there was any news of Stephanie,' she says. 'I told him Henri had seen her, but she hadn't come home. He brought Tomas a present.'

It's the rocking horse. And, by the look of it, Fabien's given it a makeover. He's even painted 'Tomas' on the saddle. Tomas is thrilled and is already climbing aboard. Ralph is looking at it warily – he has competition.

I don't know what I was expecting from Fabien, but not the cold shoulder. Rhi is staring at me, and I know she's wondering if anything has gone on. 'It was just a kiss,' I say quietly, even though it was so much more.

We walk around to the side of the house. My back aches, but I'm determined to finish getting the plants in. If nothing else, it stops me thinking about the mess I've made of things, and backache is the very least I deserve. Maybe I should just go home. Maybe this was a stupid idea.

As the sun sets, the sky turns a beautiful shade of blue, pink, and then purple, the colour of lavender again. At least I've started to bring lavender back to the *mas*: I will have done something good to leave behind, if I go, something that didn't make more mess.

I walk into the cool kitchen and pour a glass of water. I offer Rhi and Lou wine, but no one's really in the mood.

Rhi's iPad is on the table, where she's been keeping in touch with the salon, watching customers come and go on her video link, making sure the business keeps ticking over, tutting when someone doesn't do something in the way she likes it done.

My laptop went with all my belongings and frankly, I'm in no rush to get any of it back. But right now, I do need to hear from Stephanie. I look at Rhi's iPad, open it up. It looks like the internet is actually working and I quickly log in to my Facebook page, fingers shaking. I know Rhi won't mind. I wait for it to load, hoping Stephanie has tried to get in touch that way. But there's nothing. I think about Ollie and feel guilty that he'll have to explain to people why I'm not there. Maybe I should post something. Or maybe – maybe this was a blip and I should go back. I flip to his page and see he's changed his Facebook photo to a profile of himself, not the two of us. I wonder what he's written and I'm about to look when my name is shouted from outside.

I run to the front door to see what the commotion's about. Lou is hanging out of her window, freshly showered, a towel around her. Rhi has stood up from where she was playing with Tomas on the rocking horse in the dusty driveway. She's shouting my name at the top of her voice. Ralph is barking. And then we all peer down the drive to a small figure, carrying her blue plastic bags, walking up it. She stops halfway.

'Tomas,' I say, despite the catch in my throat. He looks up at me, seemingly oblivious, and I hope he realizes what this means. I point and he looks. Rhi is evidently about to burst. And both figures stand and stare at each other. I hold my breath, as does Rhi, who's turning red in the face. The figure standing halfway up the drive still hasn't moved, and I don't want to be the first to do so. I don't want to get it wrong. I don't want to scare her off.

Then, suddenly, Tomas climbs off the horse, drops to the dusty ground and shouts, '*Maman!*'

I breathe a huge sigh of relief and tears spring to my eyes yet again, this time of sheer joy. I can see Tomas toddling towards her. She drops her bags and runs to him. He stumbles and falls, face down. Rhi lurches forward, but stops herself. I clench my fists, resisting the urge to help. As he lets out a wail, Stephanie scoops him up, and holds him to her, tightly, and he puts his arms around her, tightly, as if they'll never let each other go. And, once again, I can feel Mum close to me, making me feel that everything is going to be okay.

Stephanie kisses him over and over again, then walks towards me, abandoning her bags where they are. Has she come to take Tomas and go away again? Is this goodbye? There is nothing keeping her here.

She stands in front of me. Her eyes are big, tired and

scared. I want to hug her, but I can't. I have to let her tell me what she wants. I just feel it.

'*Maman*,' says Tomas, smiling now, making me smile too.

'*Oui*,' I say. 'Your *maman* is here. You've missed her. And I think she has missed you.' I look at her. 'You're his mother, Stephanie, and no one can ever replace you, or do a better job than the one you're doing. He adores you. And no matter how many times things go wrong, he'll never stop loving you. You're his mum. And you only need one good parent in life to feel loved. I know. I had just one.'

There are tears in her eyes as she asks, 'Can I come back, please?' She swallows. 'Back to how it was? I'll work really hard, and I won't let you down.'

'You've never let me down, Stephanie. I feel I did that to you, and I'm sorry you've been hurt.' Then I can't stop myself any longer: I open my arms and hug her and Tomas close to me. 'Welcome home, Stephanie,' I say. 'Now, go and shower and let's cook,' I say, finally releasing her.

Then Rhi hugs her and so does Lou. I get to work in the kitchen making one of Mum's and my favourites: pasta bolognese.

Later I walk outside, where Rhi tops up my wine glass, then hers and Lou's, and raises a toast. 'To Le Petit Mas, cracks and all!'

'Cracks and all!' We sip as the sun vanishes on another day at Le Petit Mas. I wonder how much longer this lovely time here with friends will last, and push to the back of my mind the question of what will happen when they go, if this place isn't up and running as a *chambre d'hôte*. And why Ollie has changed his profile picture so soon.

For now, though, I'm just going to enjoy being here, with the people I care about. I'll worry about everything else tomorrow. The cracks and all.

THIRTY-THREE

The following morning, as the sun begins to rise, life seems to have found its groove again, like the lavender plants in their rows in the field. Where yesterday there was chaos, now there is order.

It's market day. Everyone is delighted to see Stephanie back. Even Cora comes over to say hello. 'But just a word of warning,' she says conspiratorially. 'I heard you were running this business from home. Hope you have all the paperwork in order. You know what the French are like! I'm telling you as a friend, looking out for you.' She seems genuine. Would someone try to push me out because I'm not French?

Henri is serving a table of two outside, and Stephanie is telling interested holidaymakers that the bakes are made at Le Petit Mas, with lavender and love. But Cora's words niggle. What if I shouldn't be making these things in my own kitchen? What if there are regulations I don't know about, including not having hairy dogs in the kitchen? Is everyone who they seem to be?

Everything seems to be hanging by a thread that might snap at any moment. Even so, I let the morning sun warm my face and watch Stephanie and Tomas handing out samples on the plates I bought that first day in the *brocante*. Henri has told Fabien the good news about Stephanie. I wish he'd come to see her . . . or maybe I'm wishing he'd come to see me, which wouldn't be a good idea. No, it's best we keep our distance for all our sakes.

As the church clock strikes midday, we have hardly anything left. Tomas was a great salesman, making people smile. We pack up, put the table in Henri's storeroom, have lunch and walk home along the riverbank with the bees buzzing, the water flowing in and around the bright green plants growing on the bottom, past the deep purple irises and overhanging wisteria. We pass the clearing. Stephanie stops and greets the man with the long beard and hair. She seems to be thanking him. She even takes Tomas to meet him and the man's face lights up – he's apparently delighted to see Stephanie reunited with her son. She waves to him as we walk on. I don't ask who he is or where she went when she ran away.

'He helped me, when I . . . was upset,' she says.

We walk with Tomas between us. '*Un, deux, trois!*' we say, and swing him into the air.

Maybe, just maybe, life is settling down for me here. I have a small business and I could enquire about any paperwork that needs to be filed. I have help with the business from Stephanie and my friends, who have given no sign that they intend to leave just yet. Life is starting to look pretty good, even without Fabien in it. Although I can't help but wish he was . . .

'*Encore, encore!*' shouts Tomas.

'*Un, deux, trois!* Wheeee!'

I may not have everything I want in life, but I've got a lot that makes me smile. I have enough to be content.

I am definitely moving forward.

THIRTY-FOUR

'What do you mean, a man?' I say to Rhi, as I put the empty boxes and cash tin on the table in the cool of the kitchen.

'A man! Hanging around at the end of the drive!'

'What was he doing there?' I ask, concerned.

'Just sort of hanging around,' she says.

'Did you get a good look at him?' I ask.

'No. I think Ralph scared him off, though.'

'Okay,' I say.

'I mean, if there's a homeless project just down the road . . .' she says, in a low tone.

'Now you're beginning to sound like Cora,' I say firmly.

'I'm just saying maybe you should be careful.'

I think about Stephanie stopping at the clearing where the homeless gather. Surely no one from there would think of . . . No! No one would think of breaking in. Not that I've got much to take. The notion scratches at the back of my mind, but I push it aside. This is supposed to be our second chance, and Stephanie knows I can't give her another if anything bad were to happen here. I trust her, I tell myself firmly. I'm going with my instinct. I just hope it hasn't deserted me.

I clear the table and see Rhi's iPad. She seems to be finding less time to watch her salon and the staff, and less to pick them up on. Instead she's spending her time watering the lavender and Lou has been helping. Bedroom painting seems to have been abandoned in favour of the lavender field. Maybe I'll get some more plants. Keep buying them. After all, if I'm to keep going with the business, I'll need the lavender. Or was Cora right? Will I be shut down without the right paperwork in place? I wonder if I can find out more online.

I look at the iPad, then sit down. The tab for Ollie's Facebook page is still there. When did he change his profile picture? Was it after we spoke on the phone, the day Stephanie went missing? I look at the picture. I don't remember seeing it before. Thank goodness he's taken down the one of me, though. I never liked it. I don't think I've liked seeing photographs of myself for years now. In fact, I avoid mirrors if I can. I know I've put on weight, since all the treatment. I peer at the new photograph: is there anything about it to make my heart leap, make me think this was some kind of madness? No. Nothing at all. My mind turns to Fabien and how my whole body shivers when I see him. He makes me feel . . . alive. I look at the photo again. Ollie appears happy, and I'm glad for him. There's nothing left between us. It was the right decision.

I'm about to close down the page when something catches my eye. The name of someone liking the picture. The name of a woman he worked with, whom he hadn't been in touch with for years . . . not since that one time. Suddenly I feel cold, despite the sunshine outside.

My hand shaking, I press on her name. And there it is: 'in a relationship with Ollie . . .'

I stare at the photograph in front of me and feel like I might be sick.

So, this is why we left the UK. And this is why he had been planning to go back. He ran away and now he's gone back because . . .

'Are you okay?' Lou's come in for a glass of water.

'No,' I say. 'I don't think I am.'

'What's up?' Rhi comes in for water too.

'Ollie,' I say. I turn the screen towards them and show them the photograph and the byline. 'He's having a baby!'

And we stare at the picture of the heavily pregnant woman and her scan picture: 'Mummy and Daddy, finally together!'

THIRTY-FIVE

'So, let me get this right. He was having an affair all the time you were having IVF and when your mum died.' Lou is straight to the point as ever.

'Looks that way.' I sigh.

'And he suggested moving out here to get away from the situation, having clearly got her pregnant.'

'It seems so.'

'Looks like when she decided to go through with it, he felt guilty and made up a load of excuses to move back.'

'He was going to keep his girlfriend and baby a secret from you,' Rhi joins in.

'That's why he sent us out here, to check you really meant it and weren't going to come back to him.' Lou puts the pieces in place.

'So he could go public with his—' Rhi is interrupted.

'Pregnant lover!' Lou bangs the table.

'Looks that way.' My lips are numb. But my instinct had been spot on. I was right not to go back. I was right to stay. I was right that we were over. But right isn't making me feel very good. I stand up, my knees shaking. I wasn't enough for Ollie. I do the only thing I can think of doing: I start to dig over more of the earth in the lavender field, ready for new plants.

And I keep digging, under my wide-brimmed hat in the Provençal sunshine, breathing the scent of the rosemary, pine and lavender. Rhi and Lou join me and silently we work, stopping only for water. Stephanie joins us, and we dig until the sun is dipping in the sky. Eventually, I stand to stretch out my back. Ralph is suddenly barking madly and I have no idea why.

'Ralph, ssshh!' I say, feeling much calmer than I did earlier. But Ralph doesn't stop barking. I catch a glimpse of something . . . or maybe someone. Everyone stops and looks up.

'Allô!' I call. 'Anyone there?'

We move towards each other, tools from the old barn in hand.

'Allô!' I call again. Ralph is still barking.

'It's okay! He won't hurt you, he's friendly!' I say.

And then slowly, from around the side of the house, a figure appears, a young man in a baseball cap. Stephanie and I gasp.

THIRTY-SIX

'JB!' I'm incredulous.

He stands nervously, his hands thrust into his pockets. Stephanie doesn't move either.

'How did you find us?' I ask, walking slowly and carefully towards him. He backs away as Ralph continues to bark.

'I asked in the town. I told the man at the *brocante* I was . . . a friend of Stephanie.' He seems to struggle to work out what he is to Stephanie: her ex, the father of her child. 'He gave me a lift up here.'

I look around for any sign of Fabien. But there's none. I wish he'd waited.

'He was delivering some furniture,' JB says. I think of the day he arrived with mine. The day I started my new life, without Ollie. Ollie and his new life are a world away from me and mine. It's truly over.

I walk towards JB and Ralph runs around barking.

Stephanie scoops up Tomas protectively and holds him to her. Ralph barks even more excitedly as JB backs away from him again. And Tomas bursts into tears. JB looks petrified.

'Wait!' I say. He seems overwhelmed by the situation. Stephanie's face is taut with worry. I don't think she could bear to be rejected again. 'JB! Wait!'

As he turns, in all the barking and chaos, I don't hear the van pull up.

'Hey!' Fabien is there. He slings an arm around JB's shoulders and JB stops, supported now. He looks down at Ralph, who sits obediently, his tongue lolling out. Fabien bends to shake his paw. Tomas sees Fabien, stops crying and wriggles to be put down. As soon as his feet touch the ground, he runs over to him.

'So, I see JB found you! Sorry, I just had to make a delivery, but wanted to check he got here okay. He'd walked here already today but he couldn't see Stephanie and wondered if he had the right place. So I brought him back.'

Tomas launches himself at Fabien's legs and hugs them, nearly toppling their owner.

'Hey!' he says, and lifts Tomas up. Stephanie walks towards them. Fabien kisses him on both cheeks. Rhi, Lou and I don't move. My heart is leaping. *Fabien is here! He made this happen!*

The wind around us is picking up, the mistral, the wind of change letting us know she's never far away.

JB watches Fabien with Tomas. Then Fabien looks at

Stephanie, as if asking if it's okay to introduce JB to her child. Stephanie nods, wide-eyed and worried. He turns to JB, still holding Tomas. 'JB, Tomas,' he says, and holds Tomas's little hand towards his father. JB gazes at him with a mix of bewilderment and awe. He looks at Stephanie with the same expression. Then Tomas reaches for him and JB doesn't move away. Tomas reaches for the peak of his cap and pulls it towards him, JB with it, and we all smile. JB takes off his baseball cap, revealing his face. I watch Stephanie, who doesn't take her eyes off the pair. Tomas has the cap and is waving it around, then JB puts it on his son's head. Tomas whips it off and throws it to the ground, laughing. JB picks it up, puts it on his head again, and Tomas whips it off, throwing it to the ground again, laughing even louder. Father and son may just have said hello.

'Thank you,' I say to Fabien. I'm in the kitchen preparing dinner, ragout sauce with pasta, that I'll serve with a big green salad and baguettes. I sip the glass of rosé Fabien has poured for me.

'It was my pleasure,' he says, as we watch JB and Stephanie playing with Tomas from the kitchen window.

'He's already asked if he can come back tomorrow,' I tell Fabien. 'He told Stephanie he was sorry about the day she came to the house. He was just shocked. Not sure how to explain to his parents. They are quite elderly. He didn't want to upset them. But he'd thought about nothing else since she left him and really wanted to meet Tomas.'

'Good. I'm glad. She deserves some luck,' he says, turning his back to the window and leaning against the work surface. I can feel him watching me. My hands are shaking as I season the sauce with sprinkles of sea salt and a grind of pepper. Heat rushes up my neck and into my cheeks. He's still watching me as I carry the pot to the oven. There are so many unspoken words hanging in the air. I feel so distracted that I nearly drop the pot but Fabien steps in and steadies it. I can smell his aftershave, which reminds me of the lavender fields and pine trees, of being here, of home. I can feel him next to me and think my legs might give way. Fabien is here. When I need him, he's always here. And right now I want nothing more than to give in to all the feelings that are consuming my body and mind. I turn slowly towards him and look into his green eyes. I look at his lips. He's so much younger than I am, a voice says in my head. Why would he be interested in me? The nagging doubts swirl in my mind.

We look at each other, holding the big terracotta pot between us, wondering where this is going and searching each other's face for answers.

'Any more wine?' says Lou, coming into the kitchen. I take the heavy pot from Fabien and slide it into the oven.

'Of course,' says Fabien, his usual charming self.

'You'll make someone a great husband one day,' says Lou. 'If only I were ten years younger!' I blush.

'And that you hadn't sworn off men for life!' I tease her.

'I think Fabien could convince me there's a second chance out there for me!'

Out of the window JB and Stephanie are laughing as they begin to relax in each other's company, with Tomas's help. Tomas is showing JB his rocking horse and how Ralph and he play chase together. Oh, and he's moved on to his frog impression! Stephanie is about to burst with pride and happiness. This is her second chance! Fabien made it happen. It's what he does, gives broken things new life. But, will there be one for me? I think of Ollie, his new life, his baby. Did he ever love me?

Fabien is holding the bottle and tops up my glass. 'You made this happen, Del,' he says, pointing to JB and Stephanie. 'You brought this little family back together.'

'You did! You were there for them this afternoon.'

'None of us would be here if not for you. You are a very special lady and a beautiful one at that. You just have to realize it yourself,' says Fabien. 'Love yourself, and let yourself be loved.'

'Come on, let's join the others,' I say, leading him outside, batting off his words.

As the sun sets over the valley that evening and dusk turns to night, Stephanie and Tomas are tucked up in the gypsy caravan: Fabien has taken JB back to the bus stop in town and he has promised to return tomorrow. I hope he does. Rhi hasn't looked at her camera link with the salon all day, and Lou has removed the nail polish that got ruined when we planted the lavender. I can't stop thinking about Fabien's words. Did he mean them, or was he just being nice? I'm exhausted and head straight to bed.

Outside the dark sky is scattered with stars. The cicadas are chirping and I can't sleep. I think again of Ollie and his new life. And Fabien's words: 'Love yourself, and let yourself be loved.' Despite the heat of the night, I shiver.

THIRTY-SEVEN

The following week slips into a pattern: Stephanie and I work, and JB visits in the afternoons. They seem to be getting closer.

'I think it's time we went home,' says Rhi.

I'm cleaning down the old wooden work surface in the kitchen. 'Why?' I say.

'Well, we only came to try to persuade you to come home. And now we know you're not going anywhere, we should probably go back to our own lives.' Rhi doesn't seem too happy at the prospect and neither does Lou. But they're right. They can't stay here just keeping an eye on me for ever. This is my life and my home now. And I'm happy here, with or without my friends, just me, Ralph and my lavender. I'll still have Stephanie and Tomas: they're not going anywhere.

'You're happy here. We can see that. This is your home. You have everything,' she says. Nearly everything, I

223

think. I'm glad Fabien and I are speaking again, friends at least. And that's what's important. I don't want anything to spoil that. I'm not here to find a partner. I'm here to be me, on my own. I've had love in my life, and it's been taken away: Mum and Ollie. I trusted Ollie. I forgave him when he said, 'It was just a one-off.' I stayed with him then because we'd loved each other. And he was clearly in touch with that woman all the time we were out here, no doubt when he was in the car on his phone. It was all a sham. Being friends with Fabien is just about as good as it gets. It's enough. I don't want to make things awkward. This is my home. I'm lucky to have good friends, I think. The sort of friends who would put their lives on hold to come here to see if I'm okay and stay until they know I am. And I am. I have a new life and it's great.

I hug Rhi, then finish clearing up the kitchen from the morning's bakes. Stephanie has walked into town to deliver them to Henri. She'll meet JB off the bus, and they'll walk back here. He's even helped to plant and water the new lavender Serge has sold me. He's becoming almost a permanent fixture around here, looking for work so he can help support his family. They've even been to visit his parents with Tomas. And every night, as the sun sets in the purple sky and the cicadas chirp, we eat outside together, breathing in the smell of the newly planted lavender field.

'When are you planning on leaving?' I ask.

'Well, as soon as we can book flights, really,' Rhi

says. 'We can't just stay on, living off you. You have your own life now.'

'I wish you could.'

'I know, but some of us aren't as brave as you are.'

'I wish I was,' says Lou, joining us in the kitchen.

'But you are! Look at what you've been through, Lou. You lost your husband and made a life for yourself. You invested your money wisely and are comfortably off.'

'Well, I exist, more like,' she says flatly.

'And you, Rhi, you've brought up two children on your own and built a business.'

'Since I've been here, I've discovered that the business, like my kids, can manage perfectly well without me. I just feel . . . well, redundant,' she says. 'But, like I say, we're not all as brave as you, coming out here and building a new life for yourself. I wish I was more like you!'

'Me? I'm lurching from one disaster to another here!'

'No, you do what you think is right at the time. You were right about leaving Ollie and you were right to stay here,' says Lou.

'And about Stephanie and JB,' says Rhi.

'You won't go until you've said goodbye to her, will you?'

They smile and shake their heads.

'What if we had another go at getting the *chambre d'hôte* business up and running? You could stay longer!' I'm grabbing at straws.

'Well, I don't think our decorating skills are up to it. And where would the guests stay if we were taking up the bedrooms?'

'True . . .' I nod.

We gaze at each other sadly, wishing our time together hadn't come to an end. But we all have to move forward and get on with our own lives.

'What will you do when you get home?'

'Go back to the business, maybe look at expanding and getting another shop. That would keep me busy,' says Rhi.

'I might book a cruise,' says Lou. 'Find myself a wealthy man to keep me in the manner I'd like to become accustomed to.' We laugh, because if we don't, we might cry.

'And you?' asks Rhi.

'I'll carry on doing the markets, and making the desserts for Henri. And I want to bring back the lavender field so I can make essential oil and soaps.' Even thinking about being in the field, with the scent of the earth and the lavender, fills my soul with well-being and joy. I'm happy here, content, and that's not a bad place to be.

'There's an afternoon flight we can get from Marseille,' says Lou. The internet connection was obviously, disappointingly, behaving itself for once.

'Best we get packing,' says Rhi, busying herself as she always does when she's upset. There's a real reluctance in the air: none of us wants to say goodbye.

They go up to their rooms and I listen to them moving around, packing and getting ready to go. This is it. I'm cutting ties with my old life. They've been the bridge between my old and new lives. Now the bridge has been drawn up and I'm on one side and they're on the other, wishing each other love and luck. I look out again on the sunny field as I finish in the kitchen, drying the washing-up and putting it away, then doing what I seem to do when I'm not sure what to do next: I open the old recipe book that Fabien gave me, its musty smell and aged pages bringing me comfort, then settle on what to cook for dinner that night: lamb shanks with lavender, new potatoes and petit pois. I'll gather my baskets and walk into town to get the ingredients once Rhi and Lou have gone. That should take my mind off things. I focus on trying to translate the recipe.

Bump, bump, bump.

It's Rhi and Lou bringing their cases down the stairs, taking more lumps out of the fragile walls as they go. But I don't mind. Those marks will act as a reminder of the special time we've had while they were here. I won't rush to paint over them. If at all.

They leave their cases in the hall and I grab a bottle of rosé for us to enjoy in the garden before their taxi comes to take them to the airport.

'Say goodbye to Fabien for us, won't you?' says Lou.

And I blush.

Pop! goes the cork, and I let my redness be mistaken for exertion.

'Of course!' I pour the glorious light pink wine into my mismatched glasses, which I love. Life with Ollie was about everything matching, everything in its place. I like my new life, where nothing matches or has to be in a particular place. We're all just finding our own.

'To new beginnings,' I say huskily. We raise our glasses and let the cold wine linger on our tongues before swallowing it, along with any remaining sadness.

We put our glasses on the table. Rhi checks her phone for the time and is anxious. We're all lost in our own thoughts. I know she'll be worrying about getting to the airport on time. She likes to be punctual. Lou will be trying to work out where she can go next, keep moving, planning the next trip. I'm wondering what life will be like when they've gone. We listen to the birdsong and the crickets in the grass. It's so peaceful. I shut my eyes and hold my face to the sun. Suddenly, I'm catapulted out of my trance-like state by someone shouting my name. It's Stephanie.

'Del! Del!'

I stand up, knocking over my wine, which spills over my legs. Rhi and Lou jump up too. I run to the front of the house. Ralph is barking and I can't hear what Stephanie is saying. She's out of breath from running and trying to talk and to hold back tears all at the same time.

'What? What is it? Ralph, quiet!' And for once Ralph does as he's told.

Stephanie bends over, her hands on her knees, and takes a deep breath. Rhi runs out with some water. But Stephanie doesn't take it and waves it away.

'Is it Tomas? What's happened?'

She shakes her head. 'Not Tomas, he's fine. He's with JB at the clearing by the river. I couldn't carry him.' And I realize this is probably the first time she's left JB with Tomas. So if it's not Tomas, what or who is it? She takes a huge breath. 'It's Henri!'

'*Henri?*' we all exclaim, and stare at her.

'I think he's having a heart attack!'

THIRTY-EIGHT

When we arrive, out of breath and hot, Fabien is already there. The suitcases have been abandoned by the front door and Ralph has followed, running close behind us down the river path to the clearing.

'JB came for me,' he says, nodding to JB with Tomas in his arms. 'The ambulance is on its way.'

I look at Henri lying on the ground, like a giant oak tree having been felled. His face is ashen. The man I've seen at the clearing, with the long beard and hair, and very kind eyes, is kneeling beside him.

'Alain has given him the kiss of life,' says Fabien. 'Henri is very lucky he was here.'

I wonder what Henri was doing in the clearing.

Stephanie is beside me, tears running down her cheeks, her face racked with worry. Even Ralph seems to sense the seriousness of the situation and lies down beside Henri, as if to keep him warm.

I crouch and take his hand. 'Stay with us, Henri. Just hang on in there.' I'm willing him to hang on until the ambulance arrives. This man has been a lifeline to me since I moved here. And I'm not the only one, by the look on Stephanie's face.

When the ambulance arrives Fabien explains who Henri is.

'Do you want to go in the ambulance with him?' a kind paramedic asks me in French, as I scramble to my feet. He and his colleague move Henri on to the stretcher and into the ambulance.

'Um, well . . .' I look at Fabien and then Alain, who has retreated back into the shadows of the big pine tree and the sofa.

'You go,' says Fabien.

'We can look after things here, take Ralph back,' says Rhi.

'We'll cancel the taxi, change our flights. Just until things are sorted,' says Lou, with what seems almost like relief. But I feel so lucky to have my friends still here, like they belong in this community too.

I nod to the paramedic and step towards the ambulance.

'No!' Stephanie says, grabbing my arm. 'You cannot go!'

'Why not?' I ask. 'Someone should be with him.'

'No! You need to cook!'

'Cook?' I'm puzzled. This isn't a time for thinking about our evening meal.

'Not for us, for these people.' She holds out a hand and two more people, in dark clothing with unkempt hair, join Alain by the sofa and he explains what's happened.

'What do you mean, I need to cook for these people?' I'm still no wiser.

'Henri!' she says urgently. 'He has many people relying on him. He cooks for the bistro, and then everything that is left when he closes he brings here, every evening, and serves it to the people who need it.' She points to the little hut with the closed hatch. 'He was here checking for any empty bowls that got left behind after he cleared away last night, like he does every morning. He checks no mess was left behind. You have to help. Without Henri, there is many a time I would have gone without food. Same for many of these people. They are relying on him.'

I look around the clearing. 'I can't cook – at least, not for so many people!' I may have enjoyed cooking for all of us at the house, but there's no way I could cook restaurant standard food in the bistro and for the numbers Henri must feed every day. 'I'm just a home cook!'

I look at the ambulance and they're shutting one door, waiting to shut the other. The lights are flashing.

'I thought I heard sirens.' Cora appears from the other side of the ambulance. 'I heard it from the garden. I'm having some new tiles laid,' she says. 'Anything I can do to help?'

This is becoming a spectator sport, I think. My hackles start to rise. Henri is a good, kind man who is in real need.

'Who is it? One of the hoboes?' She looks at Alain, who has possibly saved Henri's life with his quick thinking and actions.

We look at her in horror, hardly able to believe what we're hearing.

'No, actually, it's Henri, from the bistro,' I say, pulling myself up tall.

'Ah, the man who feeds them all. Well,' she says, 'maybe if they're no longer getting fed here, they'll move on somewhere else and leave our town alone,' she says, with a tight smile. 'This area could certainly do with redeveloping. Something for the townspeople. I'll speak to the mayor. And chase up that CCTV he's been promising us. These people aren't from around here. They don't belong here. We need to look out for each other.'

My cheeks are flaming as I watch Cora turn and totter away on her kitten heels over the riverside path. I try to find the words to call after her, but am totally tongue-tied. We're the ones who don't belong, who moved in, I think furiously.

I look at Stephanie, whose lips are tight, and see the fury in her eyes.

'Show me to the kitchen!' I say, determination rising inside me and a voice to match coming out of my mouth that I've never heard before.

'I'll go with Henri,' says Rhi. 'Fabien, you can come with me, can't you?' she says, and he nods. We just need to get Henri off. At that, Fabien looks at me as if to check I'm okay with it – but okay with what? Not going to the hospital with Henri, going instead to the restaurant to cook, or him going with Rhi in the ambulance? But the sirens are starting to wail. Rhi steps in, followed by Fabien who gives me one final look, as if he's about to say something, but the paramedic is ready to shut the other door, and I watch as Fabien dips his dark curly head and steps in. The doors are shut. And we all stand, including Alain and the group around him, and watch as the ambulance pulls away, sirens blaring, lights flashing, all of us praying that Henri will live.

'Come on, Stephanie,' I say, the steel still in my voice. 'We have people to feed. Grab the recipe book from Le Petit Mas and meet me at the bistro. You too,' I say to JB and to Lou, who is busy cancelling taxis and flights. 'We have people who need us right now.'

THIRTY-NINE

I look around the smart but small kitchen, not having an idea where to start. It's all very well cooking short-bread, tuiles and lavender *macarons*, but this is a whole different affair. I wonder if Henri has written down the *plat du jour* he intended for today. But there's nothing.

I open the fridge and look at the contents.

Cora's words are ringing in my ears. And Henri's ashen face is haunting my thoughts.

'What can we do? Where can we start?' Lou asks, as everyone piles into the kitchen. 'I can peel potatoes,' she suggests.

'I can . . . Tell me what you need me to do too,' says JB, looking lost.

I don't think I can do this. I take a huge breath. And then Stephanie arrives, with the book, and takes charge.

'Lou and JB, you sort out the restaurant. Lay the tables,' she instructs. And they nod and leave the tiny kitchen, with Tomas, who is carrying the napkins. They take the tables outside, even though the mistral is revisiting the town, causing chaos, knocking over glasses as Lou puts them in place and snatching table-cloths. Tomas lets go of the paper napkins, which flutter skyward like red birds.

Stephanie hands me the book. I take it from her, hold it to my chest, and breathe in the scent of the pages I've come to know so well. I put it on the side and open it. This book has been my map, keeping me focused and on the right track. Each day I've turned a page and planned the next. It's been my guide, my friend, my bible. Now, I look at the pages and they blur. I have no idea what to do. I put my hands over my face.

'Don't worry,' says Stephanie, placing a hand on my shoulder. 'Trust yourself. You know what you're doing.'

She thinks I can do this. She is staring at me, willing me not to let down the people she cares about. Well, I'll just have to give it a go. I walk back to the fridge. It's time to work without the book and I push it gently to one side.

I think about the recipes Mum used to cook for me and that I had hoped to cook for my family one day. The dishes Ollie never wanted me to make because they were too calorie-laden. I think about the lamb shanks I was going to cook this evening. Well, I can't do lamb shanks for everyone, but I could do cawl, a traditional lamb and vegetable stew, which Mum would cook to make the meat go as far as possible. I check the fridge and send Stephanie out for the meat and baguettes while I start chopping vegetables. As I work, I find myself back in the kitchen with Mum and a kind of calm takes over. I'm cooking, without the recipe book, from instinct. I drop things, panic, get hot, but when we're nearing lunchtime, I dip a spoon into the broth for Stephanie to try. She sips and smiles. 'Nearly perfect!'

'Nearly?' I laugh.

I taste the cawl, wondering what could be missing. I test for seasoning. The meat is falling apart. The vegetables and potatoes soft but not overcooked.

Stephanie flips open the first page of the old recipes and picks up the sprig of dried lavender that has been there since the day Fabien gave me the book. '*Lavande!*' she says.

'Of course!' I strip into the stew a few dried flowers from the bunch that Henri has hung from his ceiling.

'Perfect!' we agree.

At that moment, regulars begin to arrive at the bistro for lunch.

'Smells good!' they mutter to each other, and I'm nervous and excited all at the same time. Lou, JB and Stephanie are helping me in the kitchen, and we serve all of Henri's customers, who ask after him as we wait anxiously for news from the hospital. As we put up the 'Closed' sign, we sit down to eat together in the little bistro window, Stephanie, JB, Lou, Tomas and me.

As the sun begins to set we take the rest of the food to the clearing, where the talk is of Henri and Alain. The regulars smile when we arrive, and I tell them it may not be as good as Henri's but it's made with as much love. They clap. As Stephanie opens the hatch to the makeshift kitchen, we put the pan of stew on the stove to keep warm and I take the first bowl to Alain. He saved a special man's life today. I promise to tell him any news as soon as there is any. He thanks me and takes the bowl from me with his dirt-engrained hands.

'*Merci*,' he says, and gazes at the small queue lining up at the hatch and Stephanie's smiling face. 'Henri would be very pleased,' he tells me in French, and I understand, on many levels.

Stephanie and I serve the food into bowls. JB and Lou take the empties, stack them and start the washing-up. They smile as every single person thanks them for the meal. Dogs are wandering around and I put out bowls of water for them, then offer their owners any leftover scraps to give to them, which is, according to Stephanie, what Henri does.

Just as we're clearing up, Rhi and Fabien arrive back from the hospital.

'He's okay,' Rhi says. 'Sleeping and as stable as can be.'

'I've let Carine know and she'll tell the mayor,' says Fabien.

'Fabien was great,' says Rhi, brimming with excitement, 'really calm. Especially when we thought Henri had had another attack in the ambulance. But they sorted him. They said Alain's quick thinking saved his life.' I look at Fabien, who gives an embarrassed smile at Rhi's sudden praise for him. There are tears in my eyes. I don't know if they're from relief that Henri is doing well, or the sight of these people, who rely on him every night for the work I never knew he did.

I go to Alain and pass on the news about Henri. I tell him I'll come with an update tomorrow.

'So, you'll be back? Here? *Demain?*' he says.

I glance at the happy faces, feeling pride in what we've done here tonight. Lou, Rhi, Stephanie, JB, Tomas and Fabien: we all did this.

'Yes, I'll be back,' I tell him.

'I'll let the others know. *Merci*, from the bottom of my heart,' he says, and I see tears in his eyes too. For whatever reason he is here, he clearly didn't intend to be.

The wind rustles through the trees, the mistral letting us know that change could be on the way for everyone once again.

'I wish there was more I could do to say thank you to Alain,' I say, over wine at the table at Le Petit Mas that evening. We're all there, Rhi, Lou, Stephanie, JB and Tomas, who is sleepy now, curled up in his mother's lap, hugging *Monsieur Lapin* and sucking his thumb. There are empty bowls with spoons in them, from the last of the cawl, some goat's cheese from Henri's fridge and the end-of-the-day bread, which won't keep, crumbs spread over the table. Only Fabien isn't here. He went home after he'd delivered the news about

Henri, despite Rhi's protestations that he should join us for leftovers supper and wine at Le Petit Mas. But he said he knew I'd want to hear about Henri, then made his excuses and wished us all a good evening. But not before telling me what a brilliant job I'd done tonight.

'Really, he would be so proud of you,' he says. And then adds, 'I know I am.' He'll be in touch about visiting Henri in the morning. I wanted to call him back, ask if he meant it. But everyone wanted to thank me for the meal and he disappeared into the night, his words still in my head. I feel a warm glow and manage to smile.

'I think I may have an idea,' says Rhi, as she pours more wine.

'For what?' I ask, bringing myself back to the here and now.

'A way to thank Alain.' She picks up her glass. I hesitate, remembering the last time we sat here and Rhi came up with an idea. She had suggested we go and find JB, I seem to remember, and look how badly that went. But then I look at him now, his arm around Stephanie, with Tomas on her lap. Well, maybe it worked out for the best.

'Really?' I say to Rhi, raising my eyebrows.

'Yup! I think I might have just the thing. Lou, you can help me.' She sips her wine, putting her feet on an upturned plant pot, as we watch the sun set over the lavender field.

FORTY

The following morning, I'm awake before the cockerel starts to crow. It's Monday, market day. There is so much to do. I rush down the stairs to the kitchen and wonder how I'm going to get everything done.

Ralph barks so I go to the front of the house and look out. I see a dark figure and am suddenly filled with fear, until I recognize the person walking down the drive, away from Le Petit Mas.

'Ssh, Ralph. It's just JB,' I say, and smile as he heads into town. He's clearly trying to disguise the fact he stayed over with Stephanie last night.

Within a few minutes, Stephanie joins me in the kitchen with Tomas in her arms. There is a sparkle in her eyes.

'Morning, Stephanie.' I smile.

'*Bonjour*, Del,' she corrects, mildly scolding me, and kisses me on both cheeks. I kiss Tomas too.

'*Bisous?*' I say, and he happily kisses me back.

'Everything okay?' I ask his mother, as the sun rises in the still morning, no hint of the mistral. A new beginning arriving with the new dawn.

'*Oui, bien sûr*, of course,' she says, not catching my eye, and I can see the faint pink blush in her cheeks.

'It's okay,' I say gently, 'for JB to stay.'

And she looks at me.

'If you're an item, and you are . . .' it's my turn to blush '. . . taking precautions.' We're both slightly embarrassed, but know it had to be said. 'We all love Tomas, but no one wants any more surprises. Much better to plan next time.' She finally looks at me, more beautiful than I have ever seen her, and happy too.

'You're a couple, and if it's okay with his family, it's okay with me . . . not that I'm your—'

'You are the most family I have ever had,' she cuts me off, and we hug each other. 'You have done more for me than anyone ever has. *Merci.*'

I feel like my heart could burst, knowing that, somewhere along the way, I may just have made a difference. I was there when someone needed me, and it feels very good.

'And about Fabien,' she says, as we pull apart. This time my cheeks flame red. 'I'm sorry,' she says, and I wave a hand, pushing away the thought of him and how he makes me feel, and trying to cool my burning cheeks as well. 'I realize now he might not have been thinking what I was thinking. I was confused. Silly.'

'We've all been silly.' I try to lighten the mood.

'If you and he were to get together, I wouldn't mind. I'm sorry I made it hard for you in the first place.'

She's giving me her blessing to get together with Fabien. Could there possibly be a chance for him and me? Would he even want it? After all, we both said it was 'just a silly kiss'. Is it too late? Has our moment passed? But what if . . . what if it wasn't just a silly kiss? What if it meant much more than we were prepared to admit? I shut my eyes for a second, remembering his lips barely touching mine before they whisked away. And then, buoyed up by the memory, I clap my hands together. 'We must get to work. We have so much to do.' I take a huge breath and force a smile.

'Del,' she puts her hands on mine, 'go to the bistro. I can manage here.'

'Oh, no, it's fine . . .' I wave away the suggestion.

'Really,' she says. 'I can handle the market. I know what I'm doing. Remember? Everyone deserves a second chance? I promise I won't let you down. And I'll bring the money box straight to you.'

'I know that!' I say, shocked that she thinks I might not trust her.

'I can cook up our usual bakes. Just like you taught me. You can go to the bistro and get ready there, opening for lunch, and we'll take the food to the riverside together later.'

This young woman has blossomed and grown up in front of my eyes.

'I can cope, really,' she reassures me.

And this time my smile spreads of its own accord. 'Of course you can.' I feel a surge of pride. I need to let her do this. 'That makes perfect sense,' I say, trying not to ask if she has everything she needs. 'I'll be at Henri's if you want me. And I'll let you know if there's any news of him.'

'Okay, go, go!' She laughs. 'JB will help me set up the stall in a bit. I'll tell him to bring back some clothes. Maybe he could look for a job in town.'

'Maybe Fabien could do with some help,' I suggest. Fabien again. Never far from my thoughts. 'Or Carine may know of something,' I add quickly. 'Okay,' I say, picking up my bag and Ralph's lead as he bounces around happily. 'I'll see you at the bistro.' And then, I can't help myself. 'You'll be okay?'

'I'll be fine, Del.' She smiles. 'It'll all be fine!'

And I hope she's right as I pat Ralph's head and step out into the early-morning lavender light to the cockerel announcing a new day, pick a bunch of lavender and carry it to the bistro.

FORTY-ONE

I stand in the little kitchen and look at the empty fridge. I'm on my own here now, doing this totally by myself. Soon people will be arriving, wanting to know the *plat du jour*, and this evening there will be hungry mouths to feed at the riverside clearing. I hold on to the fridge door and rest my head against it. I'm not sure I can do this. Then I think of Henri lying in hospital, fighting for his life. If he can get through that, I can get through this, I tell myself, and pull myself up straight. I collect the shopping baskets hanging on the cupboard door and head into the market, with no idea what I'm going to cook, but knowing that the place and its people won't let me down. I still have no idea if Henri is going to be okay. Fabien has been in touch with Henri's daughters in Australia and America. He says he'll stay in touch and they'll come over if things don't improve. My memories of Mum and her stroke haunt me. There's only one way I can get through this and that's to throw myself into cooking for the bistro and the clearing. And I just hope that while I'm cooking Henri is getting better, not worse.

By eleven, everything is in hand. I go to the chalkboard and wipe off yesterday's special, replacing it with today's. Stephanie has been working hard all morning, JB at her side, Tomas handing out samples and eating them too. People are buying. Stephanie has done a lovely job of putting the biscuits in little paper parcels, tied with some ribbon and a sprig of lavender from the field. The tourists are loving them. I write on the board 'Poisson de Provence', soft white cod, sautéed with tomatoes, olives, onions, garlic and peppers, flavoured with herbes de Provence, including a sprinkling of lavender, of course. Simple but amazingly delicious. I dust off my hands, then put the board out for customers to see, feeling proud of myself.

I glance up and down the cobbled street towards the busy market square, then the other way, across the road at the top towards the brocante. Fabien appears, and my heart lurches. It's almost as if I've conjured him up. I don't know whether to turn and walk inside, as if I wasn't hoping he'd appear, or stand and stare. Instead, I stand and look the other way, at Stephanie, my heart thumping, Fabien walking towards me in his battered leather jacket and bandanna around his neck, despite the sunshine. I can smell him before I see him.

I turn, the sun catching in my eyes so I can't see his expression. What if it's Henri? What if it's bad news? My heart is thundering now.

'*Bonjour*, Del,' he says, and kisses me on each cheek. I feel the bristles of his chin and wonder if it stays there a fraction of a second longer than I'm expecting and if he feels it too. Or did I imagine that? Of course I did. I shut my eyes and shake it off.

'How is Henri?' I ask, holding my breath. We had agreed that Fabien would be the one to telephone the hospital as he'd understand more of what was said than Rhi or I.

His face breaks into a smile. 'He's doing okay. How do you say? Holding his own?' His smile broadens and my heart squeezes.

I nod and smile. 'Good.'

'I am going to see him. Rhi has offered to come with me.' He looks at me and I wonder if he's waiting for some sort of reaction, to see how I feel about them going together.

'Of course!' I say quickly, waving the tea towel that was tucked into my apron.

'You wouldn't rather see him yourself?' he asks.

My heart is saying, 'Yes! I want to see Henri, and I want to go with you!' But my mouth says, 'No, of course you must go with Rhi! I have so much to do here.' I point back towards the kitchen, thinking Rhi could probably do it, but I want to do it for Henri, to say thank you for everything he did for me. It would be so much more straightforward if I could have fallen in love with Henri than – I'm finally admitting it to myself – with a man I have told I'm not interested because I was too scared to follow my heart.

I have to find a way to stop myself falling deeply in love with Fabien. And this is a good start.

'Go with Rhi. Have fun!' And then, 'Or as much fun as you can have at a hospital.' And then, 'Give Henri my love, lots of love. Tell him everything here is fine. And,' I swallow, 'I'm looking forward to seeing him when he comes home.'

Fabien nods slowly, as if imprinting the message on his memory. 'I will,' he says. 'In the meantime, I'm going to ask JB to look after the *brocante* until I return.'

'Oh, that's an excellent idea!' I say warmly. Why is this man just so blooming lovely?

He nods, with a small smile, says he'll be back when he's seen Henri, then walks over to Stephanie and kisses her on each cheek, like he kissed me. He kisses Tomas, who is delighted to see his friend and hugs him. Then Fabien shakes JB's hand and puts his other arm around his shoulders in a brotherly way. He's asking him to mind the *brocante*, pointing. JB looks at Stephanie, who nods and shoos them away, laughing. My heart swells, as Fabien and JB walk up the cobbled street towards the main road and across to the *brocante*. Fabien still has his arm around JB. They see me and wave.

Lou and Rhi are at Le Petit Mas. Rhi has a surprise

for Alain, she told me last night, and will meet me at the riverside clearing this evening.

After the lunchtime rush, Stephanie packs up the stall and becomes the waitress at the bistro. Tomas delivers bread to the tables and brings a smile to everyone's face. Especially when he helps himself to a piece of bread before delivering the basket, or drops a piece on the floor and tries to return it to the basket. Stephanie intervenes to the customer's amusement. Each plate goes out with a little sprig of lavender from the bunch I brought from home. A little nod to the old recipe book, which has lavender at the heart of every dish.

Then coffees are served, after I've wrestled with the machine and finally worked it out with the help of a friendly customer. The place is filled with good wishes for Henri, and I can't remember when I've ever felt so tired, so happy and so at home. After the washing-up has been done, Stephanie, Tomas and I sit down to eat together, in front of the window, with a small carafe of wine, and watch the world go by. Anyone looking at us would be forgiven for thinking we were a family finishing our day's work and eating together. I feel so lucky to have come here, stayed and met these people. And I'm going to make sure I keep this bistro going until Henri is home and ready to take over. I feel blessed to be surrounded by such love. I know Mum would be very proud of what I did today. I could hear her as I cooked, right beside me, watching over me, guiding me, just like I did with Stephanie when she was learning to make the biscuits. I may never have children of my own but I feel as if I passed on the love in that kitchen, from Mum, to me, to Stephanie, who will pass it on to Tomas. That kitchen helped us all to find our way in life again.

'Okay,' I say, standing to clear away our plates, glasses, coffee cups and ice-cream bowls. My feet and back ache and I'm shattered, but our work isn't done yet. 'Let's take this lot to the riverside clearing,' I say.

FORTY-TWO

There seem to be even more people than yesterday waiting at the clearing and suddenly I'm nervous again.

'Why are there more people?' I ask Alain, who shakes my hand when I arrive.

'They have heard about your cooking,' he says, in English, and I realize it's been a long time since he's spoken it but he clearly feels ready to try. 'They love Henri's food. But they have heard that the lavender lady who makes the biscuits is cooking and word has spread down the river.'

'And are all these people homeless?' I ask.

'Some are without any home, some live on boats or in vans. Everyone here is without a table to go home to at night. Most would if they could.' There is sadness in his eyes.

'Well, we'd better get them fed,' I say. 'I hope I have enough.' I'm worried now. I thought Henri just brought the day's leftovers here. At this rate, I'm going to have to cook more.

'Some people have no money, some a little money,' says Alain. 'It's not cheap to feed all these people. Perhaps . . .' he says thoughtfully '. . . perhaps an honesty box, where people pay what they can afford for their meal.'

'That's an excellent idea!' I say.

'But no one must be turned away because they can't afford to pay anything,' says Stephanie.

'Exactly so!' I agree. 'We ask people for what they can afford, but no one will be turned away if they have nothing.'

Just then, I see Rhi and Lou coming down the riverbank, carrying a plastic bowl and bags, waving and smiling. Stephanie opens up the little makeshift kitchen and gets the food on the hob. She puts cutlery into cups and sets them on a table. Then she finds an old biscuit tin, opens it and writes a sign encouraging people to pay what they can. But if you can't afford to, no problem: everyone eats.

'Wow! It's busy tonight!' says Rhi, beaming.

'Apparently word has got around about my cooking.' I blush.

'That's fantastic!' says Lou.

'Well, if we can afford to keep it up. We're asking for contributions. An honesty tin. People pay what they can afford.'

Stephanie turns on the fairy lights and the little

clearing looks enchanting. Not a hang-out for the homeless, but with the lovely furniture Fabien has put there, the lights, the happy atmosphere as people meet and greet each other, the dogs pottering around, it really does look like an art installation. Someone lights a fire in an old bin, adding to the warmth of the gathering.

'How was Henri?'

'Doing well. On the mend,' Rhi says. 'Fabien will be here to tell you more. But I think Henri should be home soon.'

I walk back to the hut with Rhi and Lou.

'What have you got there?' I ask, indicating their bags.

'Well . . .' Rhi seems to lose her bottle, then recovers herself '. . . I thought that, what with me being a hairdresser, and always carrying my scissors . . .' she tails off.

I gaze at her.

'I thought,' she says, suddenly shy, 'that Alain might like a bit of a trim and a tidy-up.'

'That's a lovely idea!' I say. 'I'll ask him.'

'And she has me on nails!' says Lou, looking terrified and appalled at the same time, clutching her bag of implements.

'Thank you!' I say to them both.

I go over and speak to Alain quietly, just in case he'd like to decline the offer, but instead, he is very pleased and I beckon Rhi over, followed by a hesitant Lou. She shakes Alain's hand and I leave them together. Then

I go back to the kitchen to help Stephanie. JB turns up to take over Tomas from Stephanie, and is shortly followed by a smiling Fabien, who joins Rhi and Lou, Rhi cutting Alain's hair and Lou soaking his hands in a bowl of warm water, then placing them in her lap and rubbing them with a towel.

It's almost a party atmosphere. I'm so pleased that everyone has been fed, and the tin is heavy with coins and notes. Fabien finds us and gives us a can of beer each.

'To Henri,' he says, as we touch glasses.

'To Henri!' we echo, as do many others.

'Well, really! This is too much!'

Cora is standing there, furious. 'I shall speak to the mayor! This has to be stopped!'

Alain stands up, his hair cut short, his long beard gone, his hands and nails clean. 'Why, *Madame*? Because you say so? Because we don't fit into your vision of France? We belong here as much as you do. And if you want a fight on your hands, you will get one!'

Cora stares at me as if I should be standing up for her, not encouraging the riverside-clearing population. Then she stalks away.

Lou looks as if she might pass out with pride at the transformation of a man whose hands she baulked at cleaning but has now tended carefully, helping him find the man he clearly is.

FORTY-THREE

The next day is much the same. Stephanie gets up and bakes the desserts for the bistro and I walk along the riverbank, passing the clearing, which is deserted now. I have no idea where all the people came from or where they go at night. But at least they slept on full stomachs, wherever they were. And the honesty box covered our costs and some. I must start paying Stephanie, now she's doing all the work on the stall. It doesn't seem fair not to.

Fabien and Rhi visit Henri again that day, and I throw myself into cooking, returning to the pages of the old recipe book for inspiration. Stephanie joins me just before lunch service.

'I'm going to pay you for these shifts,' I say, and pull out an envelope from my bag. 'I know Henri would want that. And now the stall is starting to make some money, I can pay you for that too. It isn't much but it's something.'

'No, no.' She shakes her head emphatically. 'You do enough for me,' she says. 'This is my way of saying thank you. To Henri and to you.' She pushes the envelope away. 'Please. There's nothing I need. You offered me food and accommodation in return for work. JB is working for Fabien now. We have enough. Maybe in time . . .'

The very mention of his name makes my heart flip over and back again. 'No, I insist!' I push it towards her again. 'Something for you and Tomas, for the future.'

'No, I insist,' she says. 'Buy more lavender plants.' She pushes it back towards me. 'For the future.' She wraps her small hand over mine, closing the envelope into my palm. 'Maybe in time, I'll need a coat for Tomas, some shoes . . .'

'Of course!' I say. 'Please, take the money.'

'Maybe in time,' she says again. 'Buy plants first.'

'Then I'll take you and Tomas shopping. JB too! We'll make a day of it. New clothes for us all and lunch!'

We giggle.

'But this week we'll invest in more plants for the farm, so that it continues to give us a home and a business,' I say. 'But if you need anything for you and Tomas, just tell me.'

At lunchtime, we're full. People have heard about the 'lavender restaurant' and want to try the local product. I even overhear them talking about how lavender was a herb used in cooking, like any other, but mostly now in toiletries. There's even a journalist wanting to write about lavender and its resurgence in the kitchens of Provence.

After service, with aching feet and backs, we lay the table in the window to eat, Stephanie, Tomas and me. As we're collecting the cutlery, JB arrives, with Fabien. And no matter how shattered I feel, suddenly every nerve ending is alive.

'Del,' he says, and my nerves fray as I wonder if it's news about Henri. Fabien kisses me on each cheek.

'How's Henri?' I say, distracting myself from the smell of his aftershave, which sends my hormones into a frenzy.

'He's sitting up and talking, and the doctors say he'll be home soon. But he must take it easy.'

'Oh, that's brilliant news!' I fling my arms around him and hug him tightly. Too tightly and too enthusiastically.

Tomas laughs and claps and, embarrassed, I release Fabien from my tight embrace, which seemed to enfold everything I care about right now. Stephanie and JB laugh too. JB is a man of few words, but he has the most beautiful smile, which we've seen more and more over the past few weeks.

'You're happy, then?' Fabien says.

'Very happy,' I reply. And then I do the most natural thing in the world. 'Come on, let's all eat. Stephanie, bring some wine. Fabien, you'll stay?' Then I falter. 'If there's nowhere else you have to be?' And suddenly JB and Stephanie look at each other, as if holding their breath. 'Rhi too!' I say quickly. 'Lou is . . . Lou seems to have gone to meet Alain. He's going to show her the riverside and its plants.' I look at my text messages.

'I didn't know Lou was into plants,' says Stephanie.

'Neither did I!' We all laugh.

'And Rhi?' I'm looking round for her.

'Rhi,' says Fabien, 'can't join us.'

'Oh, that's a shame. I'll save her some,' I say quickly. 'Why?'

'She's stayed with Henri to keep him company,' he says steadily, holding my gaze. 'It seems they have a lot in common – running small businesses, kids who have left home . . .'

'Oh!' My eyebrows shoot up. Rhi and Henri: I'm slowly processing the information. 'Right. Well, I understand if you . . .' What am I saying and why am I saying it? I look at him and I'm trying to say, 'It was the most wonderful kiss I've ever had!' But maybe it was just another kiss to him. For a moment we're tongue-tied. The words just don't come.

'It's lemon and lavender chicken,' I say, and it smells delicious, 'followed by honey and lavender shortbread with ice cream.'

'I'd love to join you, thank you, if you don't mind it being just me.' Of course I don't! In fact, my heart and stomach are doing cartwheels, with streamers and hula-hoops. I beam, as do JB and Stephanie. There's an air of conspiracy between them, and once again I find myself blushing and heading to the kitchen to dish up and hide my rosy cheeks. Wine is poured, a cut baguette is put into a checked-cloth-covered basket, and I pass around plates of lemony chicken with small roasted potatoes. Gratifyingly, Tomas picks up his spoon and tucks straight in.

'To Henri,' I say, raising a glass.

'To Henri,' they all say.

'Cheers!' says Tomas, clashing his plastic mug into the glasses.

I'm not sure anything could ruin my happy mood.

After our late lunch, we walk with the pots of food and plates of biscuits to the riverside clearing, Fabien insisting on coming to help. JB goes back to the *brocante* to put away all the goods outside and close, promising to bring the keys to Fabien at the clearing. We walk from the bistro up the street towards the river, and as we do, my eyes are constantly drawn to Fabien's to find his are drawn to mine, like bees to the lavender, attracted to the flowers, needing each other to exist.

I have a strange sense of excitement, a shiver running up and down my spine, as if something is about to happen. Something unexpected.

We turn the corner to the riverside clearing. It's busier than ever before. There's a buzz in the air and I'm not sure what's going on. And then I see it. My happiness evaporates, like a popped balloon.

FORTY-FOUR

Three yellow vests across the riverside path prevent us from getting to the hut as we stand holding the big pans.

'Cora.' I sigh.

'And there's more of us to come,' she says, lifting her chin and pulling her oversized, fluorescent yellow vest around her.

I narrow my eyes at her. 'What do you want, Cora?' Just when things were beginning to work out well.

'All of this, we want it to stop!' she says, gesticulating at the busy riverside clearing. 'This area was created for the townspeople. Not as a homeless hang-out!'

'These people have as much right to be here as you or me, Cora. Maybe more. It is their town, after all. Now, please, let us pass,' I say.

She lifts her head higher in defiance. 'When we bought our place, my husband and I, we spent a lot of money. We were investing in the town, bringing prosperity.'

'Cora, from what I've seen, you hardly bring prosperity. You don't shop locally, always going to the supermarket, and you don't support the local restaurants because you always go to the "pub".'

'Well!' She puffs out her lips. 'I can see you're ingratiating yourself with the locals.' She looks at Fabien. 'Just because we're not getting into bed with them.'

'*Madame!* Enough!' says Fabien, and Alain comes to stand behind Cora.

'I'm just saying.' She points at Stephanie. 'You know how these homeless types can be. I've told you! A leopard can't change its spots, however you dress it up.'

Fury is bubbling inside me. A fury I haven't felt before. And indignation on Stephanie's behalf.

'I said enough!' says Fabien.

And then: 'Let them pass.' Cora turns and does a double-take at the sight of the smart, neatly presented man that Alain has become.

'This lot are bringing down the neighbourhood,' says Cora. 'We're known for homelessness, these days, in this town. No one will want to buy our houses. Prices will tumble.'

'Be thankful you have a house,' Alain practically growls.

'Yes, not everyone is as lucky as you. But with people like Del helping them, they might just get a second chance,' says Stephanie, sagging under the weight of the pan she's carrying and the bread.

'Now, let them pass,' says Alain.

'This place is for everyone,' says Cora, waving her banner. 'It's for the residents.'

I have a light-bulb moment. 'It was you, wasn't it, Cora,' I say, 'who threw the beautiful blue settee into the river?'

She sniffs. 'I have no idea what you're talking about.'

I can tell she's lying. It was her, all right. Her and her cronies. But I have no way of proving it, of course.

'Well, I suggest you let us pass. There are hungry people here waiting to eat and I wouldn't stand in their way if I were you,' I say. 'You know how these "homeless types" can be.'

She looks around nervously as Alain is joined by some of the other men. 'Precisely why they shouldn't be encouraged. But I'm not here for trouble,' she says, when clearly she is, and starts to shuffle aside. 'I'm here to protest, and protest I will,' she says, waving her banner.

Just then Ralph spots the dogs roaming around and lurches forward, knocking Cora's knees as he goes. In slow motion, she teeters on the edge of the riverbank. No one moves. Her arms start to swing. The banner goes in first with a splash. She turns to reach for it too late. Her friends put their hands to their mouths and noses as she topples forward, down the riverbank, one arm out to save herself, and plunges into the water. Her friends freeze. My mouth drops open. She stands in the knee-high water, spluttering and cursing and shaking a green plant off her wet arms and hands. She is furious. Ralph, though, is thrilled at this new game and launches himself into the river, with a huge splash, adding insult to injury. And although I want to call him out of the water, I can't speak. I'm worried that the only sound to come out of my mouth will be nervous laughter.

I turn quickly to the hut, unlock it, take the big pan in and put it on the side. Outside I hear, 'Get me out! You won't hear the last of this! This is why you're not wanted here!'

I can hear a kerfuffle and a cheer, just like when they got the blue settee out of the river, and I can't help but think that just desserts have been served at the riverside clearing tonight, along with my lemon and lavender chicken.

Later, as the sun is setting, we take the empty pans back to Le Petit Mas. The plates and cutlery have been washed up and cleared away into the hut. Our diners have thanked us and the honesty box is full. Rhi is still at the hospital with Henri, and Lou is taking another stroll along the riverbank with Alain, who wants to show her the bats. She promises she'll be back soon. 'Alain will walk me home, don't worry,' she says.

JB, Stephanie and Tomas walk with Fabien, Ralph and me, Fabien insisting on helping to carry things back to the farmhouse, and although we could have managed without him, I don't want him to leave, not yet.

Stephanie and JB put Tomas to bed, and suddenly it's just me, Fabien and a bottle of rosé, looking out over the valley to the setting sun. The smell of the pines and the lavender are all around us, and the cicadas are chirping in the trees. I don't think there is anywhere I'd rather be right now, or anyone else I'd rather be with. I'm nervous, yet it's just Fabien, I tell myself.

'How's Carine?' I ask, trying to make conversation.

'Fine. Busy.' He moves his head from side to side. 'She has an active social life. Actually,' he twists the stem of his wine glass, 'she's pregnant.'

At those words my heart almost misses a beat, but not quite. Not like when I used to hear friends had become pregnant, that they had joined a club of which I couldn't become a member, when people became embarrassed to tell Ollie and me. Now my thoughts have shifted: I'm not thinking about me and what I can't have; I'm thinking about Carine.

'Who . . . who's the father?' The words catch in my throat.

Fabien shakes his head, clearly unhappy. '*Monsieur le maire,*' he replies flatly.

'The mayor! But isn't he . . . ?'

Fabien nods. 'Married.'

'And is he . . .' I swallow, thinking of Ollie and his new family '. . . planning on leaving his wife?'

Fabien again shakes his head. 'He would never do that.'

'What's she going to do?' I ask.

He shrugs. 'It's early days. She's . . . thinking through her options.' He takes a big sip of wine and looks out over the half-planted lavender field. 'I'll drop off more plants tomorrow,' he says, changing the subject. And I wonder what's going through his mind. He turns back to me. 'So . . . about that kiss.' He grabs the elephant in the room and puts it between us.

'It was Stephanie. She'd developed this crush on you and I didn't want her to think I was muscling in. I didn't want her not to be able to trust me.'

A smile is tugging at the corners of his mouth. 'And now?'

'Um . . .' I flush.

'Was it really such a silly kiss?'

I look at his green eyes, with dark circles around the irises, and I want his lips on mine so much. There is a longing in me that I haven't felt for years. A pull, a draw, a yearning to make love. I can't remember the last time I made love that didn't involve trying for a baby. Lovemaking between me and Ollie stopped a long time ago. We had sex, we had charts, injections, scans, more sex, but that was what it became . . . just sex. A means to an end and an end that became a closed-off route to us. What I want more than anything right now is to be made love to. It's not about wanting a baby, it's about wanting this man, with a longing I can barely hide. I look at Fabien, so much younger than me. I can't let myself fall for him.

'Do you think Cora will manage to close us down, at the riverside clearing?' I say quickly, trying to distract myself and him. 'She clearly doesn't want us here!'

'Ignore her! I want you here. I want you here very much!'

'Here?' Butterflies, like the bats flying in front of us now, flutter in my stomach.

'Not here . . .'

'Not here?' I say. I'm flirting! I haven't flirted and felt its buzz for so long. Is it wrong to feel wanted and to want someone, no matter what the age difference? To want them for *them*. It's not about getting pregnant: it's about wanting to be with him.

I bite my bottom lip.

'No.' He moves closer towards me, and his lips are finally on mine, kissing me. And I'm kissing him back. It is the most amazing kiss I have ever had.

'How was that?' He smiles as he pulls away.

My nerve endings are standing to attention and I just want more.

'Now, will you please let me take you to bed?' he asks, and I'm taken aback, but what's wrong with saying what you really want instead of pretending?

I stare at him, the air between us as electric as the buzzing from the cicadas on this hot night.

And then I drop my head. 'I can't,' I say quietly, trying to rein in my overexcited hormones.

'Why not?' he says. 'Is it your husband?'

'Soon-to-be-ex-husband,' I say. 'Who is having a baby with his lover.'

'Is it that?' He doesn't look shocked.

'No.'

'Then why? We both want this. We are both free to be together. And Stephanie won't be unhappy any more.'

'Because . . .' I don't know that I can even say this. I look up at his beautiful face. 'Because I'm worried I might fall in love with you,' I say, so quietly I barely know if I've said it out loud.

He reaches for my cheek and stands up, offering me his hand. 'Let's take the risk, shall we?' he says. 'There is always risk in life. You coming here, staying here. It was a risk, but you made it happen, because you are you. Taking the risk is just the start of the journey, the first step.' He smiles, his hand still outstretched. 'It has to be worth the risk, doesn't it?'

My heart is pounding, my stomach fizzing with excitement.

He's right. I took the risk the first day I stayed here and I have never been happier. I look at his hand and slowly, ever so slowly, put mine into his and let him lead me up to bed.

FORTY-FIVE

The following morning, as the sun creeps back over the horizon, the birds start to sing, not a loud cacophony, but allowing each other to be heard, apart from the cockerel in the distance, as we make love again. And, yes, it really does feel like making love, being loved and loving someone else. I actually think I'm in love. Finally, and although neither of us wants the night to end, Fabien kisses me gently on the lips, then on the nose, smiles and slides from between the sheets to make sure he is out of the house before anyone else gets up, in particular Stephanie and Tomas. We'll take our time, we agree. For now, this is our secret, and it feels like the best secret ever. As he dresses, he picks up his phone, holds his face beside mine and photographs us.

'I've sent it to you!' he whispers. 'So you can think of us together.'

'I'll look terrible!' I laugh.

'You look beautiful – here!' He shows me the picture. I'm stunned. Is that really me? I look . . . lovely.

'Now you see yourself as I see you, beautiful and amazing. Look at what you've done here, the people you've helped. Liking yourself is the first step to others falling in love with you.' He kisses me again, then tiptoes out of the room, his shoes in his hand, leaving his smell on the pillows, which I hug to me, and move into the space where he was last night, feeling him still close.

The smile on my face refuses to go away as I open the shutters and look out at the sun's rays reaching over the valley, through the big balls of mistletoe in the copse of trees. A mist rolls up from the river as the dew begins to burn off the field, and my lavender plants, on this warm mid-August morning, and I try to imagine what it will be like when the whole field is covered with them. I breathe in deeply. The smell of this place just makes me feel alive. The gentle breeze brings the scent of newly turned soil and lavender, doused in dew, rising up to meet me as I think over what just happened, replaying last night in my head, like a special memory I want to imprint there and keep for ever. I have no idea where this is going: it's as if I've stepped on to a rollercoaster, with no clue as to whether it's going to be the best or worst experience of my life. 'But it's worth taking the risk.' I hear his words, feel the touch of his hand, and remember the longing in his eyes. Longing for me. I look in the mirror and raise a hand to my face. 'Now you can see what I see.' I hear his words. And smile.

'Hello, you!' I say, as if I've welcomed back an old friend. And the friend in the mirror smiles at me warmly and I like it. I like what I see and smile back at her.

I shower, dress and make my way downstairs. It's not until I reach the kitchen that I realize I'm humming. Stephanie turns when she hears me come in and I stop humming, but the smile doesn't leave my lips.

'Someone's happy,' she says.

'Thrilled that Henri is on the mend and on his way home,' I say quickly. 'Everything is going back to how it was.'

'Not quite how it was,' she says, and I'm not sure if she's talking about her and JB or something else. I give a little cough and clear my throat, and see she has already made a start on the morning's bakes. Tomas is helping her and JB is pulling on his jacket, kissing Stephanie goodbye, then Tomas, then going off to work with Fabien at the *brocante*. I reach down and pat Ralph, who Fabien instructed to stay downstairs last night with his little dog Mimi. We didn't hear a peep out of him.

'Where do you want me?' I ask.

'You're fine,' she says. 'You go to the bistro. I have everything in hand here.'

And she does. She doesn't need me. She has everything under control, her and Tomas. 'I'll see you at the bistro, then.' I smile even wider.

'*Oui, à bientôt!*' she says, opening the oven and putting in her first tray of bakes.

'*Touche pas!*' she tells Tomas.

'*Touche pas!*' he repeats, waving a finger at me, making me laugh.

'*À toute à l'heure,*' I call, as I pick up my bag, leaving Stephanie and Tomas to cook and heading down the drive to the metal gates and on to the road towards the riverbank. The smell of wild thyme, rosemary and pine gives way to the sounds of the riverbank, as I head towards town with a smile on my lips and the sun on my face. I watch the flash of blue and yellow as a pair of kingfishers dip in and out of the river and the long grasses there, fat bumblebees buzz around the wisteria hanging over a fallen fence, and a weeping willow draping its branches in the clear, slow-flowing water, all as relaxed and carefree as I feel.

As I reach the riverside clearing, I slow down. Two men in suits are there, with the mayor, looking around the site.

'*Bonjour,*' I say, and they acknowledge me, the mayor smiling politely.

What's going on? Clearly something is, and I'm suddenly worried.

I think about Carine. I have plenty of time before I should start preparing for lunch at the bistro. I want to see how she is. Maybe she'll have time for coffee before work. Maybe she'll know what's going on at the clearing. Has Cora got her way?

FORTY-SIX

'Carine?' I say tentatively as I push open the glass door and step into the cool air-conditioned estate agency, out of the morning sun. Carine has her back to me and may be wiping away a few tears with a tissue. She turns to me, her nose red and her eyes a little puffy. She sniffs, then smiles.

'Del, how are you?' she says, stepping forward and kissing me on each cheek. 'I hear you are doing a wonderful job at Henri's – Stephanie too.' She gives her nose a quick wipe, then puts her tissue into her handbag on her neat, tidy, minimalistic desk, with its clear plastic chair, everything in its place, ordered.

'Je suis très bien!' I smile, then try to rein it in a bit. I'm not ready to share my news about Fabien with anyone. I'm enjoying the delicious memory of last night and keeping it to myself just as we agreed. Take things slowly.

'You look well,' she says. 'Clearly life in Provence and at the bistro suits you.'

I catch sight of myself in the mirror on the wall and, again, feel happy to see the old me back again. I'm hoping Carine doesn't detect another reason for my rosy glow.

'I just wondered if you had time for coffee, before starting work. I'm early. Stephanie is handling all the baking at the house, so I thought . . .' I tip my head to one side, seeing her eyes fill with tears again.

She pulls out her tissue. 'Oh, stupid hay fever,' she says, and blows her nose in a noisy, very un-Carine way. Then she puts away the tissue and looks at me. 'I'd love to come for coffee but . . .' she pauses '. . . I have an appointment. Somewhere I need to be.' She glances at her watch.

'A work appointment?' I ask.

She shakes her head. 'The doctor,' she says.

I bite my bottom lip, wondering how much more I should say or ask. 'Talking of doctors,' I break the awkward silence, 'it's great news on Henri, eh?'

'It's wonderful! The best. He's a good man,' she says, and tries to smile, attempting to put on lipstick using a small compact mirror.

'I, er, I hear you have some news of your own,' I say softly.

'Ah.' She puts down the mirror and the lipstick. 'Fabien told you?'

I nod, not wanting to tell her it was just before he took me to bed last night. 'Yes.'

'I haven't seen much of him. I'd ask him to come with me this morning, but I haven't been able to get in touch with him. I think he's avoiding me.'

'I'm sure he's not.' I don't want her to think that but neither do I want to give him or me away. 'I'm sure he was just . . . busy.'

For once Carine's sharp, shrewd mind seems not to have read between the lines. Usually she doesn't miss a thing. She's really not herself.

'Like I say, I wanted him to come with me to the doctor. Sort of hold my hand. But maybe he's worried the doctor will think it's his.' She looks down at her flat belly.

'And it's not?' I find myself wanting to double-check.

'No, no. Definitely not. Like I say, Fabien and I are friends and always will be . . . I hope. But at the moment, he's avoiding me. He doesn't know what to say to me. I think he's cross with me for getting myself into this position.'

'Why? Surely he'd be a great support.'

'I have to decide whether to keep the baby,' she says, and I go cold. 'Fabien doesn't approve of my indecision. That I have "options".' She sighs. 'Will you come to the doctor with me?' she asks. 'If you have time, will you come with me?'

What can I say? I can't abandon her now when she needs someone.

'Please!' she says. 'Just walk with me and sit with me.'

This woman was kindness itself when I decided to

stay here. I can't turn my back on her now. But neither can I think about her 'options'. I'll just walk and sit with her. That's all. There's no way I can discuss her 'options' with her. Not when getting pregnant was the one thing I wanted for so long. For others, it seems so easy, just not for me. And that dream is over for me. I know that now. I have everything I need in life. My heart is as full as it could be. But I also know Carine has to do the right thing for her. I think of Stephanie and how proud she makes me, being a mother and now starting again in life. I think of Tomas and how hard Stephanie has had to work to keep him with her, to prove to herself she can be a good mum.

'Yes, of course,' I say. 'I'll come with you.' A lump in my throat.

We walk through town, neither of us really talking, lost in our own thoughts.

We go up to what looks like a house. Inside, it's a doctor's surgery, with reception desk and waiting area. Carine lets the receptionist know she's here, then sits beside me on a hard plastic chair in the waiting area.

'You never had children, Del?' she asks, straight to the point.

The lump rises and falls in my throat. 'We couldn't have them,' I say, having said this many times before. 'Actually,' I swallow, saying this for the first time, 'I couldn't have them. My husband, my ex, he's about to have a child.'

'That was quick work,' she says.

'I think his lover, partner,' I correct myself, not knowing what the proper terminology is, 'the mother of his child was pregnant before we came here. I think he ran away here when he found out she was. And when he went home, and I didn't, I think he finally accepted his responsibilities.'

'Well, that's good in some ways. At least he did the decent thing.'

'What about the father of your baby, Carine? Does he know?'

She shakes her head. 'It wouldn't be fair. He has a wife and a family. I don't want to ruin that for him. I thought I had everything sorted, in its place, but now this is chaos! This is not what was meant to happen.'

It seems an odd way of showing your affection for someone, I think, but clearly, in her eyes, that's what it is.

I wonder if this was how Mum felt when she found out she was pregnant with me.

'You have to think of yourself too, Carine, not just the baby's father,' I say tentatively, 'and the baby . . . Perhaps you should talk to Stephanie. I'd have done anything to be a mother. At first I thought it was about getting pregnant, but I know now it was never that. It was about being a mum. Being there when they need you, being Mum. I'm not jealous of Ollie and his partner being pregnant . . . but I would have liked to be a mum.'

Carine frowns as if slowly processing what I'm

saying. 'Hmm,' she says thoughtfully. 'It would have been so much easier if it had been me and Fabien finally getting together.' She attempts a small smile.

'How do you mean?' I ask, feeling a breeze as the door opens and closes and another patient enters the waiting room.

'Fabien wants nothing more than a big family of his own. He has lots of brothers, nephews and nieces. He's probably told you. They live further north. He loves them. That's why he's so good with children. He just wants a family of his own. It's the one thing he's always wanted.'

I feel myself freeze.

'Carine!' The doctor sticks her head out of the surgery door and Carine gets up, holding her bag.

'Will you wait for me?' she asks.

'Of course!' I say, without thinking. Because, right now, I can't move. I'm rooted to the spot. The one thing that Fabien wants most in the world I can't give him. I shiver as the warm breeze blows the door open again, letting us know that the mistral is on its way back. I stand up and shut it.

FORTY-SEVEN

Leaving the doctor's, Carine says very little. I walk her back to the estate agency.

'*Merci*,' she says, and kisses me on each cheek. 'Thank you for coming with me today.'

'Are you okay?' I ask. Her usually perfect complexion is dull.

'I'll be fine. I just need . . .'

I turn to follow her stare. My heart and stomach lurch and my head goes into a spin with mixed-up emotions. It's Fabien.

He's standing just across the square, having walked from the *brocante*. He looks as if he's on his way to see me at the bistro.

'I just need some time to think,' says Carine, unlocks the glass door and lets herself in.

I turn back to Fabien, who is gazing at me with a lazy smile. He points in the direction of the *brocante* and nods towards it, telling me to meet him there, then heads back with a spring in his step.

I walk away from Carine, worrying about what she's thinking. I look towards Fabien on the other side of the road. He smiles and nods towards the *brocante* again.

I point to my watch. 'I have to get on,' I call, waving a hand.

He frowns and puts on a sad face.

'Later,' I lie, and rush towards the bistro, pulling the keys from my bag, feeling sick. Because I know I can't see Fabien any more. I can't fall in love with him, or him with me, because I can never be the person he wants me to be. I can never give him what he wants most in the world.

FORTY-EIGHT

As lunchtime ends, I look up and down the road nervously, knowing Fabien will be expecting to see me, or he'll come looking for me to join us for lunch, like yesterday. Yesterday was a world away. I was the happiest I've ever been. And now I'm as far away from that as I could be.

'Let's eat back at Le Petit Mas today,' I tell a surprised Stephanie.

'Okay,' she says. 'Is everything all right?'

'Yes, yes . . . just a headache. Wondering what will happen now that Henri is on his way home. Maybe his daughters will want to take over the bistro. You have the market stall in hand. Time to make some new plans, that's all,' I lie again.

'I didn't want to take over—' she says.

'Not at all!' I stop her. 'I love seeing you taking on

the business. I'm proud of you.' I pull her to me and kiss the top of her head. She lets me and might even have smiled.

'Oh, actually, Del, you said to say if I needed anything?'

'Yes, of course,' I say.

'It's . . . it's Tomas's birthday coming up.'

'We'll get him something. Of course! Tell me how much you need. And we'll have a party!'

'I'd just like to be able to do something for him, from me.'

'Of course. Would next week be okay? I need to pay Fabien for the furniture in the house and then I can give you what you need. Just tell me how much.'

Stephanie nods.

'Right. Let's go home for lunch,' I say.

'I'll let JB know,' she says, and as we gather up the big pan, I take one last look around the bistro. Henri will be home soon. It's time I worked out what to do from here. I pull the door shut.

We've just walked into the house when I bump into Rhi. 'There's a man in the garden,' she tells me. She's come home from the hospital for a change of clothes and is on her way back to help Henri prepare to go home tomorrow.

'A man?' I ask, putting the heavy pot on the side with an 'oomph' and running my hand over my sweating forehead. 'Again?' Stephanie pours me water from the fridge and hands it to me. I take the glass and drink gratefully, my head pounding.

'Oh, and Fabien came up with a load of new lavender plants from Serge. A gift. He said he was bringing you flowers as a gift, then dropped the back of the truck and unloaded loads of plants!'

Inside I crumple. That is the loveliest gift I have ever had. He knows me so well, yet not at all! How am I going to tell this kind, gorgeous man that I'm not the woman for him? I'll have to give the lavender back. I can't accept it.

'And who's the man?' I try to distract myself.

'Don't know. He was there when I got back.'

'What's he doing?'

'Planting the lavender,' she says.

'What? No! Wait!' I run to the terrace overlooking the sloping field.

There in the field, wearing what looks to be Lou's wide-brimmed hat, under the hot afternoon sun, on his hands and knees, is Alain, planting lavender.

'Ah, Del,' he says, getting to his feet, his shirt off. 'I hope you don't mind. Lou let me shower here.'

'No, of course not.' Lou is wearing shorts and a bikini top, and is working alongside him. I can't believe it, but it looks like she's taken off her lashes and most of her makeup. She looks lovely. Beside them is the old plough from the barn, which has clearly been used on the field.

'I hope you don't mind, Del. Alain stayed in the

barn last night. It was hot, and after we'd been for our walk, well, it seemed like a sensible idea.'

'The barn?'

'Yes, the upstairs, the old hayloft. Very comfortable.' He smiles. 'And I wanted to say thank you for everything,' he says. 'This is my way of doing so.' He is holding a trowel and waving at the plants already in the ground.

'That's great!' is all I can think of saying. 'Thank you!' I can't tell him to uproot them, that I'm sending them back to Fabien. I just can't. And there's no way I would do that to Serge either! 'And do stay in the barn as long as you need,' I say, and see Alain and Lou smile at each other. 'But, please, you could stay in the house, if you want to,' I add.

'Thank you, but I haven't slept in a bed for a long time. Not since . . .' he looks at Lou for support '. . . not since my wife died next to me. It's been a long, lonely road,' he looks at Lou again, 'but things are definitely on the up.'

It looks like love is in the air for everybody. Everybody except . . . I stop myself. I can't go there. It won't help to get maudlin. I just have to tell Fabien it was a wonderful night, but we have no future together. I have to be more like Carine, everything in its place . . . even lovemaking.

'I'll get lunch ready,' I say. I go to the kitchen where I pull out knives and forks, with an extra set for Alain.

After lunch I have a quick siesta in which I don't sleep, just relive my night with Fabien, here in this bed. The sweetest, loveliest night of my life. After that, we all walk down to the riverside clearing. Cora is waiting for me with one of her cronies. I expect the other will be on her way. They're never far apart. I don't want to deal with Cora and her bigotry today.

'I've spoken to the mayor!' she shouts, as she sees me coming. 'He agrees it's time to get this stopped.' She's waving her placard in her oversized yellow vest.

I ignore her, walking towards the little hut where I greet the queue that's forming. I reach the door and unlock it.

'Tidy up our town. Get rid of trash!' Cora shouts.

At that my fury and frustration at the unfairness of life bubbles up in me. I turn to Stephanie, then to Cora, who is smiling at me in triumph. She's here to ruin all the work Henri has put in, and to make the lives of those who need a second shot at it even harder. Alain, no longer wearing Lou's hat, starts to walk towards her. I stop him. 'Here, hold that!' I say, giving him the big pot. And then I march towards Cora, right up to her, until we're toe to toe.

'The mayor is fully aware of what's going on here,' she says, taking a step back.

In no mood for her spite today, I grab her placard, pull it from her hands and toss it into the river. I'll retrieve it later. I just manage to stop myself pushing Cora in after it.

'Now shove off, Cora!' I say, sounding more menacing than I ever thought I could. 'Or these hungry people, whom you consider trash, lower than low, will be forced to help you on your way. And you never know what people "like that" may do. I won't be able to help you.'

The group takes a step forward. Cora looks at her friend, who drops her own placard, whips off her yellow vest and runs back down the path to town.

Cora looks like she's chewing a wasp. 'You haven't heard the end of this,' she says, wagging a finger at us all. 'Savages! The lot of you!' A dog barks, Ralph joins in, and Cora yelps, remembering yesterday's dunking. She hurries off towards town, calling after her friend.

The group steps back and laughs, watching her stumble away.

'Right, where were we? Dinner will be ready very soon.'

We go into the hut and it's all hands on deck to get the plates out, liners in the bins, food on the hotplate to warm up. Alain is helping Lou and Rhi.

'Um, excuse me!' says a very English voice.

It's Cora's other friend. The one who always looks like she's longing to get back to the UK.

'You've missed them. They've gone. Sent packing,' I say. 'We don't want any trouble. The only person causing it round here is Cora.'

'Oh, erm, I'm not here for trouble. Actually, I was wondering if I could help. I think finding something worthwhile to do might help me settle in a bit.'

'How long have you been here?' I ask.

'Seven years,' she replies, her head hanging. 'I

thought mixing with the expats would make me feel at home, but . . . I don't.' She looks up. 'I'd like to get involved with the town and thought I could help out here, washing up or something.'

Seven years of wishing she'd never left home!

'Of course! Everyone is welcome here if they want to join in.' I smile. And she does. She rolls up her sleeves, turns on the single tap over the sink, squirts in some washing-up liquid, and watches it fill with soap suds.

As we serve dinner, the time passes in a haze. Soon we're handing over the last few bowlfuls and collecting up any scraps for the dogs. Stephanie and JB are clearing away paper plates and collecting cutlery.

We're just finishing and the honesty box is filled with people's donations, showing their support for what we're doing.

'Look,' says Stephanie, showing it to me. Tears spring to my eyes. These people have so little, but want to give something back because they're grateful for what we've done, for keeping Henri's project going.

'Hey! *Ça va?*'

'Fabien!' He catches me off guard when I'm a mess. I brush away the tears and hand the money box to Stephanie, who puts it back on its shelf by the hatch. She glances at us and decides to finish tidying in the clearing. The fairy lights are on, and a firepit is lit – it's a dustbin lid on bricks – throwing up flames, despite the warm evening. The sun is setting, the bats are coming out, and in the background, from further along the river, I can hear a frog chorus starting up.

Fabien's face glows in the lights from the trees and the firepit, the familiar face that was next to mine all night. The unshaven chin, the green eyes and that smile. My body is aching to be with him again, and as he kisses me on both cheeks, I think my legs might give way. It takes all my willpower to pull back from him and not let my lips linger next to his. He cocks his head quizzically at me, frowning.

'Is everything okay?'

'*Oui, bien sûr!*' I say quickly.

'I have news! It's Henri. He'll be home tomorrow. Rhi is on her way back.'

'Oh, that's wonderful!' I find myself welling up again.

He cocks his head even further, reading me like a book, knowing that everything is not okay.

I have to explain this to him properly. I have to tell him how much I care about him and not that I'm completely in love with him. That is why I have to put an end to this. I love him. I know it. And I want him to be happy, but I'm never going to be able to give him the happiness he deserves. I have to finish this now before we get even more hurt. But I have to explain it properly.

'Er, Stephanie, can you keep an eye on things for a moment? I just need to . . . Fabien and I, we're just taking a walk up the riverbank,' I finish pathetically. Come on, Del. You have to be stronger than this, I tell myself.

You've been married, you've had your time to set up home with someone and dream of a future together and what it might bring. You can't take that away from Fabien. He has to meet someone he can have dreams with too. I'm me. Just me. This is it. I'm not dreaming of the future any more, just living each day as it comes and, as it happens, loving it. But I can't be the person he deserves to be with, the person to have dreams of a family with, of being a father, a grandfather, even. I have to tell him. I whip the tea towel out of the apron, tied around my waist, and wipe my hands nervously.

I tilt my head towards the path, away from the group gathered around the firepit and the new sofa there, even though the blue one has dried out now. Most people are drifting away, dogs leaving with their owners, and there's just a few left. Alain is talking to them, but has no intention of staying. He has a hayloft waiting for him and an evening stroll with Lou.

We walk a little way up the riverbank, listening to the cicadas and the frogs. I gather my thoughts, and feel I have them lined up enough to say what I need to say, no matter how hard it will be. I must make sure I explain it properly. It's not that I haven't fallen in love with him. I have. But I have to let him go. He will meet someone else, closer to his own age. He can't waste time being with me while there's a chance he could still have everything he wants in life.

I can hear the laughter of the few people sitting round the firepit, the shutters going down on the kitchen in the hut, and Tomas starting to cry as it nears his bed-time, Stephanie attempting to soothe him. I hear JB too, helping her, but neither seems able to placate him. We should start making our way back to Le Petit Mas. It's been a long day for all of us. But at least Henri will be home tomorrow and there's been healthy takings at the bistro to show him that while he's been away we've kept things going and will continue to do so as he gets back on his feet.

Fabien stops suddenly, takes me by the arms and turns me towards him. 'Del? What's the matter? Why are you upset?'

I take a very deep breath. I have to tell him all of it, me, Ollie, the failed IVF, all of it.

'Fabien, I loved last night.'

'Me too.' He moves closer to me, tucking a stray curl behind my ear. 'And I'm hoping to do it all over again tonight.' He smiles and my knees nearly give way. I put up a hand to his chest, feeling its firmness. He frowns.

'But . . .'

'But?' He cocks his head again, his black curls tumbling this way and that. 'There's a but?'

I bite my lip and close my eyes, to give me the courage to say everything I have to say.

'I can't see you any more, Fabien,' I say, with my eyes still shut. It's easier if I can't see his face.

'What? Why not? I thought we—'

'Yes, I do, we do, but there's things I need to explain about my marriage.' I open my eyes. 'I can't see you any more because . . . *phfffff*! Fabien, I am ten years older than you.'

'That doesn't matter to me. Why would it?' He laughs, trying to dismiss my worries.

'Because . . .' every bit of me wants to fall into his arms but I know I can't '. . . because that will never change. I had my chance at having a family and I know that that time is over for me now. I realize I can be happy just being me. But . . .'

'It doesn't matter to me either!' he protests.

'No. It does. I know it does. Carine told me. She told me the one thing you have always wanted is a family. I can't give that to you. It wouldn't be fair to ask you to give it up for me. I can't let you.' Tears now fill my eyes and are spilling down my cheeks.

'Del, please, listen,' he says.

I can't see his face now, but I can hear the crack in his voice. 'No, Fabien. I can't. I can't be who you want me to be. I can't be with you. That's it!'

'But—'

Suddenly there's a shout.

'Del! Del!' It's Stephanie. My eyes ping wide open but my vision is blurred with tears. 'Del! Quick!'

I don't need telling twice. I turn from Fabien and stumble back to the clearing, images of Henri and the blue lights racing through my head. Fabien is hot on my heels. I can hear his footsteps, hear his breath right behind me as we run to the clearing.

FORTY-NINE

'It's gone!' Stephanie is pointing to the empty shelf by the serving hatch. Tomas, who had fallen asleep in JB's lap, is awake again and crying. Fabien and I both slow to a standstill, him right next to me. I can smell his leather jacket, feel the heat from his body, wanting him more than anything.

'What's gone?' It takes me a few seconds to catch up with what's gone on, as I try to focus my eyes. I'm just pleased no one is hurt, in particular that Tomas is safe, if tired and grumpy in his dad's arms, clutching *Monsieur Lapin*.

'The honesty box! It's gone!' Stephanie points again.

'Are you sure?' If I hadn't been with my one-night lover, trying to explain why I'm far too old for him, I would have been here, not leaving everything to Stephanie to sort out. I seem to be doing that too much. Now Henri is coming home, it's time I got more involved with the bakes again. Maybe I'll think of some new lines, move into other towns and markets. Contact some other mayors and ask if I can set up a stall in those places. But that's for tomorrow. Right now, I need to find out where the money box has gone.

We ask around. Has anyone seen it? No one has.

'I can't believe anyone here would just take it,' I say, having looked in and around the hut. But it's nowhere to be seen. Neither, I notice, is Cora's placard, which I dumped in the river earlier and meant to retrieve. I hope it hasn't floated too far away. We all look at each other, more disappointed than angry that anyone would do this to us. It was an honesty box, based on trust. I thought the people here were grateful, not wanting to rip us off as soon as our backs were turned. I shake my head, exhausted.

Fabien is saying goodnight to the people still here.

'C'est dommage,' they say. It's a shame. A real shame. They've not just taken the money, but the trust and the spirit of the project. Then I have to remind myself that it was just one person who took it. We can't let this spoil things for everyone. Tomorrow is another day, I tell myself, and turn to see Fabien walking down the path, back towards town and his house behind the brocante.

'Fabien, wait!' I call. I haven't told him all the things I needed to explain, how I don't want to hurt him. I want him to be happy. He doesn't turn back, just holds a hand up in the air.

'Wait!'

'It's okay, I understand. You don't want to be with me!' He keeps walking determinedly. And I feel absolutely wretched. How could I have messed that up so badly? How can I ever tell him now that I love him and that's why I had to finish it? It's over.

FIFTY

The walk back to Le Petit Mas is like the longest mile ever. We all feel as though we have lead in our boots. Alain is mortified that someone would treat Henri and the project so disrespectfully and steal the box. I haven't shared my thoughts about Cora yet. Not until I've had a chance to confront her. Tomas is fractious and only wants to be carried by Stephanie. JB takes her bags and she has the little boy in her arms along the path and back up the hill to Le Petit Mas, where Rhi's waiting, having made a last visit to Henri before his return tomorrow. We're now going to have to tell him about the missing honesty box and the unpleasant taste it's left in all of our mouths. Suddenly a town, a community who lived contentedly side by side, is shattered and suspicious.

FIFTY-ONE

The following morning I make my way downstairs to be greeted by Ralph, who looks to be missing his new bed companion, Mimi, as much as I'm missing mine.

I look out of the window to see Lou, in her short dressing-gown, disappearing into the barn with a tray of coffee, croissants and orange juice. It makes me smile. The bakery van has been and there are croissants on the side for us all. I roll up my sleeves and start pulling out the ingredients for the day's bakes. Stephanie is a little late this morning, but it will do her good to have a lie-in. I look around the kitchen for the book. And then I remember, it's probably in her bag – she would have brought it back from the bistro. Maybe I should start the day with a new bake. Something from the heart of Provence, I think, and my spirits lift a little. I'm trying not to picture Fabien walking away from me last night, his hand raised in the air.

'It's okay, I understand. You don't want to be with me.' Nothing could be further from the truth. But I can't! Fabien helped me remember who I used to be. I'm living in the now, and loving it, not living for the future. But I'm certainly not going back.

Stephanie's bag is on the side, and I wonder if the book is in there. I can see something bulging and sticking out from the top. Then my blood runs cold.

FIFTY-TWO

'Sorry I'm late. Tomas is teething.' She stops and looks at me, as I reach my hand into her bag and pull out the honesty box.

She stares, wide-eyed, in apparent amazement.

I feel sick. I trusted her and thought she trusted me. She can't have taken it! I know that! But what's it doing there?

The seconds tick past slowly. My heart is beating so loudly I'm surprised she can't hear it. She can't have taken it, I tell myself.

Slowly I look up at her.

'Where was it?' she asks anxiously.

'Well,' I say, 'it was . . .' I swallow again. I'm sure it wasn't her. Please don't let it be JB either! 'It was in your handbag.' I try to say it matter-of-factly.

'In my h-handbag?' she stutters. 'But how?'

'I . . . I don't know,' I say. 'Could it have fallen in by mistake? Or someone put it there for safe keeping?'

There are tears in her eyes. Hot, angry ones.

Just tell me, I think, that it wasn't you and we can find out who it was.

'You think it was me, don't you?' she says, with a steeliness I haven't heard since we first met.

'No. No. I don't. I'm just trying to work out . . .'

My thoughts turn back to the first time I met her, in her bedsit, my biscuits on the table, taking what she needed for her son. But she wouldn't do that to me or to Henri.

'You think I might have done,' she says, in an angry whisper. 'You know I'm capable.' She is ashen-faced. 'A leopard never changes its spots. Isn't that what that Englishwoman said?'

I look down at the box in my now-shaking hands. Who would do this?!

She stares at me, her face set. Her eyes darken as they did the first time I met her in that downstairs room. When I thought I was doing something to help. Of course I don't think she would do that to me.

'No, listen—' I begin to say, 'of course I don't think that,' I go to say, but she cuts me off, her chin held high.

'I understand. I understand everything,' she says, grabbing her bag, 'and if you believe I could have taken that, I can't stay here any more!' She stalks out.

'Wait!' But I hear the front door slam. Now what have I done?

She just needed me to tell her that of course it couldn't have been her. I'm just trying to work out who would have done it. And now I've ruined everything! I've tried to keep going while Henri has been in hospital. Fabien hates me and, clearly, so does Stephanie.

A huge sob escapes me, and I feel more alone now than I did on that first night here without Ollie.

FIFTY-THREE

Outside the mistral is blowing up bigger than usual, as it did on the day I decided to stay. The dust is whipping up as I watch Stephanie, JB and Tomas walk down the drive, with their blue bags. JB is carrying Tomas. He told me Tomas and Stephanie would be fine. They'd stay with his parents until they could get something else sorted, he said, and thanked me for all I'd done. But I don't want anything else sorted. I want them to stay here, for it to be as it has been. My own little family. Every part of me wants to shout, 'Stop! Come back!' But Stephanie is clearly in no mood to discuss the matter. I watch their backs as they walk to the end of the drive, a little family facing an unknown future, and my heart breaks. The wind whips up and slams the front door shut in my face.

FIFTY-FOUR

Later that morning, Rhi appears, dressed up to meet Henri and travel home with him from hospital. Lou and Alain come in from the barn and I gather them around the table and explain about Stephanie.

'I found it in her bag. She assumed I thought she'd taken it, and said she couldn't stay if I thought that.'

Each of them looks as heartbroken as I feel.

I manage lunchtime at the bistro on my own, the hole that Stephanie filled feeling like a great crater, with all the customers asking after Henri and Tomas.

Afterwards, my eyes stinging, I finish the washing-up. The door opens and my heart lurches. I'm hoping to see Stephanie there. I wish I could go to Fabien and tell him what's happened. But I can't let him think I'm using him as a shoulder to cry on when I need it. I created this situation. I have to take responsibility for it.

At the door, it's not Stephanie, but a very welcome sight that brings a smile to my face.

'Henri!' I say, and rush forward to hug him hard.

'Whoa!' He laughs. 'You'll have my heart giving out all over again!'

'Sorry, it's just so good to see you.' I sniff, tears of happiness and sadness mixed together. He looks like himself, despite having lost lots of weight and shaving off his little goatee beard. 'You look so well.'

'I feel like death! But you look . . . upset,' he says. 'Sit down. Do as I say!'

'Aren't I supposed to be saying that to you?' I laugh and sniff again and Rhi pulls out a chair.

'I've learned not to argue,' she says. 'And to stop checking on the business every five minutes and let them get on with it.' She smiles, holding the chair for me to sit in.

Henri walks back into the kitchen, as if revisiting somewhere he used to know well and taking in how nothing but everything has changed. He nods his approval and pulls out a bottle of red wine from the rack.

'Um, are you supposed to be drinking?' I ask.

'This is France, dear girl. It's practically recommended.'

I'm sure that's not true, but I don't argue. Nor do I attempt to step in as he struggles to release the cork. Eventually he succeeds, to his own relief.

He brings three glasses and puts them on the table, as if trying to fit into an old suit he used to wear. Not that I'd ever seen Henri in anything other than chef's whites, because he was always working. He pours three glasses, then sits and raises his.

'To good health, good friends,' he looks at me, 'and new beginnings.' He gazes at Rhi, who blushes.

'Now, *ma chérie*,' he says, 'tell me everything that has been happening. And I mean everything.'

Henri is back and everything will return to how it was. I feel a huge sense of relief as so much responsibility lifts from my shoulders.

FIFTY-FIVE

'So, you see,' I say to Henri, after I've told him nearly everything. I don't tell him the details of the night Fabien and I spent together. But I do tell him how I fell in love with him, and have hurt him more than I could ever have imagined. I was trying so hard not to get hurt myself that I have hurt the one person I really loved. I sigh, and so does Henri.

'She's a proud young woman is Stephanie,' says Henri, nodding.

'But I didn't think she'd do that. I just wanted her to reassure me, tell me it wasn't her, and we could find out what really happened. I should have told her I knew it wasn't her. But she didn't give me the chance. She assumed I'd suspect her. But I know she wouldn't have done it to me. I just need to find a way of making her understand that.'

He pats my knee reassuringly. 'Parenting young

adults is like trying to navigate a stormy sea. We don't always get it right.'

Is that what I've been? Like a parent to her? Henri smiles, and suddenly that's exactly how I feel. Like a parent who messed up.

'It will be okay, Del. Just give it time.'

I sniff, take the paper napkin Henri hands me and blow my nose. Then I straighten myself, feeling like a boxer who has been knocked sideways and is still reeling. I'm wishing I could fight just one more round, but I'm not sure I've got the strength or the skills.

'Del, you have done such a wonderful job here,' says Henri.

'I'd hardly call it wonderful. You've heard what's happened. I've had yellow vests blockading the riverside clearing, had our money stolen . . . and found again in the worst place, and lost the best employee you could ever have known.'

'And Fabien,' he says.

'Yes, and Fabien.' I clear my throat.

'All I can see is what a great job you have done, with your business, my business, and with Stephanie, JB and Tomas. Rhi and I know what it's like to bring up teenagers. They love you, and they leave you. But they always want to come back.'

'But you don't understand! I let her go – she thought she had to!'

'These things have a way of sorting themselves out. Be kind to yourself. You did a great job. It's how life is,' he says, topping up our little wine glasses. Somehow having two *petit* glasses doesn't seem as bad as having one big glass at this time of day.

'So . . . I have a proposition for you,' he says, taking another swig of wine. 'Rhi and I have decided it's time to hang up aprons . . . and scissors.' She nods in agreement. 'We plan to go on a holiday, a long holiday.'

'What? Rhi?' I'm filled with joy for my friend, who has broken out of her life back home. She has chained herself to her business since her children left home, yet it runs itself without her, as she's discovered by being here. I stand up to hug her. 'I'm so delighted for the two of you, I really am.' And I hug Henri again. I always knew he would make someone a lovely partner. But not me: I had to go and fall in love with the one man I can't have and now he can barely look at me.

'But we can't make that happen if I'm running this place and Rhi is overseeing her salon. We've spent my time in hospital realizing what we have and what we need to do to change our lives.'

'I'm sure the kids will hate us for it,' Rhi puts in, 'but I'm older than you, Del. The kids have gone and only get in touch when they want money. But it's time we made the most of what we've earned, not just build up their inheritances!' They smile understandingly at each other.

'So you're selling up?' I ask, sad to think that this place, which has been my anchor since I arrived here and for all the people at the riverside clearing who depended on Henri, will close down. But now, after the incident of the honesty box, word will have got around and the mayor is bound to want to close the riverside clearing. One way or another, Cora has got what she wanted. Everything that has become home to me has gone. I'm right back where I started, only this time with a huge hole in my heart: I've lost not just a partner but a family. The wind whips up the awning, knocks over the chairs out there and shakes the wisteria growing up the wall.

'No, I'm not selling,' he says, and holds my gaze. 'Be my business partner, Del. Come into the bistro with me. Run the place. I'll take a back seat.'

I have no idea what to say. I've made such a mess of things. He could go away and come back to no business at all. He's trusting me with his whole livelihood. What if I ruin it?

Suddenly the door flies open and crashes into the wall.

'Fabien!' He has a habit of turning up just when I'm thinking about him. Or is it just that I'm always thinking about him?

'Del, I need to talk to you, urgently!'

FIFTY-SIX

'So, I went to see Carine,' he says, after greeting Henri, welcoming him home, saying they'll catch up later, and agreeing with him that I've done a brilliant job. Henri and Rhi make themselves scarce, going up to his little apartment above the bistro.

'Fabien, let me explain,' I say. I need to tell him the last thing I wanted to do was hurt him.

'No, please, Del. Hear me out. It's important. I went to see Carine, after we talked. She told me . . . well, that doesn't matter now. But I told her about the honesty box. And guess what she told me? That the mayor has given in to the Englishwoman's demands,' he says.

'He's going to close down the project!' I wail.

Fabien shakes his head and smiles. 'He had CCTV fitted!' he announces.

'*What?*'

'He has everything filmed now!'

Fabien's smile broadens and my heart melts.

'It means there is proof that Stephanie didn't do it.'

I jump up, the chair flipping back and clattering as it hits the floor, making a subdued Ralph bark. 'So who did?'

'*Monsieur le maire* is waiting for you with Carine!'

FIFTY-SEVEN

'So,' says the mayor, sitting at his desk in the *mairie*, his new CCTV cameras showing footage on the computer screen in front of him, 'I can see what's happening all over the town now. Four new cameras.'

We stand behind his chair and stare at the screen. Fabien, Carine and I are silenced by what we've just seen.

'Cora!' I say eventually. 'I knew it was her all along. I just wanted Stephanie to tell me it wasn't *her*.' My fists are tight with fury. 'But she needed me not to ask.'

'You can see it clearly,' says the mayor. 'Here.' He points to the screen as he reruns the footage. 'She appears round the back of the hut, just as you are walking away with Fabien. Stephanie and JB are with Tomas, who has had enough for one day.' He seems to chuckle. 'She takes the box and slides it into Stephanie's bag, there, by the door, where she dropped it when she went to Tomas.'

I'm so angry I can hear the blood whooshing in my ears! Not just angry with Cora, angry with myself for even questioning Stephanie or JB for a second!

'She even takes her banner back as she leaves,' he points out. She's leaning into the water and dragging it out. 'No doubt intending to be back with it again tonight.'

'If only I hadn't walked away,' I say. 'If I'd stayed at the clearing until we'd locked up, none of this would have happened.'

'You were dumping me, remember?' Fabien says drily, his joy at finding Stephanie conclusively innocent forgotten, his hurt evident. My cheeks tingle and burn – I'm not sure whether with embarrassment, regret or fury about Cora.

'Yes,' I say, hanging my head. 'Very badly if I remember it correctly. I'm sorry.'

'Sorry for dumping me or sorry for doing it so badly?' He raises his eyebrows, his lovely green eyes shining again.

'Both,' I croak.

'Okay, well, let's sort out Cora, and then you two need to talk,' says Carine. 'Talking is always the best option.' She smiles at the mayor and I wonder what decision she has come to and hope it's right for everyone. 'And to think it was Cora's idea to put in the CCTV, to get rid of the homeless in the town.'

'I think we can agree she's about to be, er, hoist by

her own petard!' says the mayor. 'You leave Cora to me and my police officers,' he says.

'In the meantime, there's probably someone else you should speak to before you talk to me,' says Fabien. 'Would you like a lift?' he says kindly. It's all I can do not to hug him.

'Please,' I manage. I just hope Stephanie will agree to see me, because if she won't, I don't think I'll be able to stay around here any longer. My time at Le Petit Mas will be over and all my happy memories destroyed. Which may be exactly what I deserve.

FIFTY-EIGHT

We barely speak on the way to JB's parents' house. I have no idea exactly what I'm going to say.

As we pull up at the house, I have no idea if she will even see me, let alone talk to me, and I couldn't be more nervous. If Stephanie won't see me I'm not sure I could bear it. I stare at the front door. The same door she knocked on when she came to find JB, who sent her away. I stare at it and wonder if the same will happen to me, presuming, of course, that they're here. My heart is pounding.

'I'll wait down the street,' Fabien says. 'Take as long as you need.'

I open the door and slide out from beside Ralph, who is happily reunited with Fabien's Jack Russell, Mimi.

I walk slowly up the road, in through the front gate and through the neatly tended little garden up the crazy-paved path to the sage-coloured front door.

I stare at it. Right now, everything that matters is, hopefully, on the other side. I raise my shaking hand and knock. My new life in France hangs in the balance.

FIFTY-NINE

JB answers the door and, to my relief, invites me in and introduces me to his parents, who seem a little guarded, understandably so. I handled things so badly. I feel wretched.

We stand in awkward silence as JB goes to tell Stephanie I'm here. He runs upstairs in the small modern house, which is now filled with four adults and a toddler and seems very cramped.

My hands are sweating and I feel light-headed.

Finally I hear footsteps on the stairs and Stephanie is coming down with Tomas in her arms. My heart leaps at the sight of them, then plummets as I remember this could be our last goodbye.

JB's parents are still looking at me from their position on the sofa, surrounded by bags of nappies and a plastic car. Through the window, I see a football in a neat flowerbed in the back garden. Everything was clearly in its place before Tomas arrived, but they're delighted to see him now. I'd ask to have a moment alone with Stephanie, but I don't think there's anywhere we could go to be on our own.

'Stephanie,' I say. It's a start. She accepts my kiss on both cheeks and Tomas too. He holds out his arms to hug me, as if I'm a special aunt who's come to visit. And that is exactly how I feel, not like his mother, but a special aunt, and it's lovely.

I clear my throat. Everyone is looking at me. Stephanie's eyes are guarded and dark.

'Have you come to tell me you're reporting me to the police?' she says, like a cat backed into a corner, spitting and hissing. 'To tell them I'm a thief.'

Her words sting.

'No,' I say. 'I've come . . .' now I have to find the words '. . . because I cannot believe how wrong I was. I knew you wouldn't have taken the money.'

'Oh, really? How did you know? If I had told you I hadn't done it, would you have believed me?'

'Yes, of course! It was Cora all along. I should've realized it straight away. I'm sorry. She was trying to set you up so that I would think it was you and the riverside clearing would be closed down. She wanted to hurt us. To get us all to leave, and leave her town "picture-perfect".'

'Looks like she succeeded.'

'I couldn't feel worse about it. I never really thought it was you. Not even for a second. I'm sorry.'

She raises her eyebrows.

'Not even for a second? Me, the thief! Who could never change her spots!'

She lifts her chin higher just like when I first met her and I wonder if it's to stop any tears leaking from her eyes.

I shake my head.

'Not even for a second.' I need her to believe me. I knew in my heart that she wouldn't do that to me, no matter how much Cora wanted me to think that.

Stephanie says nothing. Nobody says anything. That's it. It's all I can say. I could tell her how much I've loved having her and Tomas in my life, JB too, about how wonderful she is with the business. But I just need her to know that I really am sorry. Nothing can repair the damage I've done here. I turn to JB's parents and bid them *au revoir*. I'm unlikely to see them again. I say the same to JB. I want to hug him and tell him how proud I am of the dad he's become. There is so much more I want to say to Stephanie, how I wish her all the luck and love in the world, and how proud I am of the person she is and wish I was more like her.

But I can't say any more. I can't speak for the lump in my throat. Instead I nod, walk towards the door and open it. JB holds it as I step outside into the wild, windy, warm afternoon. I feel like I've been picked up and spun around – I'm not sure which way I'll end up facing when the mistral leaves again. I hold my arm over my eyes and walk down the path, hoping Fabien hasn't deserted me altogether for my foolish behaviour.

'Del,' I hear faintly. 'Del!' It's Stephanie's voice. I turn back. She's standing at the door. I walk towards her. She steps outside under the porch, pulling the door to behind her.

'Del, wasn't it you who said that everyone deserves a second chance? You gave me one when I stole from you. You gave me a second chance, no questions asked, no looking back. But you said there wouldn't be a third!' she says firmly.

'Yes, I know. But I thought—'

'Everyone deserves a second chance, you said.'

I nod. I did.

'I'm giving you a second chance,' she says, and a smile pulls at her lips, 'but there won't be a third!'

Did I hear her right?

'I accept your apology,' she says. 'I understand why you might have thought it was me, why you asked me. The money was in my bag, after all. I should have just told you it wasn't me. But I was too proud.'

'I know but—'

'No more buts. Cora was clever. She got what she wanted.'

'I'm not going to let her win, Stephanie. She nearly did. She nearly broke us.' And I open my arms. This time Stephanie steps into them and I hug her, like I'm welcoming her home after a family meltdown, when things are said, and people act before they think.

I should have trusted my instincts and from now on I will!

'How did you get her to confess?' she says, pulling away.

'CCTV! The mayor had it fitted at her insistence. He was trying it out before he announced it to the town. That's who those people were the other day when I passed them at the riverside clearing.'

'Ha!' Stephanie laughs and so do I. We laugh out of sheer relief as the wind whips up and around us. When the laughter dies down, I think of Mum. 'Least said, soonest mended': her words are loud and clear in my head, like she's right here with me.

'Come home, please?' I say.

I watch her face as she considers her answer.

SIXTY

'Room for a few more?' I ask Fabien, as we run back to the truck having packed up all of the little family's belongings. JB's elderly parents are delighted to get their home back but they, JB and Stephanie promise to visit each other and not to be strangers. They thank me for keeping an eye on the three of them and for finding JB work. Looks like bridges have been built here too. They have a grandson and an almost-daughter-in-law as well as their son now.

Fabien looks as ecstatic as I feel to have got his workmate back as he ushers the dogs into the truck, while Stephanie and Tomas tuck in beside them. Tomas is delighted to be reunited with Ralph, who pants happily that his friend is back.

At Le Petit Mas, the wind begins to subside and behind it the sun shines through the clouds, pushing

August aside as September rolls in. We unload the family's belongings into the gypsy caravan. I offer them rooms in the house, now Rhi seems to be spending her time with Henri: I'm presuming her room is free. But once again they refuse: they prefer the caravan. I'm sure one day they'll need something bigger but for now that space is theirs and they love it. The three of them together.

Finally Fabien and I walk back to his truck, unspoken words filling the air. The wind settles and I hold my face to the sun, feeling its strength. It's time I told Fabien everything, this time without interruption. I open my eyes and look at him.

'Fabien, about last night at the riverside clearing,' I say, wanting him to understand I never meant to hurt him.

'*Oui*,' he says sadly.

'Oh, my God! The riverside – dinner! I completely forgot. We have to get there! There will be people waiting to eat!'

'Get in the truck,' he says.

'No, it's quicker down the river path,' I say. 'I'll run.'

'I'll get the food and meet you there,' he says.

'Stephanie!' I call.

'*Oui?*'

'Service! At the riverside!'

'*Merde!*' She runs out of the copse of trees.

'Language, Stephanie,' I say, and feel everything

slip back into place, as if I am a big sister, an aunt, a friend – who knows what I am? It feels very special. It doesn't need a label. It just feels like family.

When we see the riverside clearing, we slow down, Stephanie and I. JB has gone with Fabien. We're out of breath when we come to a complete standstill. The fairy lights are on, the firepit is lit.

Cora is standing there, as are her two friends, but they're not beside her. There's a big crowd and, if I'm not mistaken, the mayor is there too. The hatch is open and there is Henri, his hair tied back in its usual ponytail, with Rhi. Everyone is welcoming him back and shaking his hand. Alain and Lou are laying out the cutlery and paper plates. Lavender, in washed tin cans on the makeshift tables, fills the warm evening air with its scent.

Stephanie and I walk up to Cora side by side.

'You won't stop this happening, Cora,' I say, as she stares at me.

'We all have a right to be here, no matter how much or little money we have,' says Stephanie, and I'm filled with pride again at the confident young woman she has become.

'I know.' Cora drops her head. 'I'm sorry. I've come to help out, if you'll have me. My way of making amends, so to speak.'

'We welcome everybody here, Cora, rich or poor. We are a community. We have to look out for each other,' says the mayor, unwittingly using her own words back at her.

'We all deserve a second chance, don't we, Del?' says Stephanie, nudging me.

I have a lot to learn from this young woman. 'We do, Stephanie.' I smile, and out of the corner of my eye I see Fabien appearing from the other side of the clearing wearing his leather jacket, with JB and Tomas behind him. I just wish there was a way that he and I could have another chance, but I know we can't. I drag my eyes from him and back to Cora.

'We all deserve a second chance, Cora.'

'But not a third!' Stephanie and I say together.

Her friend takes her off to start washing up, bickering about who washes and who dries.

'Ladies and gentlemen,' says the mayor, 'in English so all our guests and residents can understand. I am happy to be here tonight, welcoming you all back to the riverside clearing and the wonderful meal that awaits you.' There is a cheer. 'And more than that, to welcome back the man who has been here for you all and set this up at the very beginning. Henri!' Everyone gives a loud cheer and claps.

Henri holds up a hand and quietens the crowd. '*Merci, merci,*' he says. 'But I am in fact here for only one night. After tonight, I shall be hanging up my apron.' The crowd is very quiet now. 'But, don't worry, I am hoping to find a replacement before I go. I want to leave you in good hands, the best in fact.' He looks at me and raises an eyebrow. Everyone turns to me. I'm very nervous. Could I say yes and stay here, knowing that Fabien and I are never going to be together? I'm not sure I could, seeing him every day and knowing I'm not with him. Watching him meet someone new and bring up a family with her. I want to say yes to Henri, but my heart is torn in two. I would love to run the bistro. I wonder what my younger self would have said? I look at Stephanie, who smiles, and I know exactly what my younger self would have said: 'Of course!'

But I'm not my younger self, and I don't want to stand in the way of Fabien moving on in his own life, in his own town. What should I do?

'This is your home as much as anyone else's,' Henri says, as if reading my thoughts. 'Will you be my business partner?'

Could I walk out on all this now? Could I walk out on Stephanie and Tomas? I don't think so.

I nod, and the crowd cheers.

'Now, *à table*, dinner is served,' says Henri, one last time, and rings a little brass bell by the counter. The diners slowly move towards the serving hatch. And Fabien comes to me. Is he upset that I've decided to stay? Cross that he will have to see me, after I've hurt him?

'Del!' It's Lou and Alain, hand in hand. She's waving at me. She barely has a scrap of makeup on, her face tanned, freckled and happy.

'Del!'

Fabien stops in his tracks. I just hope he'll still be

there when I've spoken to Lou. I owe him an apology and must tell him I'll try to stay out of his way.

'You two look happy!' I smile.

'We are!' Lou says, and Alain's beautiful smooth face beams too. 'Alain and I, we're . . . Well, I'm going to stay on in France.'

'Oh, that's lovely news,' I say and hug her.

'Not with you. We're going to get somewhere of our own. And we'll look for a business. A small house with some land, so we can grow things and sell at market.'

For a moment I'm dumbstruck. Lou, my friend who hasn't committed to any relationship since her husband died and who hasn't worked in years, let alone ever got her hands really dirty, is going to look for a smallholding to buy with Alain.

'Aren't you pleased?' She seems crestfallen.

'Pleased? I'm stunned and delighted!' I throw my arms around her again and the fragrant-smelling Alain.

'He's loved working on the lavender plants so much that we want to do something ourselves,' she says. I can't believe how much my dear friend has changed in such a short time. 'We'll be neighbours. We don't want to go too far,' she says.

'And you're welcome to stay on at Le Petit Mas until you're sorted,' I say. 'In the barn or the house, whichever suits.'

Alain smiles. 'I'd like that. In the house would be very acceptable, thank you,' he says.

He's finally able to move back into a bed, alongside

Lou, and they're making a new life for themselves, putting the hurt of the past behind them.

'Now go and eat,' I tell them. 'If I know Henri, there'll be plenty.'

Fabien is talking to the mayor. He sees me and beckons for me to join him on the river path once more. I nod. And as I do, Carine is there. '*Chérie!*' she says. 'I've found you at last!'

'Carine!' I look for Fabien, who shakes his head and laughs.

'I wanted to tell you. I have made my decision,' she says quietly, against the hubbub of contented diners, cicadas, and the frogs in the distance. The sun is setting, silhouetting the cypress, pine and oak around us as summer draws to its end. The bats are flying in and out of the trees across the water, catching their evening meal of midges. I hold my breath.

'I'm keeping the baby, Del,' she says, and I let out a sigh of relief. 'I saw Stephanie with Tomas, how much she loves him, and him her.'

'I'm so pleased. For what it's worth I think it's the right decision,' I say.

'I know how lucky I am to have this chance. You made me understand that,' she says. 'It may not happen again.'

I nod.

'And the mayor?' I raise my eyebrows.

'We've talked. We are going to end our affair. I've been wrong. I thought it put everything in its place, but it doesn't. It just messes everything up for everybody.'

'Oh!'

'He's going to support me and the baby. But we will keep it to ourselves and he will spend more time with his wife from now on.'

Not an ideal situation, but better than the alternative.

'Maybe it's time I let a little disorganization into my life for once,' she says, putting a hand to her stomach. 'Oh, and look at this!' She thrusts her phone at me. 'I had a new instruction today!' I look down at the photograph of a house for sale. Cora's house. 'She's going home,' says Carine. I smile and kiss her on both cheeks, then turn to see if Fabien is still waiting for me. But he isn't. He's gone.

SIXTY-ONE

At the clearing we wash up and shut the serving hatch.

'*Bonne nuit.*' We all wish each other a good night. The fairy lights go out, but the firepit still glows, lighting the faces of those still sitting there, and again I realize how lucky I am to have a house to go to.

I pull out my phone and take a picture, then flick to Facebook, Ollie's page, where he's announced the birth of his baby boy and his own arrival into the 'sleepless nights club'. I look at Ollie and the baby, and discover the pain has gone. Today I felt real pain when I thought I'd lost Stephanie, Tomas and JB for good. Pain like I'm feeling about Fabien. But the hurt of the dream that never was with Ollie is gone. In the darkness I look at the bright screen and type, *Congratulations. Wishing you all the very best*, and I mean it. Let Ollie wait till the teenage years kick in to find out what sleepless nights are really all about. I know – I've been living with a teenager.

I follow the little family up the riverside path, Lou and Alain kissing Henri and Rhi as they head back to his flat above the bistro. And as we walk, watching the bats flit this way and that, I can't believe how lucky I am. I may not have Fabien in my life, but I do have all of this. And you can't have everything, can you? Enough to be content.

SIXTY-TWO

Back at Le Petit Mas, we all walk up the drive and I see a glow. We all slow down. The terrace is lit with candles and someone is waiting there. I hope it's not Ollie, running out on his new family already. We walk slowly up the path. It isn't Ollie. My heart gallops. It's Fabien.

'I guessed the only way to get to talk to you was away from crowds,' he says, a bottle of rosé on the table with two glasses.

Stephanie says goodnight, kissing me on both cheeks, as does JB, and I kiss the sleeping Tomas in his arms.

Lou disappears into the house with Alain. And now it's just me and the *brocante* man, standing on the terrace looking back at the town over the lavender field that is filling the warm night air with its scent. Something about that smell and this place seems to heal people. I hope it can heal the hurt between Fabien and me.

'I hope you don't mind.' He cocks his head in the way that he does and his black curls fall to one side.

'No, no, I've wanted to talk to you,' I say.

'You're in demand, Del. A popular lady.' He pours the wine into the glasses. The light pink liquid tumbles joyously out of the bottle, glowing in the candlelight. 'Perhaps now you understand why I find you so attractive. You attract people, Del. People are drawn to you. You are a very beautiful person, inside and out,' he says. 'I can't apologize for falling in love with you.'

I catch my breath.

'In love with me?' And there and then I want to just kiss him and never stop. But I can't.

'I loved you from the moment I saw you. But I understand you think I'm too young for you. Perhaps you are still in love with your husband.'

'Oh, no.' We sit down and look out over the field at the bats flitting through the trees. I take a large glug of wine. It hits the spot with its refreshing cool flavours that reflect the sunny *terroir* in which it's grown here. I breathe in the lavender. It's time to explain why I can't be with him.

'No,' I say. 'I'm here to stay. I'm going into business with Henri. I was never going back to Ollie. Our journey ended a long time ago. It just took me a while to realize it.'

'Then what?' He looks confused.

'We . . .' I hesitate. 'I couldn't have children. We spent years trying diets, alternative therapies, and then

IVF, which left me depressed, as if the old me had moved out and left just a shell of me behind. I felt I'd been excluded from a club that everyone else was allowed to join. But out here, on my own, I started to find me again, and I like her.'

'I do too.' He smiles gently. My heart and stomach shift and resettle.

'And then . . . I met you. And I . . . fell in love and made love for the first time in years. I felt loved.'

He says nothing.

'It's my fault. I shouldn't have let myself fall in love with you.'

'But I fell in love with you too!'

'But I can't be with you, Fabien.'

'I don't understand!' The candle flames flicker and light his face.

'Because I can't give you the one thing you really want, and that's a family. You have to meet someone who'll give you everything you want in life, and that isn't me. It's best we stop this now, before we—'

'Fall in love? Isn't it a bit late for that?' he asks. 'Del.' He stands up and looks across the lavender field, breathing in the night air, then turns to me. 'I loved you from the moment I met you, when you arrived at the *brocante*. When I heard you were here alone and trying to make life work for yourself.' We both laugh. 'Then you set up the stall, gave Stephanie a home, took on the bistro and the riverside clearing project, and you took on Cora. My love for you has grown.'

'But you need to be with someone who can—'

'Give me a family? Carine told me what she said to you. She hadn't realized we were together for the short time we were. When I thought I had finally met and got together with the woman I wanted to spend the rest of my life with.'

I'm hot, my heart racing, and I feel like I'm looking down from a cloud at the life I want to have but can't quite reach.

'Yes, it's true, I have always wanted a family. But you have shown me that you don't need a baby to have a family. You, Stephanie, Tomas, JB, that's family, isn't it?'

I nod slowly.

'And you, Stephanie, Tomas and JB are all the family I need. Everything I want in life is right here, right now, with you. I want you as my family. Isn't that enough?'

'It is for me. More than enough,' I say quietly.

'And for me,' he crouches beside me, 'it's much more than enough to be content. It is everything! I would be a rich man! You are my family, Stephanie and Tomas too. We may not have children, you may not have given birth, but you have created a family, here and in the town. I want to be at your side until I'm old, sharing family life with you.'

Without thinking, I reach out and touch his face, because I can't not. I hold my hand to his cheek and he kisses my palm, keeping his lips there, sending fireworks through my body, like Bastille Day celebrations, when the French rejoice in a new dawn in France's history. And this, I think, is mine. I can't fight it. I can only celebrate it. This is my new dawn with a man I love and a family that has come together through love and trust, and that's enough.

'Now,' he stands and I wonder if he's leaving, 'will you please let me take you to bed,' he says, picking up the wine bottle and the glasses, 'and let me enjoy starting our new family life together? I don't need a baby to want to spend the rest of my life with you, Del. You are all I need.'

'Really?'

'Trust me. Because we do at least have that.'

I smile and take his hand. I have everyone around me that I love, and that is more than enough. I know that Mum, looking down on me, would agree as the sun disappears over the horizon of the lavender fields, preparing for the new dawn.

EPILOGUE

There is lavender everywhere, in milk churns, across the terrace over an arch at the clearing with the lavender field behind it. Everything is set. Cream and lavender ribbons blow in the breeze.

'I want Ralph to come with me,' says Tomas, in his thick French accent, now totally bilingual and impressing his teachers when he started school.

'I'm not sure Ralph would make a very good ring-bearer,' I say, attaching a small lavender corsage to his buttonhole.

'I want Ralph!' he says, and his face starts to crumple.

'Okay, okay, Ralph can come too!' I don't want anything to spoil the day as we make our way out into the lavender field.

Everyone is there, on the white chairs from the *brocante*, in the cool of the spring sunshine.

The music begins and Tomas, holding Ralph's collar,

leads him down the aisle to the lavender-covered archway, where the celebrant, the mayor, is waiting and smiling.

'*Bonsoir*, and in English for all our guests, good evening. Welcome to Le Petit Mas,' he says, looking up from his notes. 'I am delighted to welcome the families of the bride and groom here today, JB's family and the family of Stephanie, the beautiful bride.' Stephanie turns to me and grins at the row of eclectic family there. Fabien and me, Lou and Alain, Henri and Rhi, Carine and her new baby: Stephanie's family. And I couldn't have felt prouder when Stephanie asked me to be by her side today, her witness at the *mairie* earlier and now here, holding Tomas's hand as he walks down the aisle as ring-bearer, feeling like her mum on her wedding day. As I let go of Tomas's hand and find a tissue, I'm crying a mix of happy and proud tears, very different from the sorts of tears I've cried over this year. They blur my eyesight and will probably turn my nose bright red but I couldn't care less. I have everything I need here. This is my family and I love them all.

As the service ends and they prepare to exchange rings, Ralph runs off through the lavender field, Tomas just behind him.

'Bring back the rings, Ralph! The rings!'

And we all laugh.

I stand and kiss Stephanie.

'He may not have been planned, but he is what brought us all together,' she murmurs.

'He did! And life has a way of not going according to plan,' I say. Stephanie looks at me, beautiful in the dress from the *brocante*, which we have made over, as we did the chairs, the white tablecloths, laid with a fabulous buffet, and even the wrought-iron table. Because everything deserves a second chance.

'Talking of plans,' says Stephanie. 'Good job this one was!' She lays a hand on her stomach.

'Huh?' I exclaim. I couldn't be more excited.

'You're about to be a grandmother all over again!' she says. And although I'm not sure I'm quite ready to be called that, feeling as if I'm mum to Stephanie is the best thing in the world. That, and sharing it with the man I love, because we all deserve a second chance at life and, thank God, I got mine.

'So, how do you feel about being a grandfather already?' I ask Fabien.

'More toys to find and do up from the *brocante*.' He kisses Stephanie on the cheek, then me on the lips. 'I love it!'

ACKNOWLEDGEMENTS

Writing and producing a book is a team effort and I want to thank my fabulous new team at Transworld for their lovely welcome to me in my new home. To Francesca Best for coming to find me and Sally Williamson for taking over at the helm so seamlessly and helping make this book the best it could be. And in particular the fabulous Vicky Palmer for making it all happen. And, as always, my brilliant and lovely agent David Headley for his hard work, guidance, friendship and fun.

This book wouldn't have been possible without my love affair for France, which started at a very young age. Annual holidays in the Renault 14 and camping throughout France were followed by summer holidays on parent-free PGL holidays canoeing the Ardèche gorge and camping in the chestnut forest. It is also the place I most associate with my Dad. I can picture him now, holding his face to the Provençal sunshine, back in his happy place despite the difficulties his illness brought. I can see him and Mum, him in his wheelchair, her showing him the wine list and holding up his glass for him to drink. No matter how bad that illness got, there were still pleasures to be found in life in Provence, in the sunshine amongst the lavender fields and with a good bottle of wine and a bowl of *moules marinière*. My biggest memories of these times were the meals we shared at La Garde-Freinet, at Rose's pizza place which always holds a special place in our hearts, for the food and the wonderful warm welcome we always received, and to my final birthday meal with my Dad, sitting in a pop-up restaurant, on the beach, in a huge thunder storm, the sides of the tarpaulin flapping, enjoying every moment of the food, wine and company. Happy memories that stay with me. It was here my love affair with France really began and on leaving college I went to work just outside Saint-Tropez as a waitress. It was such an adventure and a time when I felt life could have taken different directions, but it seems it led me right back here, to Provence, in the pages of this story. Of course, then there were the many trips to the old watermill in Brittany, but that's for another day! So, returning to Provence to write this book was an absolute joy.

Thank you to my wonderful travelling companion Katie Fforde for coming on the journey again, and to my Mum, for starting the journey and joining me on it too. Hope you enjoy this trip to the lavender fields of Provence, and if you get to go there yourselves, do take a trip to the wonderful Musée de la Lavande, the Lavender Museum in Provence . . .

www.museedelalavande.com

Their lavender oil and the wonderful sleep it brought me not only helped me through tricky nights but brought back the wonderful memories I have of this region and inspired this book, *Escape to the French Farmhouse*.

Read on for recipes that will take you back to the heart of Provence

Lavender shortbread

Follow this recipe to make delicious lavender shortbread cookies, just like Del in *Escape to the French Farmhouse*.

Ingredients
75g softened butter
30g caster sugar
100g plain flour
1 tsp fresh lavender buds
A pinch of salt

Method
1. Preheat the oven to 190°C (fan 170°C), gas mark 5 and line a baking sheet with baking parchment.
2. Cream the butter and sugar together until light and fluffy. Chop the lavender buds (leaving some whole for decoration later).
3. Mix the chopped lavender and a pinch of salt into the flour then combine the dry ingredients with the butter and sugar mix until it has the consistency of breadcrumbs.
4. On a lightly floured surface bring the dough together into a small ball, then wrap in cling film and leave to rest in the fridge for at least 20 minutes.
5. After the dough has chilled, roll it out on a well-floured surface to about 4mm thick and use a cookie cutter to stamp out small circles.
6. Transfer the biscuits on to the lined baking sheet and return to the fridge to chill for a further 15 minutes.
7. Bake in the preheated oven for 12–15 minutes or until pale golden. Allow to cool on the tray for 5 minutes before moving on to a wire rack to cool completely. Serve with the remaining lavender buds sprinkled on top. You can store your biscuits in an airtight container for up to one month (or eat them immediately!).

Apricot jam sponge cake

A classic jam sandwich sponge cake never disappoints, but why not try it with Apricot jam and a sprinkling of lavender to bring the taste of Provence to home?

Ingredients
4 eggs
Self-raising flour
Caster sugar
Butter
1 tsp vanilla extract
Apricot jam
A few lavender buds, chopped

Method
1. Heat the oven to 180°C (fan 160°C), gas mark 4.
2. Grease two 20cm cake tins, and line the bases of each with baking paper.
3. Weigh the eggs in their shells and then weigh out the same amount of flour, sugar and butter.
4. Cream the butter until soft and then add the sugar and beat together until light and fluffy.
5. Add the eggs one by one, mixing as you go. Then add the vanilla extract and stir through.
6. Sift the flour into the mixture, then gently but thoroughly fold it in.
7. Divide the batter equally between the cake tins and bake in the oven for 25–30 minutes.
8. Leave to cool in the tin for a couple of minutes, then turn out on to a wire rack to cool completely.
9. Once cool, spread one cake very generously with Apricot jam then place the other cake on top.
10. Dust the top of the cake with a touch of extra caster sugar and a sprinkling of lavender.

Lavender lamb

Two lovely spring and summer flavours in one! Serve this delicious dish with potatoes and some seasonal veg.

Ingredients
1 kg leg of lamb (approx.)
6 garlic cloves, peeled and cut into slices
A handful of lavender, chopped
Salt and pepper
1 tbsp lavender honey

For the glaze:
4 tbsp lavender honey
1 tbsp olive oil

Method
1. Preheat the oven to 180°C (fan 160°C), gas mark 4.
2. With a sharp knife, make incisions in the lamb then push the garlic and lavender into the openings.
3. Put the lamb in a roasting tin, season with salt and pepper and brush with the honey, and cook for 40 minutes.
4. Meanwhile, make the glaze. Warm the honey and oil in a saucepan until runny, then beat firmly and quickly until emulsified. Put in the fridge for a few minutes to cool and thicken.
5. Once you've removed the lamb from the oven, brush the glaze all over the lamb.
6. Put the lamb back into the oven for another 20 minutes, brushing on more glaze every few minutes until it is used up. The lamb should be tender and the juices running a pale pink when pierced with a skewer.